The LAST ROOM *in* MANHATTAN

Books by Kathleen Rockwell Lawrence

Kathleen Rockwell Lawrence

The LAST ROOM in MANHATTAN

New York

ATHENEUM

1988

This is a work of fiction. Any references to historical events; to real people, living or dead; or to real locales are intended only to give the fiction a setting in historical reality. Other names, characters, and incidents either are the product of the author's imagination or are used fictitiously, and their resemblance, if any, to real-life counterparts is entirely coincidental.

Copyright © 1988 by Kathleen Rockwell Lawrence

Atheneum
Macmillan Publishing Company
866 Third Avenue, New York, N.Y. 10022
Collier Macmillan Canada, Inc.

Library of Congress Cataloging-in-Publication Data
Lawrence, Kathleen Rockwell.
    The last room in Manhattan / Kathleen Rockwell Lawrence.
        p.   cm.
    ISBN 0-689-12010-9
    I. Title.
PS3562.A9128L37 1988
813'.54--dc 19   88-21944.   CIP

10 9 8 7 6 5 4 3 2 1
Printed in the United States of America

For Nora Rockwell Lawrence,
with love

Also, my gratitude to her for permitting
the use of her haiku:
"Deer Grows Up"

The LAST ROOM *in* MANHATTAN

Chapter

1

Exec-Career is a headhunting firm, of the modern white-collar tribe of headhunters, specializing in the well-trimmed head of the stockbroker. The nationwide headquarters of Exec-Career is a studio apartment in a luxury building on Park Avenue near Forty-fifth Street in New York City. The stationery of Exec-Career calls this apartment Suite 1144, but the word "suite" is misleading. So is the Park Avenue address. So is the stationery, wide and weighty and water-marked. Though it is an efficiency apartment, a thin wall has been thrown up to separate what was meant to be the bedroom alcove from the rest of the space. The bedroom alcove is the bedroom as well as the office of H. Hank Housepian, the founder and head headhunter. ("CEO" is next to his name on the stationery.) H. Hank's office contains a desk on ball bearings, a computer, and a Murphy bed, often still opened and rumpled during business hours. There is a walk-in closet between H. Hank's office and the bathroom. H. Hank's entire wardrobe is stored there, as well as his golf clubs, his barbells, a spare tire, several sun visors with corporate names on the brims, a broken answering machine, a small white Dynel Christmas tree, and much, much more. His jockstrap hangs on the hook behind the bathroom door. Only H. Hank uses the bathroom. His employees eschew it, preferring to go down the hall to the penitent paperless pissoir made available to them by their friends and neighbors, the employees of VibraColor Filmworks.

It was ten-fifteen, a Wednesday morning in early February. Karen Carmody had just arrived at Suite 1144 and was stuffing her Persian lamb jacket, a recent purchase from the Planned Parenthood Thrift Shop, into the broom closet in the kitchen nook. Annie's cranberry wool coat and Michael's trench were already crammed in. So were the broom and mop. Karen, Michael, and Annie were staff headhunters, stationed in the living room, or "outer office."

Karen had been with Exec-Career for eight months, having gotten the job through her friend Annie, who had worked there several years. Karen liked working with Annie, but didn't like Exec-Career. "Exec-Crable" was what Karen called it. She said H. Hank's Murphy bed was a corporate casting couch. She said headhunting was the moral equivalent of musical chairs. Witty and most wanton were her complaints about the profession, which she voiced whenever she knew H. Hank Housepian was out.

He was out this morning. "He's *out*?" Karen asked rhetorically, gleefully, as she sat at her desk next to the kitchen. Annie and Michael, already dialing, nodded.

How they knew: The door to H. Hank's office was closed and the circular sign affixed to it which was headed "Hello! I am . . ." had its plastic arrow pointing to the pie wedge that read "at a meeting!" The other pie wedges read "out to lunch!" "in . . . enter!" and "on

4

the phone!" " '*At a meeting,*' " said Karen, delightedly, arms outspread. She turned back to her friends, laughed, and said, "Hey! Don't you think there should be wedges that say 'jerking off!' or 'on the pot!' I mean in the interest of accuracy and all?"

Annie, who had just slammed down the phone in some pique, managed a small laugh at this.

Karen went on. "Ol' H. Hank's probably out stalking heads or head in the Beverly Hotel's lobby—isn't that where they're holding the Merrill training seminar? Anyway, thank God he's not here. I've got to find me a place to live starting immediately. Lisa the actress is coming back!" As she spoke, Karen opened a *Village Voice* to a well-marked page headed UNFUR-NISHED APARTMENTS MANHATTAN."

"Aw, Karen," said Annie, with such real sympathy that Karen had to fight back tears. Annie was Karen's good, good friend. In fact, once, when Karen found herself between apartments, Annie had taken her in for three months, and Annie had only a studio. Though Annie had been generous, it was too tight for two. After that, Karen vowed that she would never put her friends in that position again. After that, Karen knew she had to live alone. She was thirty-three now, too old to adapt, too old to be dependent, too old to be anyone's roommate.

Karen feigned interest in the *Voice* until she got control over her voice. "It's OK, Annie, I'm fine. Yeah, Lisa called me last night from Johannesburg, God knows what time it was there. Anyway, I have to be out by Sunday night."

"Doesn't she have to give you more notice than that?" asked Annie.

"No way. She has the lease. Well, actually some social worker has the lease, but he retired to Sicily and Lisa has the official sublet. Sub-subletters have no rights, you know that, Annie." Karen had gotten the place last year when Lisa signed on to go around the world with *A Chorus Line*. A long run, but not long enough for Karen. During her tenancy, Karen never failed to check *Variety* before she made plans that included her sink and her toilet. News that *A Chorus Line* was sold out for three months in Cairo had sent her into raptures. "I mean, I should have been prepared. I knew that pretty soon *A Chorus Line* wouldn't have any place else to go. Probably everyone in the world has seen it by now." They laughed. Karen bit into her corn muffin, raining crumbs down upon the classifieds. She scanned the page, her lips moving silently, counting.

"Twenty-three. I went out last night at twelve-thirty to get the *Voice*, then I went home, circled twenty-three listings, slept for a little while, then started calling as soon as it was light. Nothing. Can you believe it? The line was either busy or the places were already taken. Anyway, that's why I'm late."

"I thought you said you'd lived in New York for a while," Michael said to Karen.

"Yeah, nine years."

"Nine years and you're *still subletting*?!" he exclaimed, his blue eyes swimming in a sea of incredulity and thick lenses. Michael sat next to Annie, across from Karen. Karen liked him. She liked to look at him. He looked like a "Masterpiece Theater" extra with his sleek center-parted brown hair, his round horn-rimmed glasses, his mustache, his suspenders and crisp bow tie. Sweet-faced. Impeccably neat, even his desk. From another world. "You could have been rich by now!" he said. Karen looked at him blankly. "I mean, trading up!" he explained.

Karen's look remained blank.

"You know," he said, "*Co-ops.*"

"Oh . . . yeah . . . you're right, Michael. Absolutely. I mean, even if I weren't rich, I maybe could've been at least a yuppie by now." She grinned broadly at Michael, who was a yuppie, and knew what he was, and never minded Karen putting him on a little. "I mean, don't you think, Annie?" But Annie was now on the phone, intent. She waved her hand in front of her face, and mouthed "Shut the fuck up" to Karen.

Karen sighed and picked up her phone to continue her home hunt. She dialed "14 St. E. (Ave A) Rent Stabilized Studio $750 Parquet Floors" and got an answering machine. "Taken" was the entire message she heard before it clicked off. She combed her fingers through her inch of blond on top, tucked a straying strand of longer side hair behind her right ear, and stared hard at the page. An apartment for $1250 was listed as "Perfect Share." Its number had been busy for the last half-hour. And anyway, Karen didn't want to share.

Karen dialed yet another listing. Busy. She had to admit that Michael was right, in a way. There had to be a reason why she spurned what was within her grasp. It was perfectly clear now that she had done it to herself by not keeping jobs and not trading up.

Annie hung up the phone. "Salimoni wants Thompson Moore! He said the interview went great yesterday. But personnel there is stringing me along. You know Evonne in Personnel with her fake-o British accent. Christ! I've called her twice. 'Oh, yes, Annie, dahling. It is positive *mayhem* here. I'll have to get back to you.' " Annie exhaled and crossed two hands' worth of fingers. "I hope he gets it. He was such a sweet guy."

"Careful, Annie," said Karen. "You're personalizing things again. Remember, you want Al Salimoni to get this job because you want your commission. I'm telling you, if you look at it that way, it's easier. I mean, what really is the difference if this Al Salimoni guy gets placed with Hutton or Smith Barney or Thompson Moore? Will he be better off? Will Hutton be better off? And is it really that important to you? Is Salimoni your brother or your lover or your husband that you care so much whether he gets the job instead of the next guy? What's Salimoni to Hecuba anyway, you dig?" Karen often lapsed into a put-on hip phrasing.

"Al Salimoni's married," said Annie, and Karen heard the regret in her non sequitor.

Michael cradled the receiver in his hand and said brightly, "Don't worry, Annie, Al Salimoni can get divorced and marry you! Aw, gee, but then he'll have to pay Al Salimoni's alimony."

Both women groaned. Michael was in his mid-twenties; the women in their thirties. It was his first job, Karen's ninth. Though he joked with them, he took it very, very seriously. The job ate at him. Karen could tell by the way he cleared his throat before he began each dial, by the cigarettes, by the staccato jerking of his foot in thin air each time he began, "I'm Michael Ottley of Exec-Career and I have some suggestions for your career that you might want to consider . . ." The foot had begun jerking again. Michael was on the phone constantly. He was getting an M.B.A. nights at NYU

8

and saw this, unaccountably, as a steppingstone to a future career on Wall Street.

The job did not eat at Karen, partly because she had such fun bitching about it, partly because she was older and had something Michael didn't have—a kind of situational confidence. It applied here, on this job, though not in some of the other areas of her life. Not with men, for instance. But calling someone you never met and reciting a kind of script was easy to Karen. "Just dial and smile," she advised Michael, so often that he called her Ms. Dial-and-Smile. Well, she was good on a phone. Not that she got so many appointments with brokers, not that she made all that many placements, not that she believed any of it, but she sure could spew forth the company line.

Actually she had an appointment today with a broker. For lunch. She told Annie.

"You gotta be kidding," said Annie, "He's probably a P." She picked up her phone on the first ring.

P was their cruel code for Pathetic, that rare thing: the truly unsalable broker. For, the sad truth was that there were some brokers who, for whatever reasons, were P's. The names of P's most often crossed their desks as recommendations from H. Hank. A friend of a golf buddy or a woman he had met in the weight room of the Health Outlet. If Annie couldn't place one of H. Hank's P's, he would give the name to Michael or to Karen. And so they used the code with each other in hushed tones: "Don't touch that one! Don't take him on. He's a P."

This guy probably was a P. He hadn't been recommended by H. Hank. She'd gotten his name from the list. Still, it was unheard of for a broker to make a lunch appointment. Brokers didn't leave their desks during market hours. They met headhunters for breakfast or for a drink after work. Never lunch. But Mark Pitofsky from Merrill requested lunch. A broker who takes lunch! The guy had to be a loser. She was tempted to cancel the appointment, especially in view of the fact that she was under so much pressure today.

A shriek from Annie. The call had been from Evonne at Thompson Moore. Al Salimoni had the job! Annie had fifteen hundred smackers! Annie was on her feet, already assuming her position for the ritual Broker Placement Dance. She stood in the center of the small space, eyes unblinking ahead of her, her hand in a smart salute. Michael quickly finished his phone call and pulled out his harmonica. Karen came around, put all of their phones on Hold, leaned against her desk, waited for the tone from Michael, then began singing:

> *The toyshop door is locked up tight,*
> *And everything is quiet for the night,*
> *When suddenly the clock strikes one,*
> *The fun's be-ee-gun!*

Annie, in high heels and holding her rigid salute, was executing the Military, a dance she had learned in Marcy Flynn's dance class in Bethesda, Maryland, when she was five. Annie was now thirty-five. Nothing was as easy as it had once been.

Slide-step-slide-step-slide-step-slide-step, went Annie, counting and breathing heavy as she did so, her legs straining against her straight skirt. Short, sexy, lovely Annie, breasts bouncing in her black sheath, black because it was slimming, black stockings, slimming too, heels because they gave her height; Annie flushed and laughing now, her thick lips parted, her dark eyes flashing beneath the salute, her abundant hair falling over one eye.

Karen went on, singing without mercy:

> *Hear them all cheering,*
> *Now they are nearing,*
> *There's the captain, stiff as starch!*

The phrase "stiff as starch" required that Annie jump saluting, open her legs in midair, then land with a smart click of her heels. This she did faultlessly, ignoring the peril to her skirt and her ankles, thinking only of the fifteen hundred.

> *Here they come! Here they come!*
> *Wooden soldiers on parade!*

How had they discovered that Annie knew the dance and Karen, (who had grown up far from her in Poughkeepsie, New York) knew the song? (Karen had gotten it from a McGuire Sisters album.) Michael asked that question whenever they launched into the Broker Placement Dance. (Michael had never heard the song before Karen started the job with them and it became the Broker Placement Theme, but Michael could play anything on that thing.)

It was one of those serendipitous moments in a friendship, that was all, one of the links in their female bonding. It was entirely possible, Karen allowed, that she had actually been *singing it* one night in the presence of Annie and a bottle of Scotch. Or, had Annie been humming it and doing the dance? (Annie didn't

11

know the words.) That was possible, too. They had been friends ever since Karen had come to New York, too long a time for them to remember such particulars.

They laughed and applauded and went back to it. Annie called Al Salimoni immediately with the good news, made a celebratory pot of coffee in the kitchen, then began making cold calls anew. Karen continued calling the *Voice* listings, with no luck. When the coffee stopped dripping, Karen poured three cups. Even Michael took a break.

Throughout the morning Karen regaled them with news from the real-estate front. "This old man I just called said he got one hundred and four calls this morning," Karen said. "He wants everyone to write a five-hundred-page essay entitled 'Why I Deserve This Apartment,' to be postmarked no later than midnight tomorrow. Also, he wants everyone to tell the truth."

"Don't you think he just wants mail?" asked Michael.

"Or maybe power," said Karen. "Probably some lonely old geezer who just takes the same ad out every month. It'd be worth it, right, to get all those phone calls and then letters with everyone telling you their stories?"

"So what's so great about this apartment?" inquired Annie as she applied a squirt of hand cream.

"Well," said Karen expansively. "This apartment: First of all, this apartment is located on beautiful Avenue C. It has a living room/kitchen/bed nook *and* a bathroom *and* an eye-level view of the East River Drive. He said he'd throw in his loft bed for the winning essay. All of this for a mere $800, plus a thou for the fixture fee! Yaahhhh! I cannot bear it! Hey . . . what's this . . .

what's this?" Karen pulled at an Exec-Career letterhead that had been covered by the *Voice*. She read it quickly.

Annie and Michael exchanged a glance. They had seen it when they first arrived. It was H. Hank's latest memo, signed with HHH and a smile face. They knew Karen wouldn't go for it.

"So now we've got to *log* every broker we call on these ridiculous forms! We're supposed to call *hundreds* of brokers a week, and we've got to stop and document each call besides!

"Productivity Control," said Michael, in stentorious Housepian tones.

"Do you think he would stoop to calling guys we said we called to see if we called them? Isn't it enough that we don't get a salary, that our livelihood depends on the commissions?" But Karen spoke to no one, because Michael was back on the phone and Annie had begun her expense account for the previous month. She held her hand up again.

Annie was right, she knew. She had to shut up. She had to get going. She had to call her hundred brokers today. She had to get a home today. But right now, she had to stop everything, put her jacket back on, and go out in the cold to meet the P for lunch.

Karen Carmody sat at the counter before a cup of coffee, on the watch for Mark Pitofsky.

"What do you look like?" She had asked him on the phone yesterday, concerned about finding him in the press of humanity that is Burger Paradise at noon.

"I have no distinguishing characteristics," he said, and laughed. "I am of medium build, with dark hair and dark eyes. Oh . . . well, yes. I do have a chicken pox scar on the bridge of my nose, but I suppose that doesn't count for a marking beyond a few meters."

They laughed.

"I'll wear a white carnation," he said.

"Don't bother. I know a broker when I see one." They wore the uniform. Dark suits, highly polished plain black Oxfords, Burberry trench.

"I'll wear a white carnation," he repeated cryptically.

The waiter cleared the place next to her, swept up his tip, and threw a quick glare down into Karen's coffee cup, which she had taken care to leave one-third full. The vacant stool was quickly claimed by an elderly woman wearing a wool ski helmet and a tweed coat, who almost slipped as she raised herself up. Karen made a reflexive grab to steady her. At first the woman seemed alarmed to be touched, but then, seeing Karen, smiled and nodded her thanks. Karen turned away, but felt the woman's eyes upon her, and, shortly after, a tugging at her sleeve.

"Would you like a pass to the Van Gogh show at the Metropolitan?" the woman whispered, then interrupted herself to order a Bordeaux burger from the dour waiter. "My son's a curator there. I get 'em *free!*" The cheerful visage that presented itself through the hole in gray knitting was deeply wrinkled and white and dry as paper, though rosy from cold.

Karen accepted, knowing this permitted the woman both an expression of gratitude and a sharing of pride in her curator son. More important, it permitted Karen the Van Gogh show, which she had been wanting to see, but resisted because she resented Ticketron having control over her communion with the artist.

14

This sort of encounter was not unusual for Karen. Indeed, it was not uncommon for her to be stared at, smiled at, spoken to, and asked advice as well as directions by perfect strangers. And sometimes, though not often, to be singled out as the object of someone's demented wrath.

It was her face that did it, she knew. Almost a peasant face, direct from every Slav on her mother's side of the family. "I've seen this face a hundred times," Great Aunt Gloria was reputed to have announced when she held baby Karen. A family story. Karen often wondered whether Aunt Gloria had hurt her mother's feelings. All that work just to be told you had given birth to another one of those faces.

The face: large of bone, high of forehead, strong of jaw, wide and open. Wide open. Though the rest of her was not that big—she was of average height, just a little overweight, maybe—her head, her hands, her feet were big. The only hat she ever wore was the one she was wearing right now, a black wool beret, one size fits all. She had long since given up on finding a chic felt number in her size. Karen thought maybe the expanse of face made it easier for people to focus on it in a crowd of smaller faces, or that folks thought there was room there for them, that she could take them in. Or maybe the clearness translated somehow as honesty. She had once been told that she looked like the mother on "Little House on the Prairie" if, instead of her bun, the mother on "Little House on the Prairie" had worn a blond modified punker cut. Well, then. Karen had never seen "Little House on the Prairie," but that certainly could explain things.

Also from her mother's side: a nose that veered just slightly to the left in a modified deviated septum, noticeable only to herself, her mother, and her brother Bill, who shared this congenital defect. "Get the Operation! Get the Operation!" he would urge. "You won't believe it. Breathing can be fun!" He had had the Operation after a football injury that had smashed his septum along with the rest of his nose. But Karen resisted the Operation because it hurt, cost money, and because she only occasionally found breathing to be burdensome. Besides, a lean to the left lent interest.

From her father, who had been handsome but who was now dead, she had her eyes. Thick-lashed and large, with hazel irises which were spotted with dark and rimmed with indigo. Because they turned down at the corners and were shadowed by heavy lids, they were eyes that looked sad even when the rest of her was happy.

She had good carriage, owed to a back brace her father made her wear as a child, and this gave a false impression of confidence. Also, her nasal way of speaking, partly deviate, partly upstate, came off as confident in Manhattan. It sounded strong to people because they did not know it. Because they did not know her.

Karen smiled now and thanked the woman, putting her Van Gogh ticket in the pocket of her jacket. She raised the coffee cup to her lips and feigned a sip as she looked toward the door.

"He always did like art," said the woman. "When he was only two, I came into the kitchen and saw that he had made seventy-eight tiny *o*'s with a red crayon on a paper plate. I counted 'em. That's a sign of real artistic skill, you know, when you have the control to make such small figures at such an early age. God knows where he got his talent from . . ."

Karen nodded to show interest, but continued gazing in the direction of the door.

"He's gay," said the woman. Karen looked back at her. The woman's clear eyes were glistening. "I'm so worried about him."

Karen put her hand briefly on the tweed sleeve. "I'm sure he's OK . . . really. The media has exaggerated everything so much." Karen said this but didn't believe it. "You'll see," she said. "He'll be fine." They sat in silence then.

"Excuse me," Karen said at length, adjusting her slouchy shoulder bag and putting a dollar on the counter, standing as she did so. Because a man of medium build and dark hair had just entered Burger Paradise. This man was wearing a white carnation. A good thing, too, Karen thought, as she inspected him from this distance.

"Nice to talk to you," Karen said to the woman.

"Oh, yes, yes," she said, nodding. She smiled from her frame of gray. "Good-bye, dear."

Karen weaved through other diners in the narrow space between counter and tables toward a most unbrokerlike figure standing on the short line near the door. A long striped scarf was hanging loose from his neck, beneath and between which was visible a shirt and tie. A shirt and tie, yes, but this tie was too short and too narrow and a few shades too green. Also, this tie was squared off at the bottom. He was not wearing a suit jacket or a trench. The carnation was flopping from the mouton collar of an open well-broken-in brown leather flight jacket. A tan porkpie cap covered most of his dark hair, which was a little too long and not a little shaggy. His eyes were darting quickly, casing Burger

Paradise, until they focused on the young woman nearing him. They had a chicken pox scar between them.

"I'm Karen Carmody," she said, and shook his hand.

"Delighted to meet you, Miss Carmody," said Mark Pitofsky, with almost a bow, a courtly clip to his words, though his eyes seemed to be beyond his control and were looking her up and down in a manner that belied his cultured speech. There had been a time when Karen had been offended by this sort of once-over from men, but now she wasn't sure, the way she wasn't sure about a lot of things anymore. Maybe men who did that were made helpless by women, and should be forgiven. Or maybe even embraced. Because, perhaps, they were the men who really did love women. He had spoken the truth, she could tell by his eyes and by his half-smile—he was indeed delighted to meet her. Well, there were sometimes men who were.

"Karen," she said.

They waited briefly until the Burger Paradise hostess nodded to them and held up two fingers above a small table. He removed his cap, and Karen saw that the dark hair which seemed so full had been the victim of a serious recession. She liked it that the cap was the only covering for this fact. He did not comb it over. They draped their jackets on the backs of their chairs and he placed the paperback he had been carrying on the table: *New American Poets*. One of the ever-vigilant Burger Paradise waiters was upon them immediately: two beers, a brie burger and an artichoke burger.

"So," said Mark Pitofsky, still half-smiling, the big

striped scarf still draped over his neck, "This is your meeting. Why ever did you call me?"

"You were on the list of newly registered Merrill brokers."

"You mean you didn't single me out?" he said in a disappointed tone. "You hadn't heard of my accomplishments?" She wasn't sure he was kidding.

"Sorry," she said, and smiled at his hurt expression. "Look . . . uh . . . Mark . . . to put it bluntly, which I shouldn't, other houses try to steal new Merrill brokers away because they've had such good training at Merrill's expense. I'm the intermediary."

"The Tokyo Rose of Wall Street," he mumbled, smiling again, still studying her, his hand holding his chin, three fingers tapping against his mouth.

"Huh?"

The hand moved to support his temple. "Well, it's a rather unusual job, isn't it? Even the name: head-hunter. I never knew there was such a thing!"

"I have to ask you some questions," she said, ignoring him. She had too many doubts about her line of work to entertain his.

"I am at your disposal."

She produced a small legal pad from her purse, and he was amused at this, too, she saw. "Do you have a résumé?"

"No. I've never needed one."

"How did you get this job, then?"

"I'm wired," he said.

"You are?" Not many people admitted being wired.

"My uncle's an executive VP. I'd worked at the

liquor store on Greenwich Street for thirteen years. It was a great irritation to him. He has no children, only a few nieces and nephews. I'm the only one in New York. I suppose I did it to oblige him." He shrugged. "He's getting old . . . it pleased my mother."

"*Thirteen years* at a liquor store? But you're a college graduate, aren't you?"

"Indeed. An English major." He was defensive, she saw. It had been thirteen years of his life, after all. "Why not a liquor store? A job as meaningful as most others. You cannot know the urgency with which some of my patrons greeted my raising of the gates each morning."

"Forgive me," said Karen in mock exaggeration, smiling in spite of a growing annoyance. "Liquor store clerking is not what one normally goes to college for."

He held up his index finger. "Clarification: I was *the manager*."

"Ah!" said Karen.

"And besides, who goes to college to become a broker? Did you ever hear a child say he wanted to be a broker when he grew up? It's a job. Period. I'm a broker by accident. It's how most people live their lives . . . by accident. I don't intrude, and brokering is a most intrusive enterprise. One must break in, call little old widows and clerics and tell them what to do with their assets. I suppose I'm a fraud, biding my time until the SEC finds me out: a broker without ambition."

Their food arrived. Karen sipped her beer and began eating her artichoke before realizing that Mark had not begun. Instead, carefully, almost ceremoniously, he was rolling up his shirtsleeves, completely unmindful of the fact that she had stopped to watch the procedure. Also, to watch his forearms, the tendons, the veins, the accidental show of male skin and sinew and strength, unexpected here, in Burger Paradise in a New York winter, unexpected from a broker. When he felt the silence and her eyes, he looked up, self-conscious, and flushed as he reached for the ketchup.

Karen looked quickly away, but said, "Do you always do that before you eat?"

"I don't know. Maybe so." He stuck a slice of onion atop the brie. "You don't like it, do you?"

She was quiet. They ate for a time in silence. She liked it and she didn't like it. What she liked about it were his arms. He wasn't married, she found herself thinking. He wasn't kempt enough to be kept. Also, whenever she met a male broker for a drink, he got in about his wife in the first five minutes.

"There's no real difference, is there?" he asked at length. "Purveyor of liquors or stocks and bonds . . . hunter of heads."

"Money's a difference. Isn't that why you came to see me today? Money? The chance that I could get you a job with better commissions?"

"More money would be nice, of course. It would mean I could retire earlier to the Gulf of Cadiz. But I don't have any real hope of your getting me a better job, much less a salary that would change my life. Mainly I came to see you because you asked me to come. An invitation . . . a free lunch . . . meeting someone new. I don't get a lot of invitations. You could say I'm here under false pretenses."

She hadn't taken a single note. She played her pencil on the pad, alternating eraser and lead. "You don't look like a broker," she said.

"I *don't?*"

"No. And if I got you interviews with places, you'd probably go telling them all about the Gulf of Cadiz and how you don't intrude." She sighed and shook her head, smiling. "I should have known when you suggested lunch instead of a drink. Brokers don't take a lunch hour."

"They *don't?*"

"You mean you haven't noticed? Usually I have to meet brokers for breakfast or for a drink during the day. Aren't you afraid you'll miss a call from Paloma Picasso or somebody while you're here talking to me?" Brokers only go pee before nine and after four, she almost told him, but didn't. They laughed. She leaned over her plate. "The truth is, you're wasting my time."

"Oh, *please* don't say that! We can talk. That's never a waste. You can tell me where you're from that you speak with those funny flat *a*'s. You can tell me what movies you've liked recently, what kind of things you read. You can tell me about your husband and children. You can even complain about them if you want to. That's what strangers are for."

"I don't have either," said Karen.

"Oh. Me neither. I mean, I'm divorced. Well! So we'll talk about movies, then."

The Burger Paradise waiter was hovering, though they had barely finished. There was a growing single-file line of hungry workers in down coats in the tight aisle. The one o'clock lunch crowd had arrived. "Let's go," said Mark, rolling down his sleeves. "I'll buy you coffee in the park." There was a vest-pocket park next door.

"The park?"

"It's lovely."

She didn't know men who said "lovely." "It's freezing."

"It's lovely in winter . . . all still and hoary and bare-branched."

"Coffee?" intruded the waiter. They got the check instead. Karen signed on behalf of Exec-Career.

"You don't look much like a headhunter, either," Mark told her as she donned her jacket. He briefly fingered her frayed wide fur cuff. "I like this," he said. There was a tuft of dark hair on his wrist. His hands were no bigger than hers.

Even Paley Park's coffee concession knew better than to be there in the winter. The lone occupant of the small ivy-lined park was a woman with two shopping carts filled with bags and blankets, newspapers and rags, empty deposit bottles and cans. There was a cardboard sign on one cart that read FEED THE HUNGRY BIRDS. She sat on the low stone ledge between concrete buckets of holly, rocking and feeding pigeons from a stale crust. Karen sat on the opposite side, shivering in one of the white wire chairs before the wintertime waterfall wall while Mark ducked back into Burger Paradise for coffee. He was back in a moment, but before he approached Karen, he stopped and gave a neat white bag to the homeless woman. A sandwich and some coffee. Karen watched him as he spoke briefly to her, then nodded to her as he had to Karen earlier. And again Karen thought: courtly. Not of this time. A kind of bow.

"That was nice," Karen said, when he returned. He

shrugged. "What do you do when they ask you for money?" The woman had eaten half a sandwich and was carefully rewrapping the other half.

"I give them money," he said. "Not much . . . a buck. I just don't believe that anything is really being done for them. What do you do?"

She laughed. "I assess each situation and make a decision."

"That must take a lot of time, running a character evaluation for every person that stops you for money! How long does it take you to get to work each morning? And what criteria do you use?"

"The usual: are they gonna blow it on booze—"

"What if they do? What do you care?"

"Spoken like a true ex-manager of a liquor store. Anyway, do you want me to go on?"

"Indeed." He seemed greatly amused.

"I think, is this guy gonna grab my wallet if I pull it out? Is he carrying a weapon? Are there enough people near me? Am I carrying my briefcase and groceries? Am I in a rush?—"

"God, I hope not!" said Mark.

"—Is his story about needing a token to get to the Bronx to see his sick mother too slick? Is he really a con artist? Or, does he really look poor? Is she really blind? Or, has she asked me for money before? Or, you know, sometimes I don't give if they seem too pathetic, if they grovel too much. And the worst, what I *really* hate, is if they've got a little kid with them, helping them beg, like something out of Dostoevsky . . ."

"So you don't give them anything if they have a raggedy little child in tow . . . makes sense. Absolutely." He had one dimple which was working very hard. "You want the Platonic idea of Poor Person."

"Precisely," said Karen, laughing. He had leaned closer during their conversation and now his hand rested on the back of her chair. She shivered, and raised her frayed fur around her ears. "And besides, a buck is too much. A buck is a lot."

"For them or for me?" asked Mark.

And so they sat there in the cold, steam of breath mingled with steam of coffee. They talked of the homeless in their city and the cranes that were everywhere over them all, and about the construction scaffolding that darkened the sidewalks below. Karen told him that she was trying to find a home. He was sympathetic, but had no suggestions. Rents were astronomical, they agreed, though he was one of the fortunates, having lucked out on the Lower East Side some years ago. He paid very little. Of course, he lived on the same block as the Hell's Angels, but one had to make concessions. They talked about the Gulf of Cadiz, which was quite beautiful he said, and warmer and far less costly than New York. Why were they here, they wondered, but they knew why they were here. Which led them to ambition and the vanity of human striving, which reminded Mark of a poem in his book. He stood before the waterfall and read it to her. He read very well. They were freezing. He read her four more.

They shook hands on Fifty-third Street. He wasn't wearing gloves. "I look forward to hearing from you . . . about the interviews," he said. He gave her the same appraising look he had given her in Burger Paradise. "I'm *very* interested," he said, then seemed embarrassed.

"I know you are," said Karen, and smiled broadly. "Can I have that?"

"What?"

"Your carnation." It was hanging upside down from his collar, half-covered by his scarf. He unpinned it and presented it to her. He didn't bow, but he seemed to.

She was very late getting back, but it was only one of the reasons Karen was fired that afternoon.

H. Hank Housepian had only been kidding when he pointed his arrow to the wedge that read, "at a meeting!" It was part of his Productivity Control plan, along with his new memo. He had been in all morning, spying behind his closed door and thin wall. He had heard Karen's wisecracks. He had heard Karen come in late and then spend the rest of the morning looking for a new home. Also, he could not believe that Karen had taken lunch, and such a long one, with a broker. "Brokers don't take lunch," were H. Hank's last words to Karen.

There was one other reason, which he did not mention. He had to make room. A new headhunter was starting immediately, Annie whispered to Karen, who was dazedly collecting her effects from her desk. Her name was Virginia Stubbs. They all knew the name. Virginia Stubbs was a P, and had proved impossible to place anywhere. The P did not refer to her pectorals, however. They were just fine. H. Hank had met her at the Health Outlet.

Chapter
2

The Corps had been through while she was at the Laundromat. Home had been messed with. The dingy twelve-by-nineteen-foot room in the Corps of Light's Arcadia House was home, after all, and had been for nearly two weeks. It was where she had landed after ninety-eight calls to real-estate listings proved futile. She felt the violation first in her right eyelid, which began its twitching even as she stood in the doorway.

She dropped her laundry bag and checked things out with her left eye as she massaged the right lid into calm. Her clothes had been rearranged. Instead of covering the surfaces of both beds, they were piled high on the near bed. The bed that had been unearthed in the excavation was now covered by clean linen and a worn but clean chenille spread. There was an invisible line down the center of the brown/tan/orange shag carpet. A vacuum cleaner had been in and mowed only half the shag. The other half was as long and limp and dirt-entwined as it had been when she went out. One of the fake Ethan Allen dressers had been cleared and polished. The other was laden with all of Karen's effects: hair mousse, Noxzema, a scattering of Pepperidge Farm cheese goldfish, her nephew's picture, pennies, nickels, dimes, and all the tiny containers of things she had gotten free at cosmetic counters over the years when she made a $6.50 purchase.

Most compelling, however, was the window treatment perpetrated by the intruder. An old *Home and Loft* she had found in the lounge recently had an article on window treatment. Only she knew this wasn't what they had in mind when they said windows should be dramatic. Though this *was* dramatic. Daring, even. The near window was still draped in the pattern of orange and yellow marigolds that had become familiar, though no less dreadful to Karen. But the far window's marigolds had been removed and replaced by drapes of blue and green stripes, accented with Aztec designs. Karen checked the bathroom, but could take no solace from the fact that the five-hundred-year-old shower curtain still hung in quiet mildew from its rusty metal hooks. The tub had been scrubbed!

Terrible to contemplate what these changes meant.

Well she knew what these changes meant.

She was to have a roommate.

"Shit!" was what she said.

She was to have a roommate even though she had been promised a single by Mrs. Sergeant Major Rawlins at her intake interview. Karen had told Mrs. Sergeant Major that she was an artist and needed her space. She had put $400 down as security and agreed to pay $150 each Thursday, but now she would be paying the same money for half the space. And, she would be living with a total stranger.

Of course she was getting a roommate. The Corps of Light only cleaned for you once.

"You will have a drink in just a minute," Karen promised herself. "You will have a drink, sweetie, just as soon as you get these fucking boots off." She sat on the bed, pushed back the sweeping arms of the Persian lamb, and grunted as she bent over to the boots. It was very important to get her boots off. They were heavy-duty boots and they were only three days old. Stiff leather lace-ups, combat style, black. She had seen them in the window at Kauffman's Riding Store. They were on sale, a great buy; she needed boots and she knew she'd have these babies forever. She might need them forever, she thought now with rue. They would be her last big purchase for some time.

The problem was, they hurt like hell, even though they hurt less now than they had three days ago. She had calluses around her ankles where the boot tops rubbed as she walked. Still, she was determined to break them in. She was coming to see it as a kind of challenge. It would be an achievement. She would have these really distinctive boots that were also comfortable. Also, she had this motivation: it was February, and the only other shoes she possessed in working order were her headhunter heels, sensible pumps in black and brown. "Ah!" she said to all ten toes. "You like that, don't you, darlings?" They wriggled with delight inside their sweat socks.

And now, the Scotch. Where was it? The closet door was ajar. She closed it from behind so she could get around it for a look. Her sleeve caught on the doorknob as she squatted to check the recesses. She released it, but in doing so bumped her head on the doorjamb. She rubbed her head and looked inside. No Scotch. She stood back, closed the door again to pass between it and the foot of her bed. She sat sideways on the bed and opened her bureau drawers, putting her feet off to the right to enable her to get at the bottom drawer. No Scotch. She moved to the foot of her bed and bruised her shin as she always did on the right angle of the metal bedframe which jutted out further than the narrow mattress.

She found it, finally, under her bed, where she had forgotten she'd left it. Man, she was losing hold for sure when she couldn't remember where she hid last night's bottle! She was twice glad to find it: for the drink she would have as soon as she located a glass, and for the fact that its presence there meant it had not been found by the Corps of Light. Strict rules against alcohol at the Arcadia House. She didn't know how many reprieves, if any, one got before eviction, but what with the housing crisis in Manhattan, the Corps could probably pack the place with folks who took the Pledge and meant it.

Karen found a glass, removed the ChapStick, safety pin, mint dental floss, and pencil, and poured herself a drink, a stiff one. Still wearing her jacket, she sat down on the newly made bed. She had to go easy on the Scotch, she knew. She was not a practicing alcoholic, but it was there, in the genes from her father. A latent legacy. She was not an artist either, though she was given to an occasional artistic flight. She had been other things, though.

She looked idly at the mismatched curtains and began, unaccountably, to laugh. A hundred and fifty a week, including breakfast and dinner, was nothing in Manhattan. There were women here who paid it gladly. Many were young, just starting in the city, who knew they would not be in the Arcadia long. They would be out soon, they knew, with bright apartments, men, and careers. They were twenty-two and had expectations. Karen wished them well. Karen was thirty-three and far less certain. It was hard to find herself here after nine years in Manhattan.

"*S*tay with me, goddamnit!" Annie had said over a beer at the Cedar Tavern the night Karen announced her intent to move to the Arcadia. But Karen had been insistent.

"What is this place, anyway?" Annie asked. "The Arcadia? I've never heard of it. You don't have to do this, Karen! It's ridiculous. You're a person with *friends* in this world."

"Yes, and I want to keep them," Karen had replied firmly. "Remember the last time, Annie? The curdled milk . . . the Tampax I forgot to flush, and the sanitary napkin I *did* flush, and the two days we waited for the plumber?"

"Ah yes, I remember it well," said Annie. They laughed.

"And what about the time you forgot I was there and brought that gorgeous Nordic hunk-o home? You are too sweet-natured, Annie. How can you forget what it was like, living with me?"

"Well, live with Joan, then. She at least has a one-bedroom. Or maybe Kevin . . . Hey! His parents are going to Europe for a month! You could housesit in Scarsdale! You know they'd be really happy . . . they like you and all, and you could take care of Rusty and Nibbles. So why not?"

31

"Because," said Karen. Which meant: She needed to do it on her own this time. She didn't want to be dependent on anyone. She was allergic to guinea pigs. She wanted to be alone. Annie knew what "Because" meant because it was the third time they had been through all of this. The waitress brought their dinner.

"But, Karen, you were born middle-class! How can you go live at some homeless shelter?"

"Christ, Annie! It's not a shelter for the homeless. It's a residence for women. I pay money for it, see?" But Annie didn't see. After two weeks she *still* didn't see. She called Karen every day at the Arcadia. When Karen wasn't there, she left pink "While You Were Outs" in her mailbox: "Check out Charlie. Eva just moved out." Or, "Michael says he has an aunt with an extra room in Bay Ridge."

*K*aren took off her jacket, pulled the pillow out from under the chenille, admired the crispness of new laundering, and arranged it so that her head would be raised only to such an angle as was necessary for imbibing. This she did with no little expertise.

$150 a week . . . It was the last room left for her in Manhattan. There was not another place that would have her for that money on this island. "Beggars can't be choosers," her mother had said always, and always in a cheery singsong. And so she was in this place she had not chosen, a beggar in her chronological prime.

As opposed to her real, true prime, which had probably been her eleventh year, when her family still seemed happy, when she had been happy: in sixth grade with Sister Dorothy, secure in the knowledge of every state capital, best friend to Marjorie Ohlinger, happy summer swimmer in the waters of Chodikee Lake . . .

No! She would not give into it! She would meet the Corps head on! She must rise up against this ruthless invasion of her territory! She would confront Mrs. Sergeant Major without further hesitation. The booze helped. She drained her glass and set it on the bed next to the bottle, left her jacket where it fell, slipped on her boots without tying them, and clumped into the hallway to the elevator. "Damn!" she said, and stopped, turned, walked back to the room, fumbled in her pants pocket for the key, opened the door, and found her Tic-Tacs. Only four left. She shook them all on her tongue and clumped back out, laces flying.

Mrs. Sergeant Major was in her office behind the front desk, wearing the Corps of Light's dress gray uniform trimmed with black braiding, her gray toque hairpinned with great certitude atop a rigid brown pageboy. Karen had seen her earlier in the day and knew that she was wearing her A-line skirt and Oxfords. She alternated between the skirt uniform and the pants uniform. The only time Karen had been in this office was for her interview, and she had somehow missed an extraordinary collection of glass hippopotami on display in the corner étagère. A hippopotamus wearing a stethoscope, one wallowing blissfully in a plate of ceramic mud, a nuclear family of hippos, a clown hippo. The smallest and, to the current state of Karen's mind, most offensive hippopotamus was flamingo-colored and carried a banner with the exhortation, "Have a hippy day!" Vomit, thought Karen, and ahemmed for attention.

Mrs. Sergeant Major was proofreading one of her Letters to Residents, making swirls of omission and carets of inserts with great import. Behind her on the wall was a poster of a blond woman wearing a burlap babushka embracing a blond child with a silicone tear on his cheek. The child was holding daisies. The poster said, in feathery angular script, BLESSED ARE THE POOR IN SPIRIT. Upon every item of any worth, unless you counted the hippopotami and the lamps, was affixed a red plastic strip with raised white lettering proclaiming Mrs. Sergeant Major Rawlins to be the owner.

When at length she looked up from her reading, Mrs. Sergeant Major feigned surprise, though Karen had by now cleared her throat three times. "How may I help you?" she asked.

Karen tried to approximate the bereft expression of the poor-in-spirit poster woman. "I'm Karen Carmody in 742," she said, then realized that Mrs. Sergeant Major knew exactly who she was. "I was promised a single!"

"Ah. Yes." A silence, awkward, which Karen refused to do anything to relieve. She would not yield, say anything. She would stand in dignified quiet, worthy and bereft before Mrs. Sergeant Major. "But Ms. Carmody, you must understand that the situation has changed radically, even in the short time since you've been here."

"But you know Room 742 isn't a double. It's much smaller than the other doubles! That's why you said I could have it to myself."

"But the fact is, it can and does accommodate two beds."

"Barely."

"But there have always been two beds there. Room 742 is one of our *emergency doubles*. She leaned toward Karen, confidingly, and, with a certain delight said, "We are *in crisis*." Karen knew that by the "we" Mrs. Sergeant Major Rawlins meant herself, Congress, the governor, the mayor, and all the City Council, united in this fight to save Manhattan.

"We are filled to capacity, and still I get calls all day long from women who would be *such desirable residents*." Her tone of voice made it plain that Karen suffered by comparison. Karen tried to put down the feeling rising in her, the same one she always got when she was a child and her mother would say something like "Isn't that Susie Glover pretty? And such a good reader, too!" Mrs. Sergeant Major sighed about the desirable residents and shook her head. Every hair went along with it. Mrs. Sergeant Major's hair fascinated Karen in spite of herself.

"Yes, Mrs. Sergeant Major, I understand that things are terrible. But we had an agreement. That's why I came here. If you recall, I told you that I'm an artist. I need quiet. I require solitude. I need my own room."

"Oh, I'm so sorry we can't accommodate you, Ms. Carmody, but the tenets of the Corps call for a sharing and a spirit of community. In a time such as this especially. Also, the housekeeper tells us your room was in shocking disorder. Please try to correct this for your own morale and that of your roommate . . ."

Karen had a vision of a cadre of intelligence agents

operating as a mild-mannered housekeeping staff. It amused her until it seized her with a combination of fury and paranoia. Paranoia won out over fury, and had to do with her Scotch. Had the housekeeper found it? What if she told Mrs. Sergeant Major?

"I'm sure you're aware that housing is at a premium in Manhattan at this time," Mrs. Sergeant Major was saying as she inserted a pencil into her stiff coif, and used it as a hair pick.

All too aware, Karen thought grimly, running her finger absently over the red plastic strip which laid claim to the stapler.

"We try to honor requests whenever possible, but our first responsibility is to provide decent housing for as many women as we can accommodate."

"Of course, and I certainly appreciate the Corps' humane commitments. But, Mrs. Sergeant Major, I'm facing my first one-woman show! It opens next week at the 11th Street Gallery and I don't see how I can make it if I have any distractions . . ." She was becoming a pathological liar.

Even as she was telling this one, she was racing ahead to invent an art form for herself, with rather more zest than the lie required. Paintings would be too large. You couldn't even get one decent-size canvas in that room. Same with sculpture. Papier-mâché was nice and contained and easy . . . you did it in nursery school. Papier-mâché tiger lilies! Karen thought suddenly. Sort of a homage to Georgia O'Keeffe. And there were so many varieties of tiger lilies! Her hands almost ached to be slopping around in a pail of glue and paper, the shaping and then the waiting, all the while listening to music and sipping coffee; and after, the patient painting and repainting, applying coat upon coat of lacquer. Shades of pink and purple—yellow and ochre and bisque—a quick and shocking red.

But Mrs. Sergeant Major was indifferent to Karen's art. "I'm sure we can count on your cooperation," she was saying as she stood and braced her arms wide apart against the desk in a most dismissive manner. "Do not hesitate to come to me whenever you have a question. You know I have an open-door policy."

"Thank you," said Karen then, and smiled weakly before leaving, according to her passive-aggressive wont.

Back in the lobby Karen did a rote check at the mailboxes against the far wall. Another message from Annie? Or maybe a letter? She felt a kind of hope, though hardly anyone knew she was at this address. Hope was unfounded, of course, as it normally is, given its nature. It was only Annie: "Your mother called me . . . wants you to call. *Urgent*." Though Karen always had her doubts about her mother's "Urgents," she dutifully checked the pay phone, which was located between the front desk and Mrs. Sergeant Major's office.

There was no booth around this phone. It was on the wall, right out there, and so were you when you used it. A woman with a new perm and an old sweat suit was using it now, saying, "He's got to stay married, though, because his wife comes from a rich family and the apartment's in her name. He needs to support his saxophone. I mean, I can respect that . . ."

It was just as well, since Karen had used all her quarters in the Laundromat. "Later for you, Mom," she mumbled as she idly scanned the bulletin board. The week's menu . . . an announcement of a piano recital by one of the residents . . . several postings requesting roommates, apartments, sublets . . . a notice about the evening service in the lounge. Two women were waiting at the elevator. One, with large dark eyes and a too-small nose job, was saying, "We used to be friends once, but now she won't speak to me. And I saved her marriage, too."

"How?" asked the other woman, who had a fuzzy cloud of white-blond hair. The elevator doors opened. They waited for an elderly woman with a walker to get off.

"I slept with her husband," said the woman with large eyes.

The fuzzy blonde's eyebrows rose. So, involuntarily, did Karen's. "Well, I was really safe for him, that's all. He's still with her, isn't he? She doesn't understand it, though." The women got off on three. Karen closed her eyes, leaned against the handrail, and thought of the broker she had taken to lunch. She found herself thinking of him sometimes because she was lonely, she knew that was it. Because she was here.

She opened the door, kicked off her boots, and stumbled upon her laundry bag. She dragged it over to the clean bed and nearly sat on her glass. She picked it up, poured another drink, and sat back down to drink and sort and compose a new country-western song called "You So Mean an' Ugly Your Hair Afraid to Move." "You so mean an' ugly you ain't never been in love / You so mean an' ugly I wanna give you a shove." (Poetic license.) The refrain was real easy: A long and slow "Mis-sus Sar-geant Ma-jor, Mis-sus Sar-geant Ma-jor, Mis-sus Sar-geant Ma-jor."

This new song gave her a certain satisfaction, as did the growing pile of clean underpants on the bed. Karen was the owner of thirty-two pairs of underpants, only three of which were recent, sexy string bikinis, white, and 100 percent cotton. These three she wore first, naturally, and moved on to the progressively more ragged ones through the next twenty-nine days of her wash cycle. She came by this impressive number through careful husbandry. Underpants were not thrown out until the elastic was so stiff with age that it stayed where it was when you stretched it. She wore them through holes and through period stains. Always clean, just stained. She never wore dirty ones, which was the point. The point was she couldn't bear dirty underpants and she couldn't bear to do wash, so she needed plenty of them. Also, it was not beneath her to take home the occasional pair of strange underpants she found lonely in a dryer. One current pair of unknown unders said "Calvin Klein" around the elastic, a purchase she would *never* have made, but as a found object they were OK.

Her wash also included several large men's V-neck undershirts, some big T-shirts, two bras, many socks, and four pairs of black pants. They were all the pants she owned. They were all she needed these days: two pairs of sweat pants and two pairs of skinny straight pants. Her pants were skinny though she was not. She was firm, but she was full.

She was wearing a headhunter skirt right now, long and tailored and gray flannel. It looked a little weird with her V-neck undershirt, she had to admit, especially with the combat boots, but she'd needed something to wear to the Laundromat. There was no one to see her, anyway. Her folding was done and in neat piles on the made bed. She laughed, took a sip, and wondered who might qualify as someone seeing her. What was the reluctant broker's last name? She decided this was something to consider further, and so lay back on the pillow. "Mark . . . Pizoski . . . Petrofsky . . . no . . . Pitofsky," she said aloud. She tried to summon his face but could not, just remembered dark eyes, the chicken pox scar and a one-sided dimple. Also, his body—she remembered the forearms.

Christ! It was almost dinnertime, and she needed to lay in more Tic-Tacs to face the gang in the dining room. She could not afford to miss dinner. She got back in the boots, tied them, picked her jacket off the floor, and pulled her black beret down low on her forehead.

She walked out past the elegant square, quiet in the frigid twilight without its children and nannies. She strode briskly past joggers and dog walkers and a man in an electronic wheelchair, past the graceful brownstones and private clubs—temples of wealth that stood in mocking juxtapostion to the Arcadia and its inhabitants.

As she turned onto the avenue, she became aware of someone keeping pace with her. He was rather short and very black, and his cheeks bore scars of a tribal past far removed from this cold city. The old Army jacket he wore hung thin and loose on his small frame.

"I think that it will snow," he ventured in an accent that Karen decided was resonant of deepest Uganda. He smiled tentatively.

And she had been avoiding eye contact, too. It frightened her sometimes, this inclination of folks toward her. She knew she had to be careful. Some people could hurt you. And anyway, there were such a lot of them. But this one was so harmless and so sad.

"Yes, maybe it will snow," Karen replied, wondering how much snow he had ever seen.

"What's your name?"

"Karen," she said, after a brief hesitation, and then—what the hell?—sometimes people needed to say their names, "What's yours?"

"Joe." She nodded at him. They walked in silence for half a block. She looked straight ahead but felt his eyes on her. "I go now to the AA. It's only five blocks from here."

"Well, good luck to you," said Karen, and considered that Joe had been an angel sent to warn her against afternoon drinking, to tell her where she could get help.

"I am not alcoholic," he said.

"Good," said Karen.

That makes two of us.

"I just go there to pass by the time. I never once drank."

"Oh, that's very good," said Karen as he turned off.

"Good-bye," he said.

Karen waved. But curiosity or her heart caused her to stop in front of Lamston's to watch him. It was a mistake, because when he looked back and saw her there, he misunderstood and started back in all simplicity and delight toward her. In a fright she saw years of yearning flash across his face. She turned quickly away and into the store.

She had meant only to get Tic-Tacs and change, but as she was on line, a display of amaryllis bulbs caught her eye. Oh, she would love to have an amaryllis breaking through, surging upward in that crummy room! All of the cold Februarys in her mother's house had been brightened by brash blooming amaryllis. If she had one, she could put it on the table between her bed and her roommate's, only it would be hers, and she would see how it had grown each morning. Four bucks. The florists charged twenty and theirs were already grown and blooming and therefore ridiculous to buy when the whole idea with an amaryllis was to start with a bare bulb and witness growth so certain and strong and exciting. She would have to buy potting soil, too, not to mention a pot. No, she could find a pot in the kitchenette and that would save a few bucks. She got off the line to look for potting soil.

 T he dining hall, just to the left of the lobby, was open when she got back, so she went straight in. It was a split-level dining hall. Karen walked up a few steps to the higher level of tables, which was never as populated as the lower. She found an empty table and dumped her jacket, the Lamston's bag, and the *Voice* on a chair, then went down again, through the lower dining room to the cafeteria line. She played a Tic-Tac against the roof of her mouth as she moved along the line, placing a plate of chipped beef and a small plastic bowl of grapefruit sections on a cracked turquoise tray that was shot through with an abstract silver design.

Karen had scorned the dining hall the first night she was here and went out to dinner with Annie to a fish place they liked in Chelsea. But she saw that her funds would not hold and that she'd have no choice but to partake of the Corps' rations. Even at that it was gonna be a good trick making her savings last until she got something else. She had $623 in the cash machine. Period. She had always blown her money—good eats and drink, movies, travel. And there were other things that had eaten at her savings, like the time last year when her brother had gotten hepatitis and couldn't work and of course had no health insurance, being a Social Freethinker. . . . Well, anyway, there was her Visa card, which she had already abused beyond repayment. There was a little left on the $5000 line of credit Visa had mistakenly awarded her when she became a headhunter, maybe $350, but at 19 percent interest. She could use it, maybe, but then she would really be on the edge.

She would know humility. She would eat in the dining hall and like it. She would know what it was to pirate out a carton of milk or a cherry cobbler, its sticky red seeping through the napkin, as she had seen some of the women do. She looked down her future, a sleazy succession of sneaked snacks.

Karen chewed her chipped beef as little as possible and marveled yet again at the room's decor. "Eclectic," is what *Home and Loft* would call the dining room, combining as it did Mylar patterned wallpaper with a pastoral mural of cows, sheep, and frolicking shepherds and shepherdesses. On each table was a paper doily. Centered on each doily was a milk-glass bud vase sporting a dusty plastic rose. At the far end of the room, between two large lamps with globes of hand-painted flowers, stood the Corps of Light flag in all its seedy majesty, its blue, purple, and silver reflected in the huge gold-specked mirror behind it.

BLOOD AND EARTH read the motto under the appliquéd silver moon, which was stained brown with something—blood, perhaps, or earth. Karen wondered if she alone among the residents knew the flag's motto. Blood and Earth—it made her think of her sister Sarah, who had once been the singer for Mother Earth's Own Blood, a rock band she had formed that had only played their basement on Congress Street. Sarah, braless in a purple T-shirt, with faded cutoffs and a bandanna headband, belting out "Get Offa My Cloud" to Karen and a few of her friends, who were young enough to be coerced to sit on the pool table and be a proper audience. Sarah was a nun now. Karen checked her watch. Sarah would have finished Benediction and her evening meal by now, and would be meditating in her cell for another twenty minutes before vespers.

Karen realized that someone was heading for her table, homing right in, when there were at least three other tables that were completely empty.

"May I join you?"

"Sure," Karen said, and shrugged. The woman was in her early sixties, Karen figured, her long hair plaited and pinned back. She was wearing a housedress with matinee pearls and canvas boots. As Karen was doing this sizing up, she realized that the woman may have picked her, Karen, to sit with because she was so attracted to Karen's Laundromat outfit.

She set down her tray. Did she really have to sit right next to her, not across? Karen removed her bag from the chair. The woman was wearing a name tag that said "Audrey." She sat down and twisted the pearls into a knot. Karen resolved to eat as fast as possible.

"May I ask you something?"

"Uh . . . sure."

"I just got back from a conference on Jane Austen in Denver. There was a luncheon, and I sat next to a young woman. To make conversation, I said, 'This is very good water. I come from New York. New York has very good water, too.'

"The young woman said, 'Which do you prefer?'

"I could tell she was being ironic, so I decided to play along: 'I'm not sure which I prefer. I'll have to let you know.' But then she said, 'It's no concern of mine which you prefer.' I was stunned! This was at a Jane Austen conference, too, and as you know Jane Austen was very ironic. But I was clearly an older woman and she was so rude. And then I find out that she was one of the moderators. And the discussion was on *Emma*. It's true that Emma was rude to Mrs. Bates. So what I wonder is, should I report her?"

Karen was furtively lifting her jacket from the back of her chair and quietly slipping it on. "Report her?"

"Well, *yes*," said Audrey, "to the Jane Austen Conference. She was clearly not in the spirit of Jane Austen, and here she is, the moderator."

"I don't know what to tell you," said Karen. She was standing now, hastily collecting her tray and her bag. "I think that's something you'll have to give a lot of consideration. Excuse me. I'm sorry. I have to call my mother."

The phone was free. Karen dropped in her quarter. Collect to Poughkeepsie, New York. Four rings. Margaret Carmody accepted grudgingly. It irked her like crazy to get collect calls from her children, and be thus rudely reminded of their sorry economic status. She had friends whose children could place their own long-distance calls, and could even afford to send flowers on Mother's Day! She had friends whose children were actual adults in this world. She was, on this account, short with Karen now.

"But, Mom, you called me. I'm just returning your call. And besides, you've got that long-distance deal. Anyway, don't you love talking to me? Wouldn't you pay any price to hear my voice, Mama?" Karen jollied her mother, which was her function, how they got by.

"How come you weren't at work? I got your friend Annie . . . she said you were sick."

"Yeah, I was . . . some bug . . ."

"Then why don't you stay home, if you're sick? You're never there either when I call, and then I got this strange woman, Lisa somebody, who said you moved. Karen, have you moved in with some guy and you're not telling me? Not a loser like that Phil, I hope."

Karen felt a lump rising. "Why did you want me to call, Mom?" Karen asked, her voice controlled. It was hard to avoid looking into Mrs. Sergeant Major's office when you used the phone. Mister Sergeant Major was there tonight, so uniquely himself, with scrambled egg braiding on his shoulders, his thinning brush cut, the red line across his narrow forehead from the too-tight uniform hat that now rested on his lap. He sat near the door in a chair that had a tie-on tufted pillow of American eagle print. She could see the solid block of

Mrs. Sergeant Major's hair unanimously bobbing up and down in emphatic agreement with whatever he was saying.

"I want you to come home this weekend," said Margaret Carmody to Karen.

"But I was just home."

"That was Christmas."

"But this is only February."

"I need you home this weekend, Karen." She paused. "Karen, if you must know, I'm moving! I'm having a garage sale and I *need . . . your . . . help.*"

"Where are you going, Ma?" Karen asked weakly, and massaged her right eyelid.

"Far. A new life. We'll talk when you get here, Karen. If you can't come home, I have no idea when I'll see you again. I'm counting on you. Your brother says he'll be there."

Well. Bill was coming. She must mean it if she's getting Bill there. Bill never went home anymore. Still, she couldn't believe her mother was really moving.

"Christ," Karen muttered as she hung up, at once angry and helpless at her mother's manipulations. She would go, of course. It might do her good, the train ride along the Hudson, so majestic now with its ice floes, its long-ago lighthouses, its banks lined with snow-bowed boughs of pine.

She stood for a long moment in front of the phone and thought of calling the broker. It could be very matter-of-fact, businesslike, to say she'd been fired but it was nice doing business with him. "I Just Called to Say I Got Canned," she sang softly to the tune of a Stevie Wonder hit. She had more quarters. No, she couldn't. Too late. She knew his office number, but no way would *he* be working late. Besides, someone was waiting for the phone.

The elevator was there. She raced for it. The closing doors separated her from her Lamston's bag. As it happened, Audrey was at the helm and pressed OPEN DOOR with alacrity. Karen smiled her appreciation, then closed her eyes and put a cool hand on her right lid until they reached the seventh floor. "I do not intrude," he had said, and those words played back now in Karen's head. Even his looks were not intrusive: shaggy brown hair going quietly bald, intelligent dark eyes that missed nothing. She remembered that under the bulk of scarf and jacket he appeared to be slim of waist and solid of chest. The arms. What she wanted right now was an affair with a man who did not intrude. What terrified her was intrusive sex. Insistent, arrogant, demanding men terrified her. But *had* this man intruded on her, that she thought of him still, nearly two weeks since she had seen him?

She unlocked the door to 742 with every intention of taking to her bed and thinking of sex with the odd broker.

She reached inside for the ceiling switch, but realized it was already on. In its dim light Karen saw that she had startled a large woman with long flowing hair standing beside the made bed. She was wearing a maroon down jacket, a denim skirt, knee socks, and loafers. On the floor beside her were two canvas bags. One said "Adidas" and one said "Vision Realty."

"I'm sorry," she said to Karen. "I thought this was 742, but I think I made a mistake."

"This is room 742," said Karen, and threw the Persian lamb down.

48

"But I asked for a single!" said the woman, bending to pick up her bags, then setting them down again, bewildered. "I'll have to go down and talk to them . . ."

"You can call from here if you want." Karen indicated the no-dial phone. "Just click down a coupla times." She put the amaryllis bulb and potting soil on her bureau, then sat on her own bed, switched on her lamp, and pretended to read the *Voice*. In the brighter light, Karen saw that the woman had a bad dye job, too harsh a red. She turned her back to Karen as she talked, and hunched over the phone in an attempt at privacy. She looked to be a woman of fifty.

Karen set the paper aside, stood again, and went over to the other bed to smooth out the pillow. She pulled the spread over it and tucked it in.

"Goddamnit!" the woman yelled suddenly, and slammed the receiver violently, near tears. Karen started. "I'm sorry," she said to Karen. "I'm very sorry. It's just that I had been really counting on a single. No offense."

"None taken," said Karen, collecting her Scotch and her glass and her underpants, transferring them to her own bed.

Chapter
3

Her name was Martha Leonard and she had come in from Ohio, she said. She said she was sorry again. "It was such a long bus trip. I'm just tired, I guess." She began putting her things into the empty bureau.

"Don't worry about it, really," said Karen. So this was the person she would be forced into intimacy with. They would see each other nude, they would endure each other's flossing and farts, catch each other's colds, know each other's habits. It was frightening, the amount of ire she had been able to work up for this unknown woman who was crowding her. And was that how this Martha person felt about her, about having to share with her?

Karen sat on her bed and assessed the woman from behind a magazine. She didn't have much with her, only those two duffels. Was that all she owned? Even Karen had more. Hadn't she accumulated anything in Ohio? A family, say? A life?

"I tried to take a nap on the bus, but I couldn't. Every other person had earphones, so there was this constant tinny blasting. It's almost like I can still hear it. I mean, how can you tell someone to turn it down when the point is you're not supposed to be hearing it? I mean, not the words, just this kind of by-product that keeps ringing at you. But I tried. I leaned around to tell the man behind me. He had these dark glasses on and didn't move when I spoke to him, like he was asleep and didn't hear me, but I don't think he was. That got me, you know . . . I knew he was putting on, so then I pressed the button on my armrest and leaned my seat back. Power!" she turned and laughed. "The seats are so close anyway. He forgot that he was supposed to be asleep and muttered something when the seat hit against his knees, but he kept his damn tape blasting. If he had turned it down, I would have put my seat back up. It's funny. I still heard his earphones, but it didn't bother me after that. Vengeance!" She laughed again.

Karen happened to share Martha's opinion of too-loud earphones, as well as her enthusiasm for vengeance, but merely grunted her concurrence. If they did have to be roommates, couldn't they do it honestly, grimly? Couldn't they can the chitchat and reserve talk for what needs saying, like, "You seen my Right Guard anywhere?" or, "You got a pen I can borrow?"

But no.

"God, that view is beautiful, the Square down there and all! And what are those buildings in the distance, those ones?"

"The World Trade Center."

"Just to think I'll be able to lie in bed and look out at it all!"

Martha was aware that she was ranting, but she couldn't help herself. She was giddy after being on the bus so long. She was disappointed to find this young woman here, this girl—not much older than her daughter, and so a girl to Martha. Martha was forty-seven, though she wasn't supposed to be. She wasn't supposed to be over thirty-five. The brochure for the Arcadia clearly stated it. "A home for young women eighteen through thirty-five years old." Thirty-five seemed so young to Martha. When she was thirty-five, she had been someone different, her children still with her, her life still unchosen. Now she was alone in a great city. She was exhilarated. She was scared. She talked.

"I guess this is the only game in town, eh?" Martha had taken a large plastic peanut butter container from one bag. She took off the top and dumped its contents, hair rollers . . . costume jewelry . . . makeup, into her top drawer. She stood, looking for a place to discard the container. "The Arcadia?"

"Uh, yeah. Guess so," said Karen. "Hey! Can I have that?" She indicated the container. It would be perfect for the amaryllis.

Martha, too preoccupied to be puzzled, handed over the container and continued talking. "I thought at first that I'd go to the Barbizon. When we got out of high school, my best friend Ursula came to New York to go to Katharine Gibbs. I remember writing to her at the Barbizon. That was the place where women alone stayed. Reasonably priced . . . clean . . ." Martha paused in thought as she smoothed out a sweater before refolding it and placing it in her drawer. The Barbizon had seemed some paradigm of freedom and happiness to her then, the place where Ursula stayed, the place Ursula had left for when they were both eighteen, but when Martha was nine months' pregnant and newly married in Ohio. Hadn't Sylvia Plath stayed at the Barbizon, too, when she was still a girl in New York? Martha had always thought of the Barbizon as a tower of gleaming white, probably because it was supposed to be so clean and safe, or maybe she was just thinking of the clean white gloves Ursula said she had to wear, along with a hat, to Katy Gibbs each day.

"Well," Martha continued, "I called the Barbizon, but it's not the Barbizon anymore. It's the Golden Tulip Barbizon, a luxury hotel, right? Nightly rates start at a hundred fifty dollars, exactly what this place costs a week, and we get meals!" She stopped talking suddenly, worried that she had given away her age by this business about the Barbizon. Who knows, it might have been years since the Barbizon was a residence for young women. She had to be careful. She had to be in New York. She had to thirty-five. Anyone could report her. This girl could report her. It would be in her interest to get rid of her. No! She was just being paranoid, as though all the cautions she had heard about the city had seized her spirit now that she had arrived.

"Not exactly the place for struggling secretarial students these days," said Karen. She punched a hole in the bottom of the peanut butter container with a ballpoint, then lined it with pennies for drainage since she had no pebbles. Maybe the pennies will grow into a money tree, Karen thought.

Martha studied her roommate. Though she was very strangely dressed, she was rather pretty. Quite guarded, though—the way she held her arms across her body, the way she checked her smile. Those boots she wore, and her haircut, so short on top—she couldn't tell whether it was a kind of New York style or meant to put people off. One thing. She had the most extraordinary eyes, Martha had noticed them immediately, large and strangely colored. Eyes that could rivet you and hold you there.

When Karen glanced up, Martha looked away quickly and went back to her work. She took a large, worn, well-stuffed manila folder from her bag, looked at it, hesitated, then placed it in the drawer with her sweaters. "So then I called a Y . . . I got the Sloane House on Thirty-fourth Street," she said. "Singles there are twenty-nine dollars a day, no meals, no kitchen, and the maximum stay is only twenty-five days. It's a lot cheaper here. You know what was weird, though, about the Y?"

"What?" asked Karen, feeling calmer now that she was up to her wrists in potting soil.

"They asked me to bring a passport or a driver's license to prove I'm not from New York. Isn't that odd? Isn't a New York Y supposed to look out for New Yorkers first? What's wrong with being from New York? I mean, the whole state must be filled with undesirables!" Even Karen laughed. "I'd always heard that the city was, but this was news, about the state."

Karen took the bulb from the box, happy to see that a green shoot had already broken through. "Yeah, well, they probably think, if you let a New Yorker in, there's a good chance you'll find syringes in the room when he checks out."

"Well, I must say, I *did* start to wonder what I was headed for if a New York City Y excluded New Yorkers!"

"So, how did you wind up here?"

"It was listed in *New York on Ninety-five Dollars a Day*. I called and had my intake appointment over the phone." Martha wondered whether Karen had had to make the same promises to Mrs. Sergeant Major: that she was a woman of good character, that she wouldn't drink or entertain men in her room, and agreed to a security deposit of four-hundred dollars, to be held in an interest-bearing account in her name. And, over the phone, Martha had volunteered these two lies: that she had never been married and that she was thirty-five. "She *promised* me a single," she said aloud and then, quickly, "It's fine, honestly, just a little small."

"It's tiny," said Karen, dragging her fingers around the bulb, making little tracks in the soil. Karen wanted to ask *why* she was here, in New York. Instead, she asked, "How do you like the curtains? They did that in your honor."

"How sweet," Martha said.

Karen set the plant on the windowsill near her bed. *Sweet*! Christ! When was this woman going to cut the Pollyanna act? You have to take a break now, Karen told herself, then did. She went out into the crisp night and walked uptown for several blocks before coming back to Ralph's for a beer.

"*I* have a roommate," she told George, the bartender at Ralph's.

"Uh-oh. Yeah, I had one of them once," George sympathized, "but the litter box started to stink." She ordered a draft, which was only $1.50. She paid it, hesitated, then counted out change for George's tip.

Ralph's was a block away from the Arcadia, a bar Karen had actively cultivated since her arrival. Karen was a firm believer in having a bar of one's own.

Especially now. She had noticed, to her chagrin, that other denizens of the Arcadia shared this belief. She avoided them when she saw them at Ralph's, having no wish to know the sad parts of their lives. They were in it together, but she wanted to be out of it. If you didn't know them, then you couldn't be them. She knew what she was doing, avoiding them. Like they were all scrambling for the same lifeboat or something. If you kept yourself clear, didn't talk to them, didn't socialize with them, they couldn't drag you down, you wouldn't be submerged.

A bunch of P's for Pathetic. Ah, but it had come to Karen harshly in recent days that there were women at the Arcadia who were less P than she! Many of them seemed to have jobs, or a pretense of employment, and went out each morning with a briefcase, an artist's portfolio, or a backpack of books. There were women there who had a place to go and something to carry each day.

Still, there was no way she would drink with them or play bridge with them in the lounge. No way would she become one of them, laugh at their jokes, or go out in a group to D'Amato's on Friday night, never mind, (she did mind; she minded greatly) that she didn't have the price of dinner at D'Amato's. Salvation was in separation. She would not be of them.

George delivered her beer, foam frothing over the iced mug. George was small and neat, with fox eyes and fox features. He always wore a crisp prepster button-down, with a clean bar rag tucked into pressed jeans. His straight brown hair was on the long side, combed carelessly back. George's stated ambition was to get enough cash to buy his own place. Karen saw that he was accomplishing this in part by stealing from Ralph's till. She'd watched him enough in two weeks to realize the game he was playing with the cash register, ringing up the price of a draft when he had actually served and charged for a shot of Chivas, then keeping the difference. Or sometimes, if she paid careful attention, Karen saw George play a game called Five for Ralph, One for Me, the tab for every sixth drink going into the jeans pocket under the clean bar rag. She did not let him know she was on to him. Should she judge him, or was this the way the never-present Ralph had come by this place, the time-honored career path by which a bartender becomes a proprietor?

Damn. The man on her left was smoking a cigar. He was heavyset, with thick neck, thick mustache, thick curly hair. A heavy breather working on early emphysema. He held the cigar in one hand and in the other a small flashlight, with which he perused a folded *Times*, resting on the bar next to a glass containing a clear liquid and two small onions. "So," he said, looking up at George. "Any good Warhol jokes yet?" Andy Warhol had just died.

"Not yet. Have some decency, man! They haven't even done the autopsy yet." George winked at Karen. "Victor here is doing a book of dead jokes."

"Oh?" said Karen. She was still sad about Andy Warhol. She looked sidelong at Victor and sipped very slowly. She had to nurse this beer.

Victor leaned his head back and blew the offensive smoke straight up. "Got any?" he asked her in a moment.

"Got any?" Karen repeated weakly, misunderstanding. Her right lid gave a twitch of warning.

"Dead jokes." She looked quizzically at him. "You know," he explained, "like 'What did Princess Grace have that Natalie Wood could've used?'"

George groaned and left to take a waitress's order at the far end of the bar. Karen wanted George to come back. "I give up," she said to Victor.

"A good stroke," said Victor. "Get it? Grace Kelly had a stroke and—"

"I get it," said Karen.

"So," said Victor, turning off his flashlight and setting it carefully beside his drink. "What about Liberaces?"

"Huh?" Then she realized. Liberace had died recently, also. Actually she did know a couple of Liberaces from Michael in the office. Liberace was the last luminary to die before she was fired. Wall Street was rife with dead jokes and Michael got them straight from the brokers. Sometimes he would repeat them to other brokers as an opener before giving them the Exec-Career pitch. She shrugged. "Uh, yeah . . . I know a couple."

"So tell me."

"I should blush to tell you!" They were vile.

"Tell me one."

"No."

"I was out of town when Liberace died, so I missed them."

"I can't."

"I'll buy you drinks all night." She didn't think he was kidding.

"No."

"You're telling me you have information that I

need for my livelihood and you won't give it to me. I've even offered to pay you."

She tried to lighten things. "No way am I gonna tell these jokes to someone I've just met in a bar. Besides, I always liked Liberace. Why should I perpetuate these calumnies?" She did. She liked a lot of these dead guys and it made her sad that they were gone. Cary Grant— the woman who was the real Auntie Mame—William Holden—Truman Capote. William Holden had been dead a few years now, but Karen still missed him.

"But there is no calumny in death! In death they belong to me. I assure you this would be a purely professional exchange." But his banter had taken on a menacing tone. She saw that he wasn't going to let up, that he was verging on hostility. She considered giving him Exec-Career's number and telling him to call between nine and five for Liberace jokes, but why should she sic this creep on Michael? She had a flash of Mark Pitofsky then, his deferential behavior toward the homeless woman in the park. Victor took no care with his smoke as he turned to her this time. "You're a woman in a bar by herself. So, what're you doing here? You shouldn't be here if you're gonna be a candyass about a little language."

"You know, Victor, I think we're at an impasse. In fact, I don't think there are any grounds for continuing a conversation. I just wanted to say this, though . . ." Victor began to protest. "No . . . I have to tell you that I think you could've picked a more . . . oh . . . *uplifting* subject for a book." Did she hear "pussy" under his labored breath as she smiled stiffly at him and turned away? He will die young, she reminded herself. She was glad to see that Elly, George's sister and a Ralph's regular had taken a seat on her right.

George came back, greeted Elly, and presented them with a plate of bleu cheese potato skins. "There's a new show at On the Wall," Elly said. She removed the soft electric blue leather gloves Karen had seen each time she had seen Elly. Lined with cashmere. Karen lusted over those gloves but didn't hold them against Elly. They had run into each other the other day at a Seventh Street gallery, so they had now had this basis for conversation. Karen expressed interest and tried to listen as Elly and George talked, but found herself tuning out of the conversation, thinking of Liberace and Truman Capote, of her sister Sarah, given to God and lost to Karen, asleep at this hour on her pallet beneath the crucifix, of her mother moving far away, of the strange woman in the room and the man who had read poems to her in Paley Park. Her mug had been empty for a while. She said good night and left. Victor did not turn around.

When she returned from Ralph's, Room 742 was in blessed darkness and Martha asleep. Karen put the pile of folded clothes on the floor, added the ones she'd been wearing to it, and climbed in. But it was early and she lay without sleeping.

The fact was, Karen was in a panic. She held herself in the dark and told herself that there was no cause. You have food, a place to sleep, clothes. You'll right yourself soon, sweetie, she told herself. Sometimes she called herself sweetie . . . Sweetheart Angel Karen . . . what Sarah used to call her when they were children, who hadn't called her anything in years.

She put her hand between her thighs and held it

there. Merely held it, not masturbating, but holding it tightly there. It sometimes calmed her. You escalate things, Carmody, but there's no reason. You're being self-indulgent. Things will change. Think of what real panic must be like. Think of that woman you read about today in the *Voice*, untended, on a respirator in a nursing home and maggots start coming out of her mouth, like something in a goddamned horror movie only it happened right here in New York. Forget about the maggots. You could be cared for on a respirator in a clean place and know panic.

She held herself and sang herself "All the Pretty Little Horses": "When you wake, you will have cake, and all the pretty little horses . . ."

What we got here is nothing, she consoled herself. What we got here is a temporary situation. So why do you insist on inflicting this permanent condition upon yourself? Think of all the young men dying in this city. Think of all those out on the streets tonight. Think of Ethiopia, think of Lebanon, think of your mouth being hooked to a machine for the rest of your days. Think of Colombia, thousands smothered in volcanic mud. That way lies horror, permanence, panic . . . She couldn't help it. Sometimes she could pull out of it, but not now. But at least she had lifted herself from indulgent ruminations to a purer plane of global dread. The end was the same. She did not sleep, she who had gotten so good at sleep, especially in recent weeks.

After some time she heard a stirring and a moaning from the other bed. A moaning though her roommate was asleep. Crying from the depths of the unconscious. Karen shuddered to think that her own body could emit such sounds, expose her so cruelly, while she lay bound and helpless in sleep. Actually she had heard this kind of spectral moaning once before, from Phil, a man she had loved for a long time and lived with a short time. He had cried in his sleep, actually wept. When she told him about it the next morning, he was angry. "Why didn't you wake me?" he demanded, furious. He told Karen then that his father had committed suicide, hanged himself. He was a child and he had found him, and his life was plagued by dreams of him. His saying that brought them closer than they had been before. Or so Karen had thought. Actually, he had not wanted to be with Karen after that.

Should she wake Martha now? Could she save her from some pain of loss or agony of longing if she just shook her awake, shook her back to their dark room and only the moderate terrors of wakefulness? Karen decided that she had to do it, that she'd want someone to do it for her. Also, so that she, Karen, would not be chilled by those ghostly sounds through the night. But, Christ! Was it going to be a nightly occurrence, this preternatural moan and Karen's morbid closeness to it? Karen sat up, ready to go to the other bed, when the crying stopped. Finally, she slept, but lightly, afraid of the deep sleep.

"Save me a seat!" Martha called gaily from the bathroom as Karen left for breakfast the next morning. As though they were college roommates. As though they were friends. As though Martha really gave a damn about talking to Karen. As though any of the other women would be vying for a seat near Karen after the mantle of secrecy she had thrown about herself in her two weeks here, her adaptation to life at the Arcadia. Saving someone a seat in this dining hall was such a quaint notion that it lifted Karen a bit from her boiled egg and coffee. (One cup, not two. McDonald's gives you a second cup on weekdays, but not the Arcadia.) The idea of saving a seat amused Karen so much that she actually would have saved it for Martha if anyone had wanted it.

Martha approached, balancing her tray, a briefcase, and a jacket. She was wearing dungarees and a black Shetland sweater, a bit pilled, a little tight across her full breasts. "Thanks," she said to Karen as she took her seat. "Looks good," said Martha. She was referring to the boiled egg, Karen realized. "Is it usually?"

"The food? Here's the menu for the week," said Karen. It was encased in plastic, propped against the bud vase. "Read it and weep! For instance, here we have tonight's mortification of the flesh and spirit."

Martha read it in silence:

Navy Bean Soup
Liver and Onions or Cheese Omelett
Harvard Beetts or Buttered Carrotts (Frozen)
Pear w/ Cream Cheese
Ginger Bread w/ Cream

"Well, she said, "I opt-t-t for the omelet-t-t, what about you?"

"Oh, definitely, but I'm trying to decide between the beet-ts and the carrot-ts. Ah, but check out tomorrow's listing!" She indicated:

Chow Mein w/ Fried Noodles
Golden Glow Salad
Asst. Puddings

They laughed, but Martha seemed distracted, her eyes surveying the dining room. She probably adores the shepherdess mural, thought Karen. But Martha was not concerned with the decor.

"Why are there elderly women here?" Martha whispered. "I thought everyone would be . . . well . . . our age."

Our age? Karen liked that. "Huh?" she asked.

Martha inclined her head in the direction of a woman, perhaps in her seventies, who had just passed.

Karen realized then. "Oh . . . you mean, because of the brochure, 'eighteen through thirty-five'?" Martha nodded. "Oh, yeah, forget that," Karen said. "There was a fire in another home the Army ran for the aged a few years back, and this place got all the refugees. This place takes everyone—young, old, retarded, artists, students, models, and nuns whose convents got made into co-ops."

Martha managed a weak smile. "Gee, I really believed thirty-five was the cutoff," she said, thoughtfully tapping her egg. Karen saw then that this misunderstanding was the explanation for the "our age," and felt a stab of pity for this Martha, who thought she had to pass to be here, and had come here anyway. She thought again of the moaning in the night.

She must want to be here in a bad way, thought Karen. But when she asked her why, Martha only shrugged and said, "The city . . . I like what can happen in the city." Martha ate quickly and excused herself. It was her first day in New York, she said. She had to get going. There was a lot she had to do.

Karen lingered for a while in the dining hall over an abandoned *USA Today*, then checked her mailbox. There was a message from Annie in her mailbox. The phone was free and she had a little change. That was all she had. It seemed like she had just gone for a hundred at the cash machine and now she would have to go back.

"Exec-Career," Annie said brightly. "Oh, it's you. I'm beginning to feel like I'm the operator on 'Lassie' and you're Timmy's mother, taking all these messages."

"So? Who?"

"I forgot to tell you the last time I talked to you . . . A guy called and said you were supposed to get back to him. I said you had left the firm and that I was handling your clients. He seemed pissed off, wanted to know where you'd gone. That was last week sometime. Anyway, he called again yesterday."

"Yeah? What did he want?"

"He wants you to call his office. He said it was unfinished business. What *kind* of business, Carmody?"

"What's his name?" She knew his name. She was smiling into the receiver.

"Some Polack name . . ."

"Be careful, I'm part Polish, y'know."

"Well, in that case, I'll say it nice and slow." They laughed. An old joke. "Ma-rk . . . I don't know. It begins with a P," said Annie, and gave Karen his number at work, which she already knew. "Gotta go."

Karen dialed his number. As it was ringing, Audrey emerged from nowhere to form a line of one behind Karen. She was holding worn copies of *Emma* and *Northanger Abbey*, tapping them with impatience. He answered, a pleasant tenor.

"Hello, this is Karen Car—"

"I know who it is. Why didn't you call me back? You aren't with Exec-Careers anymore."

"Yes, I know that," she said. "I got fired."

"Oh."

"Somebody else can help you."

"But I *liked* you. I'm rather discriminating about who I let hunt my head. Are you going with another firm?"

"Actually I'm . . . looking."

"I'm really sorry."

"It's OK. Maybe it will turn out to be a good thing. I didn't really like it. It's just that . . . getting fired does such rotten things for your self-image, you know?"

He laughed. "So. You mean it was all for nothing?"

"What?"

"Our lunch at Burger Paradise. You mean I took time from my busy schedule just to chat with you?" She was quiet, unsure of his tone. "Here I thought I was advancing my career." She laughed.

"Your first three minutes are up . . . Please deposit ten cents for the next three minutes . . ." She only had seven cents.

"I have to go—"

"Karen, give me your number, I'll call you . . ." But Audrey coughed significantly just then, and Karen caught a glimpse of Mrs. Sergeant Major's lacquered locks just inside the door to her office. She couldn't stay on and she didn't know the switchboard number.

"I'll call you again. It's hard to call me."

"Why?" he asked in mock alarm. "Are you being held hostage? Where do you live?"

"The Arcadia," she said, simultaneous with the disconnect. She'd call him again just as soon as she came by her next quarter.

Chapter
4

The lounge was a large room on the ninth floor. The far wall was taken up with a refrigerator, a soda machine, an inactive change machine, and a dispenser of such tasteless treats as packets of peanut butter on bright orange crackers. In the center there was a small pool table upon which rested a large rabbit-earred television set. Metal folding chairs were arranged in front of the television, and these same were used for evening service. In the corner opposite the refrigerator were two old brown cut-velvet chairs, once overstuffed, now losing their stuff through random rips in the upholstery. Between these two was a straw peacock chair with a red corduroy cushion. They were arranged around an old hooked rug, an attempt at home.

Next to this cozy setting stood a typing table with an old Smith Corona. A card table with four more metal chairs completed the furnishings. The beige walls were accented by oil-by-number paintings done by residents, a Matisse print, and a jigsaw puzzle of pandas, its pasted pieces polyurethaned permanent. A few acoustic tiles were missing, and some were stained where the lounge had suffered a leak. The flooring was dark red linoleum speckled in primary colors, a pattern very popular during the Korean War. Yellow vinyl tape, chosen, Karen was sure, to highlight the yellow speckles, traced over the cracks and picked up dirt at its edges. But for all its faults, the room was large and bright, exposed to the south with many windows.

Karen was there at the typewriter after her breakfast with Martha, after her call to Mark, after a quick dash out to the cash machine and to the stationery store to buy a new ribbon to replace the worn one she had found when she first inspected the ancient machine. She inserted the blank page which was to be her updated résumé. She would begin her job hunt in earnest today. So much energy and depression had been expended just relocating and adjusting to the Arcadia that to date she had had only a couple of disheartening meetings with employment agencies and a few fruitless calls to friends and friends of friends. The unfeeling digits on the cash machine lent real urgency to her task: $335.25 left, even less than she had thought. She stared hard at the page, considering how she would unify her jobs on paper, disguise them, make them look like someone's proper career path.

Why couldn't she keep a job? She had always avoided therapy, but she knew the idea of it was to pin everything on your family, your childhood. It was true she had seen about jobs from her mother's job at Hardesty and Loomis, her father's law firm, a job awarded her mother in lieu of a proper widow's wage. Her mother had been indebted to Hardesty and Loomis, and always in debt because of them. And Karen had seen how important the striving was by watching the ambitious young lawyer her father had been turn yellow and die. She had seen her mother's sustained state of surprise at the turns her life had taken. She wished she could just blame it on the death and low-lying loss and get on with things, but it didn't seem to be that easy.

Two elderly women came in and took metal seats in front of the television. Karen heard the sound track from "Gilligan's Island."

"We've seen this," said one, fragile and neat, with a very short haircut and a kelly green turtleneck tucked into baggy elastic-waisted pants. She got up very slowly and flipped the dial.

"Housewives do it for refrigerators," a prostitute-turned-author was earnestly telling a talk show host.

"Hah!" said the other woman, whose thin white hair had yellowed to a mockery of blond. She fingered a surgical bandage on her cheekbone. "So we're all hookers, is that it?"

"Well, of course, but what does that make Betty Furness, peddling refrigerators all these years?" asked the one with the turtleneck. They laughed.

The woman with the bandage bent to a striped cloth bag on the floor and removed yarn and a crochet needle. They settled in, one making afghan squares, the other whipstitching the squares together, watching the prostitute with great industry and good fellowship. Karen turned back to her task.

"I don't judge housewives," the prostitute was saying. "It's a matter of taste. Me, I'd rather order out."

Karen typed: *Fatality Specialist, New York State Department of Motor Vehicles.* How she worked her way through Albany State. Pulling the pink forms from the sheaves of yellow. Yellow meant an accident. Pink meant death. For months after, the job had held her dreams hostage. She would wake at night with images of infant heads splitting against windshields. Arms and legs hurled four lanes across the thruway. A young man decapitated on his motorcycle. Burning flesh and stinking tire in a four-car immolation. The quiet typed letters on innocuous pink Rediforms could not control the horrors for Karen. A child burning in his infant seat as his parents watched helplessly. What speed? Were they wearing seatbelts or not? How many this Memorial Day? Was it a DWI?

Once, while scanning a pink for its yield of gore, she had been forced to reread. She hadn't understood. A cow. A cow had been hit on Route 208 and carried an eighth of a mile on the hood. Someone had filed a Fatality on the cow. There was one extra person alive in New York State that day! It had been a light moment in a bleak job. She ripped the sheet into tiny pieces and tossed them like confetti into the trash bin, raised her Diet Pepsi can aloft and sang a few bars of "Let the Good Times Roll." Her fellow workers had been quite surprised at such an exultant display in the New York State Department of Motor Vehicles.

She typed in a quick summation of her work in Fatalities, then paused before typing *Employment Counselor, Labor Department*—her first job in New York. She had been an employment counselor specializing in subemployables. They were P's before anybody had ever coined the letter, chronic unemployment beaters (alleged) who were rerouted to Karen and her colleagues before they collected checks. They were, very often, truly pathetic. But some were very smart.

"I keep seeing green dots on the page," said Teresa

H., a thin, wanly chic woman, a proofreader by trade. "Whenever I start a job, they're there. They get in the way of the words." Karen had agreed that green dots on the page were a tough rap for a proofreader. "Do you see them anyplace else?"

"No."

"So, what do you do?"

"I tell the boss."

"About the dots?"

"Sure."

"Listen, maybe that's not such a good idea. Next time, tell me, not the boss. Just give me a call and we'll talk about it." Karen was able to get her a job at Tucker, Mussman, and Burstein, but worried that the proof-reading done there was too demanding. She got a call the second day from Teresa's supervisor. She had insisted he call Karen. She said there was a reason why she hadn't read any proof, but she wasn't allowed to tell him or anyone, and she wouldn't leave the premises until Ms. Carmody, her advisor, personally escorted her away. She told them she was only following Ms. Carmody's orders. She said it was her right as an unemployable to have Ms. Carmody as counsel. Karen was unemployed the next day, but after her experience there she could not bring herself to apply for unemployment. She could not even now.

She had lasted only five months with the Labor Department. How could she type that on the résumé?

Exasperated, she ripped the paper through the platen.

She was stopped. Blocked. Résumé writing should have been a snap for Karen after her jobs, and her jobs advising others about their jobs, but things got in the way: The sticking *a* key. Karen's apocalyptic view. The *n* that skipped. The prostitute's discussion of the importance of job satisfaction. The dried-up Wite Out. Did the struggle really availeth? Karen thought naught.

She stuck another sheet of paper in. This time her fingers flew over the keys.

RÉSUMÉ

Karen Carmody, *Diversified*
The Arcadia on the Square
New York City

PHONE: Incoming Only
EDUCATION: Masters in Deprecation, Destruction (Self), and Disillusion.
Honors in the One-liner.

BUSINESS HISTORY: What's it to ya?

INTERESTS: Myriad.

CAREER GOAL: Creative Avoidance of the Street and Ultimate Bagdom.

Variations of this vital vita were prepared and discarded through reruns of "Carol Burnett," "All in the Family," and "The Waltons." Karen had just finished typing "For Me to Know and for You to Find Out" as "Family Feud" ended. It was noon. She had labored long enough. It had been a useful exercise. She still had no résumé, but she came away with this: there was not a job she wanted in this world that a résumé could get her. There was a reason why she had had so many jobs. She didn't like them and she didn't believe in them. She was not of the straight working world. She wanted something else. She didn't know what yet, and she was too old to be starting, but she thought it had to do with those papier-mâché tiger lilies she wasn't making in her room, or all the movies that had made her weep, or the way she got ripped apart every time she read the poem "Márgaret áre you gríeving / Over Goldengrove unleaving?"

It has been a kind of wish, her lie to Mrs. Sergeant Major, saying she was an artist. *An artist.* How did you dare really call yourself that? It was what she wanted, though. Was it possible you started with the yearning and then found something to fill it, that it didn't come to you full-blown? She would find something, and in the meantime, she wouldn't take a job that would sap her.

Sure, what she really wanted was to direct movies and eat lunch out with Mel Gibson and get paid big bucks. Didn't everyone? But, ah! The difference between her and everyone was that she wasn't going to settle anymore. She would take all or very little. And you couldn't get to be a director or a waitress or an artist with a résumé.

Strange, she thought, how you had to live through things before you understood the bald truth of something heard so often you had dismissed it as trite. Yes, it was true! Most jobs ate at your soul. Hadn't songs tried to tell her, with lines like "workin' for the man every night and day," and "I owe my soul to the company's goal . . . " Hadn't the Sixties? Hadn't her own father, by drinking to death on his job? Hadn't Ralph Kramden and Ed Norton tried to tell her on "The Honeymooners"? She hadn't even listened, not really, when as great a personage as William Wordsworth tried to tell her, all the way back at Albany State:

The world is too much with us; late and soon,
Getting and spending we lay waste our powers;
Little we see in Nature that is ours;
We have given our hearts away, a sordid boon!

It was one of the poems she carried with her always, but she hadn't understood the poet's urgency until this moment.

Why take on another job that would eat at her soul and make it smaller? And, when it had had its fill of her, body and soul, it would spew her forth, and, for this, take its credit on her next résumé. Another job at this point would be simply a delaying tactic, not a solution. For now she would be low on cash, but large of soul. Karen shunned small soul.

Expiation had occurred. The need for the summation of her life on twenty-pound bond had been lifted from her. And now, to celebrate, she would go to the Van Gogh show with her free ticket.

After breakfast with Karen, Martha sat in the small parlor opposite the security guard, opened her guidebook to the subway map, and carefully rehearsed her way to Police Headquarters. It was to be her first subway ride and she was very frightened, though strangely elated, as she walked to the IRT. Though she knew her stop was to be Brooklyn Bridge, she asked the token clerk anyway, because it seemed an odd name for a subway stop. Yes, the stop was Brooklyn Bridge.

A blind man was singing on the subway platform as she waited—"Somewhere Over the Rainbow." His voice was dark and old, and the song, so misplaced on the indifferent platform, took on a new, raw meaning. Martha bent to put a dollar on the pie plate in front of him, hoping no one saw her, hoping no one would think she was carrying a lot of money. A cold wind, a deafening roar, a beam of light, and then the train. It was the Express. Good. She had heard that the trains would be covered with graffiti, but this one wasn't. This one was clean and shining stainless steel. Martha was disappointed that she got a seat and couldn't be a straphanger. Why were they called straps when they were made of metal?

She looked up at an ad that read ARMANDO VARGAS, VICTIMA DE HEMORROIDES. Armando, whom the ad identified as a restaurant worker, appeared disconsolate about his plight. Martha hoped he had gotten a lot of money from Preparation H. She looked out as the train came to a halt. Onion Square. No, Union . . . someone had topped off the *U* with marker. She checked her map once more. Three more stops, then it would be Brooklyn Bridge. The woman next to her was reading a newspaper in Russian maybe, or Swedish. Martha made out the word "Horoskop" in a headline, but then forced herself to concentrate on the windows so she wouldn't miss her stop.

At Brooklyn Bridge, she followed the crowd upstairs and emerged, bewildered, under a dark Gothic portico, to freezing gusts, sunlight, and the bridge just beyond, cars speeding by. A man passing out leaflets for a new beauty-aids discount store pointed out Police Headquarters, a modern brick building across the square, next to an old church.

Once inside, Martha was stopped at Reception by a young black woman wearing a pink maternity dress. Martha presented identification and received a pass:

Headquarters Visitor. M. Leonard. Destination: 1110. She removed her jacket and stuck the pass on her black sweater.

Missing Persons is located next to Arson Explosion on eleven. Martha hesitated a moment before the door, raised the strap of her small shoulder bag over her head to rest on her left shoulder. She had been wearing it more securely across her body and under her parka, a precaution for the subway. She shifted her parka to her right arm and entered. On the left was a dingy wall covered with faces of missing children, wanted posters, and a notice for the 2nd Annual Police Commissioner's Sports Dinner Dance. There was a high counter on the right, behind which a young woman sat. Her eyeglasses were Scotchtaped together, but her long hair was neatly brushed and shining. There were several phones and a computer terminal on the counter. On the wall behind the woman was a clipboard holding special forms. The clipboard was marked ETAN PATZ in large dark letters.

"I'm looking for my son," Martha told the woman.

"How long has he been missing?"

"A long time," said Martha. "Six years. But he's been seen recently . . . a friend saw him."

"Have you checked your local precinct?" the woman asked. Kindly, Martha thought. She didn't ask why she was only looking now, the question Martha always asked herself.

"I don't have a precinct . . . I'm not from here."

"Is he under eighteen?"

"Not now, no. Well, but he was. I mean, six years ago." Martha was suddenly feeling quite warm. The room was overheated, and after being outside in the freezing cold . . .

"We can take down an inquiry, but we can't follow

it up, not if he's over eighteen and been missing a while. I'm sorry." Martha took the report, four carboned sheets, white, buff, green, and blue, and began filling it out, though she knew the futility of it and saw the futility of it in the kindly gray eyes studying her from behind the broken glasses. "Name—James Leonard, Jr. Eye color—blue. Hair—sandy. Blood Type—A Pos. Scars?" Yes, he had a scar, a small one, bisecting his left eyebrow. He got it when he was a baby in the backyard, tripping as he got out of the wading pool, falling against his wagon. It had bled a lot but stopped. She didn't take him in for stitches, but was sorry later. It might not have scarred if she had taken him in for stitches. It had gone deeper than she thought.

Clothing? She didn't know about clothing, certainly he had no jewelry. The friend who saw him said he had a beard now and that he was quite thin.

"I have a picture and dental records," Martha told the woman.

"We can keep them on file, of course."

"Do you have pictures I can see?"

"I'm sorry, we only have morgue shots."

Martha paused, holding the counter against a wave of dizziness. "I'd like to see them, please."

The woman picked up the phone. "Detective Figueroa," she said. In a moment there appeared a rather short man, whose athletic build was giving way to paunch. He had a dark complexion with a light flecking of acne on each cheek, thick dark curls, and a mustache. "I don't know whether you wanna do this, lady," he said. But Martha did.

He ushered her into a room with blue walls and a

dirty gray floor, gray metal desks and file cabinets, piled with phone books, large cardboard boxes, and computer paper. A detective sat at a computer terminal, his back to them. "He's entering on the national system," Figueroa explained, then indicated a desk Martha could take. He looked over the report Martha had just filled out and left the room. Martha waited, staring blankly at a sign taped to the wall: COMPUTER WHIZ KID AWARD.

Figueroa reentered with a tray labeled "MW 1986," all white males, all dead in New York City in 1986. He brushed away a ripped Sweet'n Low packet and placed the tray on the blotter in front of Martha. It was the beginning.

Martha spent the entire morning flipping through the morgue shots, trays of them, six years' worth of unidentified dead white men. She did not notice when the man entering on the national system left. Figueroa came and went, bringing new trays. There was a number beneath each face for cross reference to the Mortuary Processing Sheet which detailed the place and manner of death. Martha did not refer to any of these numbers. None of these faces could be Jimmy's face, they could not be. Polaroid death masks, hundreds of them: old and young faces, mummified faces, rotted faces, bloodied faces, bloated faces, waxen faces, eyes closed, eyes opened, dark and empty sockets, toothless mouths, mouths closed, mouths eaten away, mouths opened, surprised by death. Faces of damned dead men framed Madonna-like in folds of morgue sheeting. Faces of dead men now buried in Potters Field on Hart Island. Buried by convicts. Figueroa told her they had to bury them standing up. He told her, then immediately apologized. Standing side by side, an army of the dead, unknown soldiers all. After the first tray she saw the impossibility of it, of finding his face in any of these faces, the blond boy's face which would have become a man's face in the years since she had seen it.

When he was in second grade Ms. Walther taught them haiku. Jimmy's was "Deer Grows Up":

> *There once was a fawn*
> *He liked his jolly mother*
> *He left her today.*

The fawn, covered brown and spotted in pencil beneath the haiku, was smiling in pencil. The mother's face was indistinct beneath brown crayon. There was a pencil line drawn down the middle, separating them.

"It's very pretty but it makes me so sad," Martha had told her little son.

"It's not sad, Mom. It's just a deer growing up."

Figueroa brought her in a cup of tea, weak and sugary, but she sipped it gratefully. "The job gets to you," he said. "We got volume here, tremendous volume. These small towns, we get inquiries from them all the time . . . this one's missing, that one . . . why didn't we respond quicker, all that. But they don't know New York. They have *no idea*."

There was something driving her to see them all, beyond reason or hope. Was it for Jimmy, or had it somehow gone beyond him, to take in them all, to be a kind of witness to them? Or was it a kind of penance for the missing years, to be sitting here now, sipping tea from a dirty cup and going down, down into it? And Figueroa, sentinel to sadness, allowed her take her time. When she had finished the last tray, she stood up, dizzy and nauseous, and reached for her jacket.

"Thank you," she said to him. She leaned against the desk to steady herself.

"I'm sorry, miss. I have kids myself." He reached in his pocket and produced a neatly folded handkerchief. He unfolded it and gave it to Martha. She took it dumbly, not realizing until then that she had been crying. She wiped her face with it, then held it crumpled and soaking. She could not give it back to him, and besides she still needed it. He indicated with a small movement of his hand that she should keep it. Martha leaned toward him, meaning to shake his hand. Instead, she hugged him, pulled away quickly and confusedly, and left.

Chapter
5

Karen stopped back in 742 for just enough time to drop off her typing paper, splash water on her face, and don her jacket and beret. She walked in the cold sunshine toward the train, grabbing a slice along the way. The Arcadia did not serve lunch. She asked for water with the pizza. "We don' sell water here," said the pizza man with some irritation. "Good," said Karen, and smiled expectantly.

He served two more people, but at length brought Karen a green-striped paper cup. He shook his head and laughed. "Thanks," Karen said, then took a sip and carried her slice to a stool by the window. As she sat down, she saw a familiar figure in the passing crowd. Martha, heading back to the Arcadia, her red hair stuck untidily into her hat, her purse strapped across her jacket, walking quickly, on guard against New York. Karen was glad she had left their room when she did.

At the Metropolitan Karen plunked down three dollars for the commentary cassette, rationalizing that she hadn't had to pay the entrance fee. The place was crowded for a weekday afternoon, people genteelly jockeying for position before each work. These were Van Gogh's last paintings, done in the asylum at

Saint-Rémy and in the town of Auvers just before his suicide. Karen looked upon his coarse strokes. Childlike, she thought, and so childlike and true in the feeling. The eerie hallway of the asylum, the sinister sun over olive trees, the terrible *Wheat Field Under Threatening Skies with Crows*.

"Was this his last picture?" the refined voice over the cassette puzzled. "Did the crows express despair or hope?" Was it her mood that she couldn't see any hope in this painting? Was she clinically depressed, as Van Gogh had been? Three roads ending abruptly, nowhere to go, stark stalky fields, dark sky and crows above. So. Where was the hope? She thought of *Lust for Life* and this man who had had several false starts before he found his art, who interpreted Christianity too literally and gave away all he owned, who longed for love and community and who was always lonely.

Searching for hope, she left *Wheat Field Under Threatening Skies* walked back, against the crowd, to *The First Steps*, a painting of a mother supporting a child who is about to leave her arms and walk across a small sunny garden to her father, who kneels waiting, arms lovingly opened and beckoning. But this picture, which minutes before had seemed happy, now made her sadder, so sad to know that a man on the brink of suicide could paint this scene of domestic bliss, feel it so acutely and tenderly, because he never had it, because he never would.

In the small grouping around *The First Steps* she felt someone looking at her. It was Phil. She had not seen him in months, but now he turned quickly when she saw him. She had loved Phil, and did a little now, since she didn't shake love that easily. Phil. Tall and angled, of bird beak nose and large dark eyes. She had lived with Phil on Thompson Street, before Lisa's sublet. He was an art teacher in a Lower East Side public school. His kids' creations were all over his small tenement: masks of happy and sad faces, construction paper farm animals made three-dimensional with crumpled newspaper stuffings, self-portraits in charcoal. Phil was an artist, but it was enough that he could stimulate his students to do poignant Magic Markings of "What I Lost" or "Something I Want to Remember." It had been enough for Karen. It was something she wanted to remember, those hot spring nights on the fire escape with Phil and a quart of Budweiser, looking out over the bocci players across the street. It was something she had lost.

She saw him now in a violet wash of pain. Hers. Hers knowing his. *"You cried in your sleep last night. What made you cry?"* A cramped walk-up, freezing in winter, torrid in summer. Neither of them had had any money, and he blew what he had on marijuana, beer, and art supplies. Sequins and sparkles for the kids, yards of netting and Mylar and cellophane, stacks of colored lucite blocks and tubes and prisms. All stuff for his students. It was manic, misplaced, this devotion to his students' art. She knew this now with time and distance. You couldn't move in the place. But at night their naked bodies would be luminous, absorbing light from prism and street lamp and Mylar, glistening bright with sweat.

"Phil!" she said.

But he had turned away and was walking quickly back to the beginning of the exhibit. There was no point in following him. He did not want to see her. Karen stood there until she was jostled by a woman backing away from a painting. She collected herself then and walked toward the exit. She stopped and bought a postcard of *The First Steps* for forty cents, handed the cassette player to an attendant, hung her earclip on the earclip tree, and left the museum.

*A*lone in the room in midafternoon, Martha rose from the bed where she had been making jottings from the phone book of numbers and addresses of social agencies. She had to get ready for her appointment with Father Hartnett of the House of Hope. In the bathroom she washed her face. Her eyes were still a bit puffy from the morning, so she held a cold washcloth against them for a moment. When she removed it, she stood and studied herself in this new place.

What she saw was a big woman in a turtleneck and jeans, ample of bone, long of waist, and wide of hip. "Good pelvis," her doctor had said, and patted her on it appreciatively after she delivered Jimmy. Doctors liked it when you saved them work. Her only lines were fine crosshatchings around eyes which were deep-set and dark. And she had recently noticed the inexorable workings of gravity in the flesh around her mouth and beneath her chin. The movement downward had begun. Not too bad, she thought, but she guessed that in matters physical she was capable of self-delusion. She had read that, in a poll, most Americans said they thought they looked younger than their age.

She was named for the biblical Martha, of Martha and Mary, and for that reason did not like her name.

Poor sad Martha, running around getting her Lord Jesus Christ's lunch together, only to be told that he liked Mary better all along. It was really a parable about how men set women up, one against the other. She could just see this Martha, smiling bravely when Christ gave her the word about Mary. She would rather have been called Eve: fallen, sexual, human, woman. Or Magdalene in her wanton state, before she got all repentant, washing Jesus' feet with her tears.

She had always been pretty, she knew. She had asked; she had been told. But recently, after the divorce, working her job at the Landlocked Dock, she had heard a customer ask the hostess for water.

"Who's your waitress?" the hostess had asked.

"The pretty one," the man had said. Martha had heard him, a frail man in a red windbreaker. There were only two waitresses on that afternoon, Martha and a rather sullen young woman. Martha was not his waitress. She would not have minded if he had said, "The young one." She was not young, but she was still pretty.

When Martha was in first grade she was obsessed. From the time she started in September, every day without exception, she had to ask the teacher this question: "Do you like my dress today?" "Very much, Martha," Miss Blaisdell would always say. Martha was compelled to do this. It mortified her mother and enraged her father when Miss Blaisdell wrote of it on a note on the back of her report card. One wet afternoon her mother had picked her up and they were already at the A&P before Martha realized: she hadn't asked Miss Blaisdell the question! She insisted that they go back, and back they went, waiting while Miss Blaisdell tidied the classroom and donned her raincoat, her mother glowering in the doorway, for the moment when Martha could ask her question.

"Do you like my dress today?"

"No, dear, I think it looks awful," replied Miss Blaisdell, wisely but too late. It was already April. Still, Martha had been cured of this particular obsession.

There were others which would follow.

She had gone to a psychiatrist and they were still there, so it must mean they were supposed to be there. They were hers. She decided to embrace them.

Always the need, always the question, asked in one way or another, of men—always men—men she knew, men she didn't know, men she loved, men she hated, men she slept with, men she didn't: "Do you like my dress, do you like my breasts today?"

She was not religious, though she had read the Bible and plenty else in her years in Cornwallis, Ohio. She knew about poor old Job and Martha and Mary and Lot's wife. Lot's wife looking back. Like herself yesterday. Looking back on a life gone, though she turn to salt. Weeping over a life gone. A husband left, a son lost, a daughter come to womanhood and living far from her. She had cried quietly on the bus yesterday, the tinny sound of little earphones all around her. But she felt better now, maybe because she had had the strength to go to Missing Persons. She carried her grief still, but she knew how to use it.

She had been married before Jim Leonard. Her first husband Brian had pleased her briefly and then died drunk when his car careened on the treacherous road near Moonwink's Grill. She was twenty-three, with a five-year-old daughter. Jim Leonard married her two years later and everyone told her how lucky she was. A college graduate. Heir to Cornwallis Electric Supply. Solid. Taking in a widow and her child, a child who had been conceived out of wedlock, everyone had known, for though she and Brian had married, they married after Leslie's birth. Everyone had known, which was why they also knew her good fortune in marrying Jim Leonard.

She had not much wanted another child. Jim's anxiety when one was not immediately forthcoming disgusted her. To seal the deal. She knew that was what it was. Produce an heir to the heir of Cornwallis Electric. Show the world that he wasn't shooting blanks. The dead Brian Kane had not shot blanks.

It was the son they had then and whom they had now lost, who had caused the dissolution of their marriage. She could not stay with her husband after Jimmy left home. She was unable, after that night, to share a bed with him or prepare food for him. She was unable to eat food, in any case, or sleep in any bed. If it weren't for Jimmy's leaving, she might have stayed with him, so inert had she become, and so fearful. For she saw now that it was an inertia rooted in depression, and a bad fear that bound her to that small place.

But she turned cold to Jim Leonard on the night, damp and dark as sorrow, the night she realized that her son would not come home, that he had left in anger and would not return.

She had wanted to search for him! She wanted to call the troopers, hire a private detective, wake up the one teacher he had cared for, or the girl he liked who had stopped by once with a homework assignment. She wanted to go out along the railroad tracks and walk beside them to see if she could find him there, waiting for a train to jump, though she didn't know if there were trains still, the kind you could jump. Then out to I-75 and drive along looking for hitchers, for a slight blond boy hitcher, for hitchers going to Saginaw maybe, or south to Cincinnati. She wanted to do anything that night. (He was gone and this was the night, not weeks from now, but now. You had to say, when something happened, that it did happen.) She wanted to do something for the grief she felt, and the guilt.

She had not been a mother to him. It had been too hard to show her love for him because he was the son of a man she had never really loved, he looked like that man, a man she felt forced to marry. She could not give him the unbridled love she had lavished upon Leslie when she was a baby. Actually she had not wanted another child after Leslie. James Leonard, Jr. Even his name was his father's.

She had wanted to find Jimmy that night, and hold him to her in the rain, show him too late that she was his mother, that his heart was formed from her heart, his pain hers. "Let's *go!*" she had said to her husband, throwing on a jacket (she later dumbly looked at the sleeve and realized it was the boy's denim jacket) and rushing into the garage.

"We are going nowhere. He knows where we are," said Jim Leonard in the doorway lit from the kitchen, framed by shelves of paint cans and turpentine and gray jars of nails. "You are not to start that car, Martha. He'll come back, but when he does, he'll have to answer for it. And if you go, don't come back." He returned to the house, as Martha leaned against the wheel. The horn honked, then stopped, and there was no sound anywhere but the sound of rain and weeping.

She looked for him after, futilely, hopelessly driving to this town or that. She was disorganized, helpless against the magnitude of the task and her loss. He didn't return the next day, nor in a week, nor in a whole year after. She went to the police after the first few days, but it seemed foolish—too late, too hopeless. She went to a psychiatrist who merely shrugged. "There's nothing you can do," he said. "He wanted to go, so you had to let him. Searching for him is out of the question. You'll upset yourself and you might not find him." But Martha didn't believe that. He was a psychiatrist doing his job, which was to make her feel less guilty. That's what they always said, "It's not your problem . . . don't feel responsible . . . you've done what you could, so don't feel guilty." Martha felt guilty. She blamed herself. Sometimes you were responsible for things. She thought of him often each day, what she should have done.

Jim had thrown Jimmy out because he found a packet of white powder in his drawer. What had Jim been doing in his drawer? But privacy was not permitted. "Get out of my house, you bum," he said, the last words he every spoke to his son. "You were never any good. You'll never amount to anything. I don't want to look at you." His words were spoken in such a controlled voice that they meant "I would kill you if I could."

And Martha had stood weakly by, staring numbly at the needlepoint she had done in the days when she had done such things. "Love one another," it said, and roses twined about the letters. "Love one another," it admonished, over the door that Jimmy walked out. She had been unable to stand up to her husband and his wrath, and she would never be able to put down her fury at her failing.

Jim Leonard had never loved the son he had been so anxious to have. He was the boy's father. The boy looked like him. But it was easier for Jim Leonard to be kind to Leslie, Brian Kane's child. It had to do with his own stern father. Oh, it was too complicated about families! It made Martha heartsick to think of it, how you could go back and back and find the same problems in every generation. Jim Leonard held himself in contempt, because, among other things, he had gone away to Stanford only to return to the place he had always been and run his father's store. He thought it was a failing. He hated himself. And so he could not love his son.

And so Martha left him. She could not sleep in the house, she told him. She stopped working at Cornwallis Electric. It was only temporary, she said. She had to be away for a bit. Friends had a converted basement, a little kitchen and bath. She could stay there. She stayed too long. He wanted her home, but she wouldn't go home. He stopped the money then and she got a waitress job. She took up with men in time, different ones, and it eased things some when she was with them. She was shameless about the men for a while, and in a small town, too, but she never thought of shame.

Though she had thought of men often enough. It

was, in fact, how she had gotten through all her days at Cornwallis Electric: lust. Literature helped, too, all the books she got from the Bookmobile and read during lunch hour. But mainly it was lust and her own imagination that saw her through; her ability to, say, become aroused by some craggy carpenter's dispassionate request for just the right female part for his male plug. Discussions of electronic couplings never failed to excite Martha, though the workmen involved did not seem to be aware of metaphor.

Martha worked at the Landlocked Dock for months which turned to years. She slept with men and saved money and told herself she would one day find Jimmy. Butch Costello, an old neighbor and a friend of Martha's from high school, came in to the restaurant one day. He had been to New York and said he had seen Jimmy there, on Astor Place. He hadn't been sure at first—the person he saw had a full beard and Jimmy had been a boy. But when he spoke to him, it was Jimmy, all right, and he asked to be remembered to his mother.

Martha grilled Butch about Jimmy and found out he had lied. The boy he had seen was Jimmy, he was certain, but so gone on something that he could not know if he had ever come from parents. Martha questioned him so relentlessly that he said he was sorry he had told her anything at all. How had he looked, Martha asked. What did he say? Where was he staying? Butch was evasive. He was so sorry. He had only made it worse for this woman he had always liked. Her son was doing very badly. Drugs—a life on the streets. It was him, no question. Butch remembered carrying little Jimmy home the day his dog had been hit by a car, Jimmy in his arms, the bleeding dog in Jimmy's arms, and Martha's face as she opened the door, frightened that the blood was the boy's. How could he tell Martha what he really had seen? He was so sorry.

But the news of Jimmy decided Martha. She must go to New York. She called her lawyer, who said she'd be getting a settlement soon, a lump sum, and she gave notice at the restaurant. She had to be in New York, to make herself available for any hope at all.

She was very glad to be here, even in this room. After a life spent in a small town, she craved anonymity. She liked knowing no one. She liked being alone. She liked being free. She liked being in New York, where anything she chose to do could be done without comment. She was tired unto death of comment.

She believed that in New York the significance of a person's being was made more so by that person's being there.

She hummed the song: "I want to wake up in the city that never sleeps." Corny. She loved it.

New York, they said—they had heard of it. Some had actually been there, and a few had been on the subways. They said don't go, you'll be alone. Even Jim Leonard dared to say don't go, you'll be alone. You're crazy, he said. He said there's a plague going on in New York right now. Would you go to a place if you knew the bubonic plague was there? Well, he said, same thing. It's only sperm now, but it will be saliva soon, he said.

They said you're not strong, you'll crash. They said you're unbalanced, and this she certainly was. She thanked them all for their good wishes and left.

She would use the money well. It was hers: the house, the stocks, the business were in both their names, after all, and after twenty-two years she had earned her share. She would get it soon, and in the meantime, she resolved to live as frugally as possible on her savings and on her temporary settlement of eight hundred dollars per month.

In spite of everything, in spite of the sadness of her mission, she didn't think she was unhappy. She couldn't suppress this feeling she had that, at forty-seven, she was starting. Almost that, in pretending to be thirty-five for the Arcadia, she had actually become thirty-five. Sometimes she tried to slap herself down, tell herself it was ridiculous to feel this way. If anyone knew, if Karen knew, she would pity her. It was her midlife crisis come late.

She donned her jacket and stood looking at the Square below. How did people ever get to live their lives in Manhattan, do dishes, buy stamps, attend the PTA? How did they accomplish the ordinary things, with curtains rising all around them, on hundreds of stages each night, with artists and sculptors and opera singers for neighbors, with newsstands and restaurants and bookstores and galleries offering excitement and variety? Wasn't the energy released by the ideas and undertaking too heady for ordinary pursuits? Even if you didn't go anywhere, didn't the choice you had to make not to do these things leave you exhausted? Even if you weren't an opera singer, you breathed her air.

She would learn, too, to live her life here, to be about her business.

You're going through the change, she warned herself, as she went out, taking care to lock the door behind her.

*　　*　　*

*T*hough it was freezing, Karen walked all the way home from the museum, down Fifth, then over to Park and through Grand Central Station. There were homeless people scattered throughout the station, in the hard pewlike seats of the waiting room, on the cold floor beside growing lines of commuters at the gates: an old woman leaning against the information booth wearing a dirty windbreaker and a new pair of argyle socks, but no shoes; a man with a knit cap pulled completely over his face rocking back and forth and moaning. They were there for the same reason that Karen was there, to escape the cold. But there were other people, most people, who were there only because they were on their way somewhere else. And all of them together beneath the vaulting ceiling of awesome beauty that illustrated the constellations of heaven in gold leaf. Gemini, the Twins, the Ursas— Major and Minor—Sagittarius the Archer. It frightened Karen to see the outcasts in this place, for she had come to see herself as a kind of outcast, when she followed her situation to its logical limits. She knew, of course, that she was far better off than these unfortunates, but she was too smart to think that she could never be of them. Karen looked at the well-heeled people waiting to get to Westport, some carrying flowers, others with their briefcases or Benetton bags. She looked in dread at the abandoned old woman, then rushed out into the street.

She began to obsess as she walked, thinking of the housing crisis in Manhattan, and her pathetic place in it. She thought of Lisa the actress's large sunny studio on West Thirteenth Street. She walked on in the cold of Forty-second Street and thought of the place that had never been hers in the Village—its tiny ancient stove, the thick layers of white paint, a half century's worth of paint, melting the molding's once-defined design. A rustic pantry in the entranceway was her only closet. Shelves rose high to the tin ceiling and she needed a stepladder to reach the flour or her thesaurus or Lisa's colander on top. Karen crossed at Lexington, mercifully unmindful, as she stepped off the curb, of her near brush with death at the wheel of a kamikaze bike messenger.

The actress had come home and claimed her place.

Was it possible to be suffused with nostalgia at so recent a state of one's existence? Too early for nostalgia, Karen decided. Call it what it is. Out-and-out grief. Nostalgia kicks in when mourning ends.

Karen arrived at the Square and walked around it to the Arcadia, nodding to the security guard as she walked toward the elevator.

As she walked down the hall to 742, she heard someone, in another room, singing "Amazing Grace" in pure-voiced simpleminded fervor.

> *When we've been here ten thousand years,*
> *Bright-shining as the sun . . .*
> *'Tis Grace hath brought me safe thus far,*
> *And Grace will lead me home.*

Karen resented how these old hymns held the power to wrack her heathen sensibility. "Adeste Fideles" was another killer. Martha wasn't there. Karen flopped facedown on her bed. Things sure were easier ten thousand years ago when she made her First Communion. Time now for the assumption of the fetal position. Sing it, sister. I hear.

The phone woke her.

"Is Mrs. Leonard there?"

"I'm sorry, she's not. May I take a message?"

The caller hesitated. "It's Father Hartnett from House of Hope. I guess she's on her way."

Karen hung up. House of Hope, eh? Martha must be checking out new digs. Maybe the House of Hope has singles. I should look into it, too. Father?— Catholic? Episcopal? If it was Catholic, they might let you drink. But you'd still have to contend with the Catholic part of it. There might be rules against lapsed Catholics checking into Catholic hope houses.

The phone rang again just as Karen was reaching for the Scotch. Amazing! And that this call should be for her. It was from downstairs, Mrs. Sergeant Major announcing that there was a gentleman caller waiting to see her, Karen, in the lobby.

Chapter
6

In the parlor a man wearing a long striped scarf was waiting uncomfortably in a small wooden chair, the knobs on its rungs at odds with the discs on his spine, even through the protection of his worn leather jacket. A small rack on a table said "Take One." He did. Inspirational literature—Self Improvement With God's Help. He folded it idly and stuck it back, then thought of the book in his inside pocket. It was probably a mistake, coming here.

"Hi, Mark," said Karen, standing in the doorway, touching her right eyelid nonchalantly with two fingers and smiling against her will, unable to hide her pleasure at his presence. "How did you find this place?"

"It was on the corner," he said. They laughed, and then were quiet.

"You never called me back," he said accusingly.

"I didn't have a quarter," she said. A quarter was easy. The truth cost more.

He rolled his eyes at her lame excuse. "In any case, I thought I would look in on you. I don't live all that far from here. I was a little concerned . . . Also, I had to drop a jacket off at a tailor right around the corner. He does excellent work—"

Karen interrupted him. "I'm glad you came," she said. She looked down at her scuffed boots, up at a Monet print, through the door to a woman at the bulletin board, then back at Mark. "The Ritz, right?" she said at length, with a gesture that took in the lobby, which now included Mrs. Sergeant Major, who seemed suddenly to have the most urgent business to discuss with the security guard at his desk.

"It's not that bad," said Mark.

"We can't have men upstairs," she said, to say something, then felt herself reddening.

"So," he shrugged, "we could go out. We could go to the movies. Would you like to?"

"I have to get my jacket," said Karen, trying to recall which underpants she had put on that morning. Too, she was painfully aware that she was still wearing the same grubby black sweat pants she had been wearing since she did her wash. The knees to these pants were out there somewhere by themselves, no longer in any contact with Karen's knees. "I'll just be . . . uh . . . five minutes."

Back in 742, Karen surveyed her clean unders. She found a pair of faded pink cotton—lace trim, a bit ripped at the seam, an errant string she dared not pull. But she deemed them acceptable on two counts: for their unstained status and for the fact that they were bikini. She stripped down, pulled them up and then a clean pair of black skinny pants, which she nearly ripped getting over her boots in her haste. "Haste makes waste," her mother always sang.

This possibility of sex for the first time in months made her reach deeper in her top drawer for the joke present Annie had given her on her last birthday. It was a small box, elegantly wrapped, accompanied by a lunatic verse of Annie's:

> FOR KAREN
> *The flaming hetero*
> *Must rein the libido*
> *As never heretofo.*
> *If you cannot refrain,*
> *Do not disdain*
> *These here*
> *Through the next year*
> *Of living dangerously.*

A box of Ramses, "for her pleasure . . . electronically tested for reliability . . . size Large."

"Only Large?" Karen had asked Annie, laughing. "Is that all you wish for me? Didn't they have Super? Didn't they have Colossal?"

"Well, you want them tight, don't you? You don't want the damn things to *fall off*, do you? I got a package for myself while I was at it. Wishful thinking, and all. But it was so *strange*, buying condoms, like the first time I had to buy sanitary napkins and this boy I knew was working at the drugstore. Anyway, it's just what you wanted, right? Good things come in small packages . . . get it?"

Karen hid the box in her purse and raced for the elevator.

She hesitated before entering the parlor, studying him, poor unsuspecting male, hunched over his reading. He was her kind: passive—private—weird—smart. Not that, if she were writing a program for her life, she would have typed this kind of guy in on her floppy disk, but she had been preprogrammed. Type "Man," press Return, and this was what came up on Karen's screen. Every time.

And, he had searched her out and come to see her in this place!

He looked up and smiled broadly at her.

He's sort of handsome, she was thinking as they went outside, but then she noticed that he was putting on gloves that had a face at the end of each finger, gloves a little kid would wear. She had seen illegal Andean peasants selling such gloves near Washington Square. Inexpensive, serviceable wool gloves, very warm, no doubt, and that's what he'd tell her if she made fun of them, but really! So foolish for a grown man! Each little face had a different primary color tuft of wool for hair. Good, she thought. I'm glad he's wearing them. It will help me resist him.

They went to the Film Forum to see *A Geisha*. His suggestion, which pleased her greatly. They stood under the marquee in the frigid early evening. "Let me pay . . . in honor of your unemployment." He produced an ancient wallet.

"No. It's against my principles." *Men Don't Pay* was the motto she might have emblazoned on her flag when she got around to commissioning one. "Anyway, you've got to save your money while you can for the Gulf of Cadiz," she counseled. "You could be in the great state of unemploy soon, the way you're not calling new retirees and widows."

"But I made a few calls today," he protested.

"Wonderful," she said.

"A couple of people asked me to send them more information." His single dimple was working now.

"Terrific."

"One guy said he was thinking of buying his wife a Krugerrand for her birthday in April. That's only two months away."

"Well, you're a damn star, Pitofsky!" Karen said, and they both laughed. "Yeah, but you wouldn't sell a Krugerrand, would you? I mean, South African investments and all."

He looked askance at her. "But don't we live in South Africa?" Karen nodded her head, considering this. He went on: "Well, there's just no escaping these difficult moral decisions in the workplace, is there? Should you sell a pint of Thunderbird to a gone drunk? Should you sell Krugerrands? Should you hunt the head of an indolent broker? Anyway, madam . . . you bought lunch at Burger Paradise, I pay for the picture show."

"Exec-Career bought lunch."

"In any case, you were the means of a sumptuous hamburger at no cost to me." He smiled. "It was a pleasant lunch, wasn't it?"

"Yes, " she said. She relented and let him pay. It was a relief. There was no way she could afford to be going to movies right now.

Men Don't Pay could have been the motto for *A Geisha*, too. All about how these geishas have to spend yen they don't have and yen their families don't have, start-up money to buy stiff clothes and heavy wigs you can hardly move in, and for what? You get to sit around all day on your straw mat waiting for a bunch of men to call you so you can jump into your duds and put on black liquid liner that makes a point, and then hobble on over to make them tea and make them laugh and then make them. Karen was raging at men when she came out. It wasn't the right movie to see with a new man.

"But it was made by a man, see," Mark explained. "So we all can't be shitheads."

"You mean Kenji is a boy's name?"

"Indeed," his dimple doing double duty. "Mizoguchi is a boy." He was delighted to give her this information.

Karen was astounded that a man had made this movie. Sometimes, though, men surprised her. "Are you a shithead?"

"Stick around," he answered, and smiled as he adjusted his gloves. "So, uh, what do you want to do now?"

It was freezing on Watts Street. Karen knew what she wanted to do. In the middle of the movie he had taken her upper arm lightly and leaned toward her, ostensibly to whisper something about the geisha's father. But when he moved away, he left his hand there on her arm, his fingers resting quietly against her breast, until, toward the end, they began a small, stroking movement, at first nearly imperceptible, then quite definite, the backs of his fingers against her sweatered breast. When this had begun, Karen leaned low in her seat and let her leg fall wide to rest against his.

Karen knew very well what she wanted to do. She wanted to lie with him. She had not had sex for so long! She wanted to be touched again, have someone feel her, make her feel, make her feel him. "We could go to your place, maybe . . ."

"But aren't you hungry? I thought perhaps we'd get a bite someplace."

She was starving.

His reluctance now surprised Karen after the backs of his fingers. Had she misunderstood, been too for ward? No. This was what men and women did all the time. It's just what Karen hadn't done in a while. He stood considering in the cold. Karen felt her ardor cooling along with her toes.

"We could do that," she responded, "or we could bring in moo shu pork."

"OK," he said. But he still stood there, considering. "Let's go, then," said Mark Pitofsky finally, and five little people grabbed her hand.

She was worried when she saw his place. Home for Mark was maybe a step above the Arcadia. A one-bedroom apartment he had rented furnished years before. The furnishings that weren't his included a couch and a chair done in a once lively, now dingy, quite horrible fern motif. The bedroom door was ajar, and Karen could see packing crates and books. He never used the bedroom, he said it was where he stored everything he got in the divorce. It depressed him. A pile of library books lay on the floor in the living room, next to a television and a VCR bearing a red "Ace Rentals" sticker. He was a minimalist before Zoran ever caught on to the scene. A wooden clothes valet held cufflinks, sock garters, a cordouroy jacket, and several ties of doubtful taste. The man seemed not to own anything but the items on the clothes valet. Karen was enough of a materialist to find his fact dismaying. She wanted one of her friends, someone, just one of them, to own something.

"Nice valet," Karen said, grinning, running a hand

reverently over the base of the catch-all dish. Mark had taken off his jacket and undone his tie. "Oh, here, let me hang that up!" said Karen, taking it and placing it carefully atop its unattractive brothers between the metal tie demarcations.

Nice body, she thought, but didn't say. Hard underneath the loose oxford cloth shirt. You could tell how slim the waist and narrow the hips by the way the shirt bunched going into the baggy chinos. And now he had begun the ceremonial rolling up of his sleeves.

"Are you getting ready to eat or are you really glad to see me?" Karen asked in her best Mae West, but was immediately sorry when she saw how her remark had stopped him, left him without comeback, flushed in mid-roll. She turned away, absently picked up a sock garter for inspection, then, realizing, put it down in mild horror.

He had been watching her intently as he opened the refrigerator and reached for a bottle of Gatorade. "You hate it," he pronounced, and didn't just mean the sock garter. He set the Gatorade on the table, picked up the bag of Chinese food and looked at it as though he hadn't seen it before, set it back down, found a glass and poured her some green. "But I can't help it. It's me. This apartment, these clothes, this refrigerator" (the door still open: ancient, frosted over, and dank) "are what I am. I have no ego."

Karen sat on the couch and sipped tentatively at the Gatorade, even though she knew it really wasn't made from alligators. She also knew alligator wasn't endangered anymore, but she had always been a bit picky about what she consumed, and this was such a strange green, maybe squeezed from Everglades slime.

And this was such a strange man, now sitting on the folding chair before her, telling her he had no ego.

"Don't give me that. Lack of ego is bullshit. I don't even know what it means, no ego."

"It means I'm free."

"Yeah, or maybe it's your first line of defense."

"Go ahead, tell me anything, it doesn't bother me, whatever you say."

"Of course not, because you have no ego," said Karen, and they laughed.

She looked at his pile of library books on the floor and thought of the old man the *Post* found dead in his apartment with hundreds of unreturned library books around him. Mark Pitofsky looked nice, but his place made her think he had mass murderer potential. She shivered a little, but the clearness of his smile reassured her.

He interrupted her maudlin musings. "So, uh . . . whaddya wanna do now?"

"I dunno, Marty, what d'you wanna do?"

"I dunno, Angie, what d'you wanna do?" he asked, real Ernest Borgnine. "What about a little moo shu?"

Damn, why is it always me? Karen wondered, but plunged ahead anyway. "Um . . ." She leaned toward him and kissed him for the first time. She kissed him again. She touched the chicken pox scar between his eyes. "What about a little do you?" she said, and swallowed hard.

"C'mon," she urged, touching her deviated septum to his perfect straight nose and rubbing her lips lightly across his. "Don't you think a little display of affection is in order?"

He obliged her as far as leaving the folding chair and moving next to her on the couch. "I thought that was what you wanted. Look, I have to tell you something," he confided. "You're more experienced than I am."

Karen shrugged. She was more experienced than a lot of men. Just not lately. "Don't worry," she said with exaggerated brightness, "I'll show you what to do."

They laughed, then were quiet. She remembered the box in her purse. Damn! "In fact," she said mysteriously, "I even brought props." She stretched and grabbed for her purse, unwilling to leave his side now that she had gotten him here.

"What did you bring?" He sounded nervous. Did he think she had handcuffs or whips?

"You might not love it . . ." She sheepishly showed him the box, and, to make things lighter, quickly explained her birthday present and recited Annie's poem.

He laughed, but weakly. "I suppose I should be flattered that you think I'm active enough to have acquired an immune deficiency."

She couldn't tell if he was annoyed, but it sure had broken the mood. "I can put it on for you . . . " she said.

"On me, you mean," he said, smiling.

"Yes, you jerk!" She put her hand on his knee and kissed him. "You do want to?" she asked.

"Oh, indeed!" He put his hand in her hair and began massaging her scalp, a little too vigorously.

"But do you want to, really?" She put her hand up on his thigh and wondered if she dared move it higher. His chinos were just too baggy to make an assessment of dilation and blood flow without a hands-on. "Because I think my ego's getting involved here. I happen to have one, and it needs a certain level of enthusiasm in situations like this. So—are you or aren't you?"

"What?" he asked, smiling, drawing her toward him.

She opened her arms and held him. "*Enthusiastic!*"

For answer he suddenly began kissing her, his tongue strong in the recesses of her mouth, his fingers running back and forth over the ribbing at the bottom of her sweater. It seemed he was. She began to lift her sweater over her head.

"No," he said, pulling it gently back to her waist. "Maybe not now." He was breathing heavily. "I'm sorry," he whispered. "Maybe another time."

Why? Karen wondered, knowing there would be no other time if there wasn't this time. As she searched his face, she felt a flash of fury. "*Yes, now!*" she whispered back at him, determined that he would at least see her. She pulled her sweater off in a kind of frenzy, she undid her combat boots, then the rest—bra, pants, socks. She wanted to be *seen*, that was part of it. She would bare herself and make him face her. So much of sex for her was the other's eyes upon her, the watching. She wanted the darkness of his eyes now. She would not be cheated of that, at least, not after so long without, and certainly not after his tongue. She looked at him until he sighed, placed his hands heavily upon her arms, and pulled her back down to the couch.

"*I*f you did have an ego," she told him later as she chomped into her moo shu pancake, "it would have been very proud of your id tonight."

"Thank you very much," he said, beaming.

And much later, as he locked his door before taking her down to the street and a cab, she stood on the landing looking at his uncombed hair, the honest bald spot, the unruly cowlick in the back, the wanton hairs that came over his upturned collar. She felt a mix of happiness and dread, knowing how deep he went.

Karen slept very late the next morning, dozing in and out, vaguely aware of Martha, sitting up and working on her made bed. She woke to feel his spirit lightly, like cirrus clouds about her. She wanted to stay in bed and think of where and how he had touched her, to think of his fingers moving slowly and repeatedly over her lips. She wondered whether he would ever touch her again. She was confused. She needed to think. She needed solitude.

But here was this lady, this intruder in her room, diligently about some kind of work. An intruder wearing a dose of sinus-zapping cologne. In truth, all colognes had this effect on Karen's deviate nose. Even if Martha did leave, her scent would hang heavily, disturbing the cirrus clouds, causing her to sneeze. Was the cologne a stratagem to drive her out of the last room in Manhattan?

Martha heard her stirring and looked up. They exchanged awkward greetings. "Hi," was how Martha put it.

Karen responded guardedly. A nod merely. She was not sure how much to read into this hi. What exactly did Martha mean? Judgment, of course, about the fact of Karen's late night. Was she some kind of Holy Roller who really belonged here, who would actually go to the Corps' evening services in the lounge?

"We missed you last night." Read: *Where were you—out screwing around with someone you just met? Do you do this often?* And who was this "we"? Karen hated it when people appropriated the royal we for themselves.

"Uhhh," said Karen. She would not offer an explanation. She did not need to account to this woman. Though she was older, Martha was not her mother. What was she thinking, Karen wondered. Did she think that sleeping out was a regular occurrence for her?

Christ, Carmody! What is your story? You're the one that's setting it up, not her. She said "Hi." You know what that means? What is this, guilt for sex, even now, even after all the sex you've come through? It's your problem, not hers. She looked at Martha, now fumbling with a metal fastener on a manila envelope. She was, for all appearances, oblivious to Karen and her proclivities.

"You know, I'm not thirty-five," Martha said now to Karen. "Actually I'm forty-seven." She looked up and smiled. There were several manila envelopes in a pile on her bed.

Karen was surprised, not by the revelation, but by the fact of the revelation, that Martha was so willing to venture when Karen had never given her any encouragement.

But it was a great relief to Martha, not having to be thirty-five, and being able to say it to someone, that is, to Karen, who was the only person she knew in New York. "I dyed my hair to come here."

"You did?" asked Karen, because something was expected. The wind moaned through the stairwell that abutted their room. She thought of how Mark had turned her over and pulled both his hands down the length of her back to rest on her haunches: "What a lovely ass you have, Carmody! Really . . . such a sweet smooth rump."

Martha continued, "Well, of course, and even then I wasn't sure I'd pass. I have a lot of gray. It's too long for my age, I suppose, but I've never felt feminine in short hair. It's against the hair rules, though."

Martha thought of her mother. "Mama, I want you to let your hair grow," Martha had told her mother, Clem Spinelli, long ago. Clem had worn her hair in a tight little bob, dyed dark, but faded in places where the sun had gotten at the peroxide.

Her mother had protested. "But women over forty can't wear their hair long. I'd look like a squaw woman with long hair and these wrinkles."

Martha was forty-seven now. Her mother was dead.

"Hair rules?" Karen was interested in spite of herself. She laughed. "Oh, you mean like 'Only great beauties should part their hair in the middle'? My mother believes in hair rules, too." She ran her fingers through her short top. "I think I got this haircut so I could avoid the question of a part altogether."

"Oh, yes, 'Avoid center parts'—that's a very important one!" Martha agreed. "Don't you wonder when you see a woman with her hair parted in the middle? I mean, how daring! To announce to the world: 'My looks are worth a center part!'" She threw her head back and her chin out in imitation of the dauntless egoism of center-parters, and, in doing so, caught a

111

glimpse of herself in the mirror. The dye had begun to wash out at the roots, but the rest was still an awful orange red, a color that had never been found in nature. "I never dyed my hair before. I never thought it was worth the mess." Clem Spinelli had been bound to the mess and the every-two-weeks' ritual. "Actually, what really made me decide not to was John Updike."

"John Updike?" Karen asked.

"Yes, one of the Rabbit books . . . Rabbit goes into a drugstore and sees rows of hair dye and thinks: 'A different smiling cunt on every box.' "

"He *does?*" asked Karen.

"Oh, yes!" said Martha, nodding for emphasis.

The line, when she read it, had chilled Martha for its scorn. There was no one in Cornwallis she could tell about it, but she kept thinking about it. Was it Rabbit's character or was it Updike's voice coming through? Though she knew the sins of a character should not be visited upon the author, she could not suppress the thought that Updike shared Rabbit's opinion of women who dyed their hair. "But I thought, isn't the whole reason women dye their hair *men*, so men would like them, you know? So why dye your hair if it's a lot of trouble, expensive, and gets you called cunt? You can get called cunt easier than that."

Karen sat up in bed. "It's true, all right. You can get called cunt in this world for practically nothing," she said, then laughed, yawned, stood up, stretched, and stumbled into the bathroom. She had to get her sweet smooth lovely ass in gear. Today she was going upstate to see her mother.

Chapter
7

"Let's make a quick stop at the Pacific Cleaners on South Avenue," Margaret said, driving her battered Falcon from the train station in Poughkeepsie after picking up Karen.

"Wha—?" Karen asked vacantly. She was thinking that her mother was really doing it. She really was selling the house, *Karen's* house, their only house, the house with the magnolia tree that bloomed outside her bedroom window, Karen's bedroom. That she, Margaret, Karen's mother, was leaving and going to a far place. "Uh . . . you got clothes at a cleaners on South Avenue, Ma?"

Margaret laughed. "No, but this cleaners has been seized for nonpayment of taxes and is now in the possession of the state!" She relayed this information with rising excitement.

"Yeah . . . so?"

"Well, they have to sell all the impounded clothes that weren't claimed by their rightful owners on claim morning, see?" Karen was beginning to see. "And . . . today's the day!" This last was said with a kind of wonder at the coincidence of one of Karen's rare appearances in Poughkeepsie with the Pacific Cleaner's tax sale. "Stuff'll go really cheap, and everything will be already cleaned and all in plastic and hanging up nice, not in piles like in a thrift shop."

Karen was the only one who had gone back to Poughkeepsie the last few years, and when she did, she and her mother had gone to thrift shops and discount stores. Shopping was a kind of bond. It was how they could be close. It was good because there was always a new outlet store or flea market or thrift shop to try. Her mother would insist on buying Karen something, though she had no money. A blouse, maybe, at K mart's flashing blue light. Love was OK, but it was bargains that saw you through.

"Maybe you could get a decent suit for work."

Karen's wince at the mention of work went unnoticed by her mother, who was pushing in the lighter and driving up the ramp to the highway. Karen felt the tug of the tax sale, the powerful pull of their bargain bonding. It could be so pleasant. They could spend their day the old way, bury their heads between the cleaner bags . . . But she had to be firm. Face it: the moment was strong against a spree through the Pacific Cleaners.

"Ma, if you're having a garage sale tomorrow, you shouldn't be buying more shit today, now should you?"

"But just to have a look around . . ." Margaret pleaded, touching the lighter to her cigarette. Karen waved the smoke away and rolled down the window in disgust, shivered, and rolled it up again.

"We've got a lot of work ahead of us, and besides, how good could the stuff be if no one ever claimed it?" Karen thought of something else. "Ma! South Avenue's *poor*. Maybe they didn't have the money to claim it, even to pay the cleaning bills to get their clothes on claim morning. Or maybe they couldn't get off work on claim morning. We'd be buying poor people's clothes, Ma! Literally off their backs!"

"All right, all right. Give me a break! You sound like your brother. We won't go, OK? Christ, I'm sorry I said anything. Enough, OK?"

"No OKs, Ma, let me finish . . ." They were laughing. Karen measured her words. "If we go, guaranteed you're gonna find some old wool coat in a color that's perfect for you . . . a . . . a . . . *magenta* wool coat that you'll have to drag with you to Arizona . . . to the goddamned desert."

They were on the four-lane now, but Margaret was driving slowly, haltingly, taken up with talking to her daughter. "You don't think we'd be able to sell it for twice the price at the garage sale?" she asked meekly, only half-joking.

"You're sick, Ma, you know that? It's a disease. I want to go home. Immediately!"

*T*he *Poughkeepsie Patriot* lay on their peeling porch. "My ad's in it," said Margaret as she retrieved it. Karen opened the front door, always unlocked, then the shuttered doors that led from the foyer to the family room.

The familiar command, issued by her brother Bill: *"Close the shutters!"*

"Hi, Bill," said Karen. She was home.

"Close the shutters, damn it!" The shutters in the archway served to keep heat in the family room, which was always where they were when they were here. Her brother stood to kiss her.

"My ad's in here," said Margaret as she plopped on the couch. Karen sat on the arm of the couch as her mother opened the paper to the classified section. "Here it is! 'Garage Sale: Forty years of accumulation!! NO EARLY BIRDS.' " There followed a listing of particulars.

Karen played with her hair as she read, then groaned as she handed the paper to her brother. " *'Forty years of accumulation,'* Ma?" She fingered the black hole in the upholstery where, years before, her mother's cigarette had smoldered, causing the family's evacuation and a brief visitation of the Fire Department. Bill hunkered back down to the floor where his work of stickering and pricing awaited him.

"Yeah, I figured that'd grab people. Nobody wants to come if they think you're only getting rid of *this* year's junk."

"*Two* exclamation points, Mother?" Bill asked.

"You like that, huh?" Their mother was beaming, happy in the attentions of two-thirds of her children. She was nervous. She was excited. She needed them here right now. After sixty years Margaret Carmody was leaving Poughkeepsie, New York, for New Age Estates, Phoenix, Arizona.

Bill put the paper aside, stood again and stretched. "Karen, now that you're here, you do the pricing, OK? It's women's work. I have a man's job to do. Or would you like to haul all the shit down the stairs?"

"You mind if I get my coat off?"

Bill gave his sister a playful punch. "Yeah, I do mind. Yer here to work, gal. I'll be right down with another year's worth of accumulation. Whaddya say to 1968, Karen? That was the year I was in love with Josie Shea." He headed through the shutters to the stairs.

"Close the shutters!" Karen and Margaret yelled in unison.

"So, Ma, what's 'NO EARLY BIRDS?' " Karen inquired, as she surveyed the room in dismay.

"Oh, you know . . . sometimes these dealers come real early and who needs that? Some guy on the stoop at the crack of dawn, trying to gyp you out of stuff that's worth something, you know, before the competition."

"Oh," said Karen, and considered that this was how her mother saw life mostly. For Margaret Carmody the world was filled with dealers of one kind or another, early birds trying to gyp you out of your stuff. That, for Karen, was the weirdest thing about this decision of her mother's. Why was her mother, after being so guarded all her life, falling for some guru and his hype, selling her house and all her stuff and running off to be with him in Phoenix?

"Sue warned me. She said a guy showed up at her place at six-thirty. She didn't even have her contacts in . . . she hadn't even finished her *marking* and this guy arrives. He bought a creamer for four fifty and later she realizes it's carnival glass." Sue was going with Margaret to Phoenix. Margaret rubbed a thick ankle after removing her boots.

"What's carnival glass?" Karen asked idly.

"Oh, you know . . . it's that stuff . . . something they used to give out as prizes at carnivals in the old days."

"You know what it looks like, Mom?"

"Sort of . . ."

"Well, jeeze . . . you could be selling carnival glass and we wouldn't even know it. It could be that cup over there you got marked fifteen cents." Her mother sighed mightily, hopelessly, and they both laughed.

Margaret got back to work. She stood solid and short and barefoot, tiptoeing precariously on the step-stool, straining for a bowl on the top of the bookshelf. The reaching hand also held a cigarette which had gone a full half-inch to ashes.

"God, you are a slob about your cigarettes!" Karen grabbed an ashtray (already priced: 25 cents) from the pile of glassware on the floor, and held it above her head for her mother, who stopped mid-reach to flick.

Karen began her work of writing prices with reckless whimsy on little yellow stickers and affixing them to all the articles of her mother's life. They worked in silence for a while, occasionally interrupted by Bill, from the attic or the cellar or the back bedroom with a fresh delivery of stuff.

Margaret was leaving them now, but they had left her a long time ago. They left her in order to live. This was what Bill said, and what Karen was able to believe, mostly, until, maybe, on a freezing Manhattan morning, the snow crunching underfoot, Karen would have a flash of herself embraced by her mother, rolling downhill in the snow in Washington Park, like one person downhill. Or a perfect spring evening would call back an image of her mother on the porch of their small frame house, waving her off to her prom, and all the happiness that came to her was from her mother's smile, not from the boy, a stranger to her in his father's car, not the corsage, the metallic mesh bow scratching her wrist, not the dress, too short-waisted and tight, the spaghetti straps cutting red into her shoulder. Only her mother. Because when she was good, this mother, she was very, very good.

 They worked on into the afternoon, filling the family room with stickered artifacts. *Rhapsody in Blue* whined over and over them from the old stereo: Da da da *da* da da da—da da da DUM . . . (It was what they had always played on rainy days at Chodikee Lake, sitting on the screened porch of their cottage, getting soaked, watching whitecaps, looking out for fishers they could call in for shelter.)

Theirs was to be an in-house garage sale, since there were no garages to any of the old clapboard houses that slumped into each other all the steep way down Congress Street to the Hudson River and urban renewal. The garage sale had become the thing itself. It was the focus of all her mother's anxiety, not the guru Simtra and the move to Phoenix. What if too many people came? What if no one came? What if someone stole something? Did she need to get more change, some rolls of dimes and nickels? Where did you get them, anyway? If she didn't charge tax, would she get reported?

If she sold everything, and this she was determined to do—wasn't she stickering each item and setting it out?—then she would have to move. Karen saw the logic of all this. You had to trick yourself into action somehow. Mark would agree.

Bill entered with two milk-glass lamps, one

cracked, pleated shades permanently dust-darkened. "3.00 for pair," Karen wrote without hesitation, but Bill was still standing there, shifting his feet in irritation.

"Mother," said Bill accusingly, with an angry jerk of his head, "there is a *fucking shitload* of stuff in the walk-in closet!" Karen groaned. Their mother looked sheepish. She'd been holding back, saying there was just a little more to do. Karen's back ached. She made herself sit up straight and stretch.

"Let's have a beer," said Margaret by way of apology. "Oh, and I got ham at Juengling's. Sliced thin." These last two words were enunciated precisely, and punctuated with two jabs of her thumb and forefinger, closed in a demonstration of extreme thinness. "I stopped by Juengling's on the way to get you at the station, Karen."

Which was why you were late, Karen thought, annoyed, as she popped the beer tops in the kitchen. Karen had been briefly irritated this morning, sitting on cold molded plastic in mid-February, staring dumbly at forgotten tinsel drooping from the ticket counter. But the moment passed to sadness for Karen now, as she thought that that was the last time she would be forced to wait for her mother's dented Falcon. Within the week her mother would be gone.

It was a command performance. She had even gotten Bill here, though to do that she had had to tell him the exact nature of her plans in advance. New Age Estates, Phoenix, Arizona. New Age Estates was a senior citizen trailer park with a twist of mysticism. Karen picked up the flyer for New Age Estates next to the toaster ($5.00, excellent condition—"Ma, aren'tcha gonna eat toast in Arizona?") "New Age for the Golden

Age" it read. There was a picture of Simtra the guru on the flyer, looking a good deal like Red Buttons in his promos for some other senior community in Florida.

Simtra. An eighty-year-old white man who claimed his wizened flesh embodied the spirit of an eighteen-year-old Apache maiden, Chiricahua, who lived on the site of New Age Estates two centuries before the arrival of the Spanish. Margaret ventured to tell them more now as they sat down to eat. Karen had not been able to bear hearing it earlier.

"Sue and I met Simtra last month at a Saturday Lunch and Learn at the high school. We both felt, for the first time, that we were at one with the cosmos." Her words or Simtra's? But maybe her mother was so at one with Simtra that such nicety of distinction did not apply.

They were at the old white tin-topped table ($150) gone to black in spots where the enamel had chipped off. Bill reached for a small foil of takeout Chinese mustard. "We have to share that," Margaret warned him, lightly smacking his hand and smiling. "I didn't want to get a new jar of mustard after I made my plans."

"You don't think a hundred fifty is a little high?" Bill asked as he squeezed out his ration.

"What, this table?" Margaret was indignant. "Hey, I got news . . . they don't make these tables anymore. Even those old *formica* dining sets are getting to be nostalgia, if you can believe it. Am I right, Karen?"

But Karen blurted out, "What, you think if you go there and swim in the pool that you're gonna turn into an Indian maiden yourself?"

Her mother sighed. "Don't mock me, Karen,

please. I can't make you understand, can I, that this goes much deeper than any yearnings for youth." She put her hands open-palmed against her ample chest. "It's like my quest has been fulfilled. Simtra has the girl god within him and there is god within each of us. We have only to find our god within. Simtra is our model only, and the trance channeler for Chiricahua. He makes no greater claims than that, but that's enough."

"Ma, please don't do it! You're too young to sign on with a bunch of old-agers." Her mother was sixty-one.

"I haven't been young since the day he died." It was their mother's life and their mother's cross, the early death by cirrhosis of a husband who, though unbalanced, was possessed of a vibrant spirit and the best of intentions. She kept all her vows to him, and even ones she hadn't made.

"No, not too young, Karen, especially when one sees what one's missed. But, you know, I already feel rejuvenated, just not the way you think."

"Why do you have to go all that way to get meaning? Isn't that sort of artificial? Why can't you get meaning right here? Why do you have to go to the desert to get meaning?" That was what Karen said. What she felt, so acutely, but didn't say was: Why do you have to go so far from me? *Mother . . . Mommy . . . Mama!* I want you here, where the Amtrak goes along the Hudson. But she was thirty-three years old and could not say it. The last time she had expressed this sort of need to her mother was in the fourth grade. Would it have made a difference anyway? Would it have changed her mother's plans if Karen had said, right now, *I need you so much?* After the events of the last few weeks, Karen needed her as much as she ever did in fourth grade. She knew that it wasn't right to keep someone available against your need, to leave them again when it had gone. And she hoped most sincerely that her need would pass. It was selfish.

Still, "I mean, you're signing your money away to . . . to some old guru nut. What's gonna happen in five years when Simtra kicks off and the place goes bankrupt?"

Bill exhaled audibly. Karen felt a quick jab as his foot connected with her ankle. He had no patience with her argument about Simtra. He held to the annoying belief that people do what they want to do and that on certain issues, arguments were futile. It was a belief that pissed Karen off almost as much as her mother's belief in Simtra. She turned to her brother. "Just because you're a Social Freethinker! That makes it OK, then, huh, 'cause she wants to? Let her go ruin her life, let her give up everything, the house, her job, her life here, everything . . ."

"What everything?" asked Margaret, bemused, looking around her, hands raised and opened in an empty gesture, daring to laugh in the face of Karen's wrath.

At another time, Karen might have asked the same question of her mother's life. What everything, indeed? Life isn't fair, she often heard her mother sing. Her mother, who certainly knew. Her mother, who had praised the Lord anyway for so many years. Praised Him for the mysterious ways he worked. Praised Him in charismatic tongues for her dead husband's soul.

Praised Him for the brother she had loved so dearly and who had been murdered by a sniper on a street in Chicago. Praised Him for the security of her twenty years of secretarial work for the firm of Hardesty and Loomis on Hillwood Street. Her mother had had very little. But Simtra sure wasn't gonna recoup any of her losses for her.

"Christ!" said Bill, nervously tattooing the tin tabletop with his delicate fingers. "Can't you just leave it, Karen?" Karen knew she got him when she knocked the Social Freethought Party. Her brother was the perennial Social Freethought candidate for mayor of Syracuse. He was the author, publisher, and distributor of the *Social Freethought Broadside*. His numerous jobs had been mere fronts for union organizing. He got fired from all of them because of his affiliation. His family suffered for it. He had borrowed money from Karen, from Margaret, from his in-laws, from friends. His wife ran the movement's day-care center. Diapers stunk from a pail in their bathroom because Pampers were bourgeois and wasteful. They lived in a dark basement apartment and they took their baby to late night movement meetings and early morning factory picket lines.

Once, Bill had almost convinced Karen to register as a Social Freethinker. After all, she'd stand to profit big if folks ever really started sharing the wealth. But you didn't let anything, an ideology, a guru, a religion become all-consuming—limit you and your family, your choice of jobs, your choice of friends, your life.

"You're not seeing this holistically, Karen," said Margaret. "The signing away of assets is an act of trust and a denial of worldly goods. I have complete trust in

Simtra." Her voice sounded funny then. "I mean, what else is there for me, really?" Karen thought she was going to cry. "No, I'm fine! Really." She grabbed the hand Karen offered and squeezed it, then smiled. A little too brightly, Karen thought.

"You don't have to go, Mama," Karen said quietly.

"No," she continued, "I see the unity of the universe now, the god within. I see that I am god and have my powers apart from any possessions. My consciousness has been lifted from traditional forms. I have been healed."

Couldn't her mother, a smart person and a grownup besides, see what jargonese that was? "Yeah, it's the old 'Go, sell what you have and come, follow me' command. Only now it's a guru instead of Christ! Ma, can't you see it? It's what Sarah did!"

They fell silent at the mention of Sarah, their sister and firstborn, who had left them and everything else to become a discalced cloistered nun. It was the logical extension, Karen believed, of the fervent and severe Catholicism in which the children had been raised, the stern faith of their dead father. Margaret had demonstrated a spiritual laxity during their father's life, then espoused the faith wholly and enforced it rigidly after his death, even to the point of becoming a charismatic—but left it in shock when Sarah took the veil.

The fact of Sarah's choice spoke volumes about their upbringing; but Sarah, who had taken the vow of silence, spoke not a syllable. Sarah, whose breathless "Here's the deal . . ." always promised a torrent of words to follow, words that would hold you, words

125

that would make you love her. Sarah, whose shoes once filled two triple-tiered racks, was now barefoot, having taken the vow of discalcedness. Sarah, whose abundant hair was lit with natural streaks, had covered it with darkness. Sarah, who had slept around plenty, had found a narrow pallet in a cell of the Abbey of the Strict Observance of the Crucifixion, Rhode Island. Karen sometimes thought it was guilt at her carnal knowledge that turned Sarah into a mute bride of Christ. She had been raised repressed, and dawned into the Age of Aquarius. Karen remembered the news Sarah had brought back after her high school trip to New York: "At the end of *Hair* they took off their clothes and stood on the stage *naked!*" Both girls had been horrified, disgusted, fascinated.

Karen, at thirty-three, was seven years younger than Sarah. They were significant sixties years, so some things were easier for Karen. Take sleeping with men. It came easy to Karen.

Sometimes Karen thought that Sarah's action had been the ultimate rebellion, the perfect manifestation of fury. Taking her parents' religion and using it to leave them forever. Even better than suicide. There were other times, though, when Karen gave less weight to Sarah's decision and attributed it merely to her choice of work before she became a nun, a sixties choice: social worker in Bellevue's detox center. The cloister probably looked good after that.

Sarah left New York to become a postulant as Karen was preparing to come to New York. Her sister would be in New York and that would make it easier for her. Karen was in her early twenties then, and stunned by the news. Because there was no denying that, in renouncing the world and forsaking shoes and all others, Sarah had also forsaken her, Karen. She had forsaken Bill. She had forsaken her mother.

Margaret left the Church after that. But leaving the Church after years of Altar Society and daily mass and charismatic prayer meetings had left Margaret empty, a void just gaping to be filled with Simtra. Just as the Freethinkers had filled Bill's void. Karen saw it plain. She despised this need, this weakness in her family. She would go through life a vessel, carrying her void with great care, as though it were the truth.

They chewed their extremely thin, nearly mustardless ham sandwiches in silence, and the taste was dry in Karen's mouth. She took a hit of beer. She ate too many potato chips. So did her mother. Margaret had let it go in recent years, eating too much, drinking more, gaining too much weight for her short body. She was still pretty, her thick hair now professionally frosted and side-parted (of course) into a loose twist, a graceful frame for the wide and open face she shared with her daughter (the nose veering off ever so slightly). But the hair was not, sadly, Karen's hair. Karen's hair was fine and thin and oily. If she had been a man, she would have lost much of it by now. Her father had lost his before he died, and he had been young. Bill had lucked out. He had Margaret's hair and features, their father's eyes and height and slimness. Karen looked at Margaret and saw her own body down the years, what it would be like.

She tried again: "Yeah, well, what about the food? I mean, admit it, you like grease, Mom. You like your chips and ham and beer. It's gonna be strict alfalfa and pita city when you get out there."

"Simtra will cleanse me of my base tastes. When you are one with your spirit-god, the bodily appetites have no meaning."

"I guess eating will be this out-of-body experience, huh?" Karen stood up abruptly, knocking over her chair in the process. She righted it. Its yellow sticker read "$9.50."

"*I*t's mind control," Karen whispered later to Bill when they took down the drapes in the dining room.

Bill stopped humming Gershwin. "You got the hammer?" he asked. And then: "At least she'll be taken care of."

"Yeah, and for how long?"

"She signed a contract with them when she turned over her assets, didn't she? Besides, what kind of assets does she have?"

"This house."

"This *house*. This *house* is gonna get nothing, Karen. It's falling apart. It's in a depressed area." He pried off the curtain rod and handed it down to her. "This *house?*" He laughed.

"Well, what makes you think somebody named Simtra honors contracts? I mean, he probably didn't sign any last name. You know what the flyer says Simtra means?—'bowl that washes itself.'"

Bill's laugh came now from behind the drapes. "Look, Karen, it's better than the charismatic stuff, dontcha' think? I mean, people do weird things."

*   *   *

Dusk comes suddenly when there are no curtains in a house. They had been working for hours. On a whim Karen plugged in and lit all the lamps that were lined up for sale. They cheered her in a perverse way, the woeful mismatched beacons of her childhood, beside her on the floor. The three of them worked on, now accompanied by Dan Rather— Karen stickering, Margaret dusting each item with paper towels, Bill at the table patiently making sense of ancient board games, sorting through all the plastic pieces and cards they'd found in an old pitcher. They discussed whether to order Red Front pizza or go out to the Volcano or maybe the South End Tavern. Friday was Corned Beef Night at the South End. The Red Front, Sicilian-style, won out. "Hold the anchovies!" Karen yelled as Bill dialed Information.

"Mom . . . I want the picture of the lake." Karen reached up for the beer Bill handed her as he came back in from the kitchen. She spoke it very casually, took a sip, and focused back on the television. Something she had been meaning to bring up, was all.

"Didn't I say she would, Bill?" Margaret was unable to mask her delight. "Hey, I got news! Your brother is way ahead of you. He asked me this morning. I told you, didn't I? I said, 'Karen's gonna want it, too.' Well, it goes with me to Phoenix and you can fight over it when I kick off."

Her father had painted it when they were children. The place they had on Chodikee Lake. The place they had had to sell when he died, and rented when they could afford to after that. The picture was hanging over the couch, though the rest of the walls had been

129

stripped. It was as though no one could bear to remove it. It was a lopsided sketch of the red Victorian cottage, barn red, with white touches of gingerbread dotting the wraparound porch. The waves were larger in the picture than they ever really got, except in a storm, but the picture's waves were sunlit waves, and they really were that color, that deep green. Karen loved the green and the dots of white. She loved it that her father had this talent, though he had rarely used it.

"I thought you couldn't look at it," Karen said in a reproach to her mother.

"I can't. So what? It makes me sick, OK? When I think what we sold it for. When I think what they could get for it now. Hundred-foot lakefront! You kids messing around in boats. That's what your father always called it: 'messing around in boats,' you know . . . like in *The Wind in the Willows*."

Of course she knew that's what her father always called it, and what the allusion was. Her mother had told her often enough.

They were all hung up on the lake. Her mother most of all. The lake had been the place Margaret was happiest, when she had been young and the wife of a handsome lawyer, the mother of three pretty children. When there had been some money and the promise of more. When there were neighbors and motorboats and parties with lanterns over dark water. Summers of bright red lipstick, and bare tan shoulders, and skirts that flared to wide circles when he turned her.

Karen would never let a man make her life, or break it, the way her mother had. She remembered Bill Carmody, Sr., in flashes: proud, all charm and distance and promise. And she remembered how quickly the charm would turn on itself, almost guilty for its ease, to become accusation and silence. In the middle of dinner, on a ride to the dairy for cones, in the rowboat on a foggy fishing morning. It didn't come often, but you couldn't know when it would come. It came often enough in the middle of happiness to leave his children ever unsure of themselves and the happiness they would find. If their mother hadn't idealized him, if he had been mere monster and never wonderful, if he had not been quite so handsome, his children would have been better off.

Anything could set him off. He would slam a fist down and hurl indictments at his wife and children: *Sinful. Selfish. No-good. Always wanting something.* He would shout at them, slap someone hard, then weep in frustration. Then it would be back to the promises to make it up: They would leave Congress Street soon for a big house in Hartswick Hills. He was going to buy a Mercedes-Benz. The girls would wear plaid jumpers and go to school at the Convent of the Sacred Heart. At Easter they would go someplace special: Washington . . . Niagara Falls . . . New York City, maybe.

Karen remembered a cashmere sports jacket he wore and how, after his death, she would go to the back of the big closet and weep into its softness. She had not found it in all this accumulation. She did not know whether she remembered him reading them *The Wind in the Willows,* or her mother's legend of him reading them *The Wind in the Willows.* What she remembered was that there was often a glass in his hand. She had been small, nine, when he died. There had been no money. Her mother had taken the job with his firm and worked there until last week.

"Then can I have Grandpa's hardware cabinet?" Karen asked.

"Uh-oh," said Bill, and then, quickly, "This Scrabble game is missing so many pieces, but its the real wood kind, you know . . ."

But his mother was answering Karen, apparently shocked by this new request. "You have gotta be kidding! You saw what it was marked." It was marked "$850," the showpiece of the garage sale, the come-on for all the dealers. It was worth it, Karen knew. Maybe more. An octagonal structure of warm oak with eighty wedge-shaped drawers meant to file various sizes of nails and screws. It rotated creakily for access to all of its drawers. Margaret's father had had it, and his father before him, in their store on River Street. And when she was a child, Karen had stored treasures and secrets in those little drawers: troll dolls, gum, the love notes she never sent to Brian Umiker, the turquoise baby ring she had chewed out of shape and turquoises, a bra she had stolen from Sarah.

"Ma, how can you *sell* it? It was your father's."

"You just want me to give it to you?"

"No, I'll *buy* it, Mom. I'll pay you money for it. I just can't pay you now."

"Karen, be practical. Where would you put it, anyway? I mean, if your new place is anything like your last place. By the way, give me your address while I think of it. And *when* are you gonna get a phone installed? I don't like having to call your buddies and wait while they take their time getting a message to you. And it's dangerous, besides, not having a phone in the city." Margaret ripped off a piece of paper towel, picked up her marker, and looked up, expectant.

Karen dictated only her street address, leaving out the fact of the Arcadia. She watched the fat letters form, ink bleeding into paper towel. Was there any real hope of this scrap of paper making it through all this accumulation to Arizona? She was in a fury at her mother for changing the subject, for pointing out her poverty. She knew too well she had no place to put her grandfather's hardware cabinet nor even the possessions she had been storing in her mother's attic. Among her other tasks this weekend would be the sorting through of her scrapbooks, autograph books, yearbooks, records, and letters. Sorting through only to throw out. The house on Congress Street would no longer be her storage facility, which was in part what home should be, after all.

Bill whistled softly, incredulous. "You live on *the Square?*"

Karen looked up, surprised, then amused."Yeah, I do. Yes." Well, it was true.

"You're kidding!"

Really, he was too impressed with the address to be a Social Freethinker. "Of course," said Karen haughtily.

"Hunting heads must be paying off big!"

Karen ignored this comment, though her mother, who didn't know from the Square looked up, hopeful, inquisitive. Was it possible that one of her children, that Karen, was finally doing well? She had naturally assumed that Karen was in yet another sublet. This was news, about it being on a square that was called the Square!

Karen smiled and said nothing. Inscrutable.

Margaret Carmody suddenly rose from her place on the rug, then returned, holding a ceramic object toward Karen. "Here, you can have this, if you want something." It seemed to be a vase, but very small; pretty, though, with dusky colors waving through it like sunset. "To tell you the truth, I never could understand why you gave me this." She looked straight at Karen, hurt weighing her eyes.

Karen avoided Margaret's gaze as she accepted the piece for inspection. "*I* gave you this?"

"Two Christmases ago. Why did you?" The pain still fresh in her voice, the insult of the wrong present.

"I never gave you that," said Karen.

"You did," her mother insisted. "It came all wrapped from some fancy store in New York."

"Oh, yeah," said Karen, remembering. She had bought it, at Bendel's, and she knew why. It was the same reason she ever bought anything at Bendel's. For the box. Whenever she was impecunious and needed to purchase a gift, she would go to Bendel's and select the cheapest article she could find and then have it boxed in the sturdy brown-and-white stripes with the brown polka dot grosgrain. The well-bred salespeople would oblige you as though they weren't far better dressed than you, and as though you hadn't just purchased the cheapest thing in their store. Karen thought a Bendel's box was a thing of beauty, rare in this world of flimsy collapsible cardboard and elasticized gilt ties.

The problem, Karen realized, was that her mother didn't know shit about presentation. She didn't understand that a crummy gift in a Bendel's box said "Love the Giver."

"Go ahead, you can have it."

"I don't want it," said Karen. "Sell the damn thing." The beer she had been drinking half the day had

134

evidently caused her tearducts to go slack. She put her head on the arm of the couch and began to cry.

Her mother leaned awkwardly toward her then, resting her hand lightly against the back of Karen's neck. Karen pulled away sharply.

"Oh!" Margaret quickly pulled back her cigarette, "don't burn yourself!"

"I didn't," said Karen. "You burned me."

Margaret knelt, grabbed Karen's shoulders, and planted a rough kiss on Karen's nape. "Let me make you a cup of tea," Margaret said, herself in need of tea, of the familiar ritual of water, whistle, pot, bag, cup, and sweet swizzle of honey. She stood too quickly, and had to grab the couch to steady herself.

"Pizza's here!" said Bill as he left the table and made his way to the door in simple gratitude.

Chapter
8

They worked all weekend on the garage sale, netting Margaret sixteen hundred dollars. Not enough. What didn't sell was put on consignment with a local auctioneer, who collected it Sunday afternoon. The hardware cabinet sold, but for three hundred. "An insult," Margaret said sharply to the dealer as she took his check.

Bill was to drop Karen off at the station Sunday night before heading to Syracuse. Margaret was to spend the night with Sue at Sue's daughter's house. Bill, Karen, and Margaret said their good-byes in the frigid twilight on the sidewalk of Congress Street, the dark small home of their family an empty shell behind them. "You take care now," Bill said to his mother, his voice cracking. Margaret shivered in her thin turtleneck. Bill embraced her roughly, pressing her face into his down jacket. Karen saw his eyes above their mother's head, focused firmly in the distance. And then her mother was coming toward Karen, where she was leaning on Bill's car. Hands in her pockets, Karen opened the sides of her jacket and folded what she could of her mother within it. Their sweatered breasts were pressed together, their mouths together, too, in a surprising lovers' kiss. They pulled away when they realized, and realized, too, that they were weeping.

Her mother fumbled with something, then put her hand in Karen's hand in the pocket. Karen felt something small and cold. "Take it," said her mother, whispering conspiratorially. "My ring. I want you to have it. Anyway, Simtra eschews jewelry, as you know. Too worldly, but also Chiricahua told him jewelry drives away entities from the astral plane and you miss out on their energy. All jewelry, but especially diamonds. So hard. Anyway, I know I'd have to sell it. You take it."

Karen fingered the ring. "Thanks, Mom." She shook her mother's shoulders. "It'll be great. You're doing the right thing." Karen knew perfectly well how to deal with the inevitable.

"You'd better believe it!" said Margaret belligerently. But Karen did not. She got into her brother's car.

Margaret Carmody would leave for Phoenix the next morning with Sue and whatever would fit in the Falcon.

On the train Karen took out the ring. A small diamond in a clunky white-gold setting. Dirt between setting and diamond. How many years of accumulation? Too small for her ring finger, too large for her pinky. Karen smiled and stuck it deep into her pants pocket. She wasn't sure if her mother had meant it for sentiment, or for the money it might bring if Karen fell on bad times. You couldn't tell with Margaret. Karen hoped she'd never be desperate enough to have to cash the poor little ring in.

She took her ticket stub and went to the club car to buy a beer. Back in her seat, she sat, drinking and thinking and staring at the river flowing cold and south along with her. She fell into a sleep. Her mother was in the sleep, and little Karen and big-girl Sarah, wearing matching smocked pinafores that maybe they actually had one time, that she may have remembered, or remembered from a picture of that time. The sleep took her as far as Croton-Harmon, where she woke, disoriented, to a formless sadness and an arm numb in the place where she had been resting her head.

When the train descended from the elevated tracks to speed beneath Harlem and Park Avenue, passengers began lining the aisle holding bags and skis and children. Karen stayed in her seat until the train stopped and the others filed out. She thought of Mark Pitofsky, using him to jog her from sleep and get off the train and back home to the Arcadia. Probably there would be a message from him in her mailbox.

She grabbed her bag from the overhead, and, ignoring the constellations of the heavens and of the homeless, she walked through Grand Central to the subway. It was after eleven when she arrived at the Arcadia. She looked in her mailbox with a kind of yearning for even the third-class mail that had not followed her to this place, all the mail-order catalogs and contests and pleas on behalf of the Third World that could lull one into feeling sought after. There was nothing from Mark, only a ghoulish message from Annie that caused her to laugh in spite of her disappointment: "Jennifer's uncle just died. He had a one-bedroom. Call her quick."

Well, maybe Martha had taken his call, and there would be a message in the room. But Martha was asleep.

Karen showered, washing the last of garage sale

138

grime from her body. Her mother's bathroom had not been all that accommodating toward the end. As she was drying, she noticed a pretty floral cup on the side of the sink, into which Martha had placed their toothbrushes. Karen took hers, used it, and left it out on the sink.

Karen slept past breakfast, so went out for a corn muffin and the *Times*. She thought of Mark again, and how she hadn't seen him in four days. Back at the Arcadia she inquired at the reception desk, but Mrs. Sergeant Major informed her that there had been no calls during her absence. She wondered idly where he had been born. How many brothers and sisters did he have? Did he ever meet his ex-wife for dinner? Where did he come in his family? There were a lot of questions she hadn't asked him.

She thought then of her mother and the Triptik she and Sue had gotten from the AAA, how optimistic it could seem, to be hitting the road, the route to Phoenix so cheerfully highlighted in yellow. There was really nothing like hitting the road, even when the destination was some ancient guru. Maybe the thing was not to take your destination all that seriously, as in the Destination, but just catch on to the joy, the fresh zest of starting. It was ten-thirty. Had Margaret and Sue started at eight as they had planned? How far would they have gotten by now? She hoped Sue did most of the driving. She could see her mother slowing down to chat in front of an eighteen-wheeler as they by-passed Chicago during rush hour.

*   *   *

139

Martha was back in the room when Karen returned. She looked up from her desk and greeted Karen cheerfully, inquiring about her weekend. Karen responded monosyllabically, and Martha went back to her work. Karen watched her, irritated at the other woman's involvement, then reached under her bed for the Dewar's. It was as though she couldn't help herself. Not the need for a drink, but the need to be badassed. "Want a shot?" she asked Martha. It was for shock value, she knew she was doing it for shock value. It is good to know your motives, Karen thought as she proffered the bottle.

Martha looked up and said simply, "I could report you for that."

Karen poured a finger. "Why don't you? You should. Then you'll have a single until they get some other P to take my bed."

"I wouldn't think of it," said Martha.

"But you did think of it."

"But I would never do it. What I meant was, why would you take a chance like that in order to test me?"

Karen was silent, and for some reason near tears, holding the Dewar's between her thighs in the middle of morning. "To test you? How 'bout maybe I wanted to get out of this dump?"

Martha shrugged. "So? If you think it's a dump, leave. Why do you need someone to throw you out? Why let someone else take your action from you?" Her words as she said them sounded to Karen like thought formed recently and hard. Karen went into the bathroom, dumped her drink, grabbed some toilet paper, and silently blew her nose.

"What's a P?" Martha asked. She eyed Karen keenly as she emerged. "You said, 'some other P.'"

"P for pathetic."

"Do you really think everyone's pathetic here?"

Karen missed her gaze. "Yeah, I do. Have you had a chance to check out the Slow Girls yet?" At the Arcadia there was a group of retarded women so euphemistically referred to by the other residents. The Slow Girls hung together in the lounge each night—watching television, laughing, hugging each other, slapping each other affectionately on the arms, talking loudly about their boyfriends. By day they attended a special program at a nearby university for their eventual certification as day-care/nursery-school aides. The graduates of this program stayed on, living at the Arcadia and working in nursery schools. Was it too bitter for Karen that even they had gainful work? "Something wonderful for coming generations, to be taught by them in their formative years."

Martha didn't laugh. "I don't find them so pathetic. They're happy, and they've got something going. Maybe they're more affectionate. I mean, they're real physical, right? They sure like their boyfriends! Little kids would respond to that. But I've met some of the other women here. Some are working on doctorates. There are actresses, models, artists, nurses. You think they're pathetic?"

"They're pathetic if they're here."

"They want to be in Manhattan if they're here, like the rest of us. They might need to be here." Martha stood then and threw on her jacket and slung the Adidas bag over her shoulder. "Hey, Karen . . ."

It was rare that either used the other's name. There

was a brief silence as Martha made her way to the door.

"What?"

Only Martha's head was visible now, her cheek resting against the open door, smiling at Karen. "You don't think I'm pathetic, do you?" She laughed. "Don't answer that!" But Karen couldn't. Martha was gone before a response was possible.

Where was she going, Karen wondered. Was it possible she had a job, and so soon? She put the bottle of Scotch on the floor, sat back on her bed, and twitched her nose at Martha's cologne. She probably considered Karen more P than even the Slow Girls. Martha had kicked it to her the way a psychiatrist probably would. Karen deeply resented having to live with one when she had never gone to one, and one who made so free with the meddle.

She held her glass carefully and lay back for a review. "You call me," she had said to Mark as they waited for the cab. "I called you before, remember?"

"Ah, yes, but I came calling, do remember that." Mark had laughed, but seemed a little irritated, shifting his feet in a cold-weather dance. "In any case, are you keeping a reckoning of this?"

Karen was quiet, looking dumbly at their mingling breath. She wasn't keeping score, she didn't think, but she did think it was important for him to call her. "I just would like you to, that's all."

"But you don't even have a phone, do you?"

"Incoming," Karen said. "And, you can leave a message. The Arcadia. We're listed . . . all of us."

He smiled. "But can I just talk to you?" He kissed her lightly on the lips. A cab pulled over. "Good," he said. "I'll call you, Karen Carmody."

She had wanted to embrace him. She put out her

arm, but he stood straight, as though nothing had gone before. Certainly nothing like passion or sex. Her hand lay limply on the belt of his overcoat for a moment before it fell away. She got into the cab. He had said that he would call. She wanted so much for him to call!

Instead of ruminating further about Mark, Karen decided to indulge in a little prenap self-pity. Nothing like it to make one feel the nap is deserved.

The name of the game would be Indignities. Let me count the ways:

1. No refrigerator. No stove. No hot plate. No heating coil. Instead, chicken chow mein, waxed beans, and turkey loaf.

2. No outgoing calls. Calling a friend was almost as big a deal as doing the wash. Making sure you had quarters, dragging downstairs, waiting in line. No name listed with New York Tel. Who would find her if there were a party? Only Annie and Lisa the actress and now her mother and Bill and Mark Pitofsky had the Arcadia's number. Not her sister who had no use for phone numbers. Not Phil. Who would call her if a job opened up someplace, or if she won the Trans Am she had bought a chance on last month? Who would find her if someone she knew once, and loved, died? She didn't know who would die before reaching her, but someone would— someone, maybe, that she had loved in childhood. She was almost sure of it.

3. No privacy.

4. No beauty in the place. But for her growing amaryllis. The other plants were plastic, the only rugs were shag.

5. So little hope. DESPAIR OF HOPE ALL YE WHO ENTER HERE. That's what should be over the door and on the brochure. Karen almost smiled.

The phone rang. It was Lisa, telling her that she owed $63.15 for last month's phone bill. Speaking of phones. Karen thanked her for calling.

The check is in the mail.

The call jarred her. No nap now. She needed money. She really had to get some kind of a job, even a temporary one. She needed to get out of this place. "We gotta get out of this place," she sang, "if it's the last thing we ever do." She would shower, shave her legs, wash her hair, blow it dry, dress, and check the classifieds. She was feeling decidedly manic.

One of her headhunter dresses was in good condition. In the bottom of her laundry bag she located a pair of pantyhose with a limited run. Even for counterculture or counter jobs you needed to wear pantyhose the first time out. She sat on Martha's bed to pull them on, but realized too late she was sitting on some of Martha's papers. She reached under to move them, but a manila envelope fell to the floor, scattering pictures, glossies, full-color eight-by-tens. About twenty-five or thirty of the same picture: a boy in his teens, sitting on the back of a boat, shirtless and tan and muscled, and though he was squinting a bit from the sun, you could see his eyes were blue. His hair a dirty summer blond. For all the young macho look of him, he was holding back with his smile and his arms were crossed tight against his chest.

Pictures like that cost. Who was the boy? Was it a shot for a model's portfolio? But it wasn't a great pose, and besides—the chipped front tooth, the eyes a little close—he didn't look model-perfect. Then why so many of them, and eight-by-tens? Was it possible that he was her son? She knew Martha had a daughter, but there had been no mention of a son. But then why wasn't she with him? He was still so young! Any why so many copies? Talk about being hung up on your kid! Karen checked it closely. He didn't look much like her, but it was only a picture, and Karen wasn't great at spotting resemblances. She stuck them back in the folder and put them back on the bed.

She finished dressing and touched up her side hair with gel. She pinched her nostrils together and pushed her nose to the right. She looked OK, pretty even. She looked like someone who had a job. She looked like someone who had purpose. She only felt like shit. She grabbed her *Times* and left the Arcadia, walking quickly past the front desk and Mrs. Sergeant Major.

It was a gorgeous day, an affront to all who felt like shit. A day ripped untimely from the jaws of winter. Mild, bright, and clear: promising, though it was February, that things like croci would soon be seen in the Square. For a moment Karen considered crossing to the Square so she could investigate more closely, to see if such things had begun. She went instead to Ralph's to read her want ads over a beer.

"I've got to get a job," she told foxy George.

He passed her a draft and began humming "Sha na

145

na na, sha na na na na, get a job . . . ," practiced-like, as though he had hummed the old doo-wop standard to a few patrons before Karen. "I was gonna get a job once, but I started considering what I was qualified for. It stopped me cold when I realized that I was qualified for absolutely everything. Hey, I'm a talented guy. I mean, how was I gonna limit myself to *a job,* you dig?" He strutted in place, his open hands gesturing emphatically.

Karen dug.

"I'm interested in everything, but not in doing any one of those things forever. It's this problem I have." He went to the end of the bar to take the waitress's orders from the tables.

Karen scanned the classifieds vaguely as she thought again of Mark and the deep attraction his kind held for her: a man who was inert from knowledge. A man who might not even call you because he knew the destination. Like George, Mark knew very well, but Mark knew more. They could drive you crazy, his kind—waiting for you to court them, to call, waiting for you to invite them someplace, to suggest amusements for them. And then, if won, this kind would be waiting for you to move in or move him out, buy the furniture or call the super about the toilet, waiting for you to have a kid or not have a kid, waiting for you to tell him when and where he would take his annual two weeks. Always waiting for you. And that was it, she figured, the attraction: He would always be waiting for her.

She forced herself back to the ads. Multilith Operator. Admin Asst. Host/Hostess. Sous Chef. Color Mixer. Refrigerator Mechanic. Secty F/T. Undercover Operative. Tax Preparer. Beggerman. Thief.

George was back. "You know, a woman comes in here, she started a business where she charges people five hundred dollars to tell them their interests. She's really thorough about it. She uses all kinds of disciplines—myth, psychology, horoscope, biorhythms—just to get at them, and then she makes a video that they get to keep. It's real complex, she says. In the end, she can tell them what job to go for and whether they like sushi. Maybe you'd be interested in starting some kind of hype like that. You could probably put it over. The competition would be good for her."

"Interest doesn't interest me much. But why are you giving this great idea away."

"Can't use it. I yam what I yam. Bartending is my life's work. It is meat and drink and art to me. I'm too soulful for anything less and too lazy for anything more."

Karen had sensed from the first that George was kin. "Yeah, well, I would like tending bar a little more than I should, if you get my drift. I guess I need to find a metaphor for bartending."

"There are some around," agreed George. "But it's tricky."

Karen spent an hour or more on want ads then, enough to convince herself that she was in earnest. It had been foolish to waste time and her last pantyhose in getting dressed. It was getting late. There was very little she could do today. She turned for further scanning to the movie page. Maybe she could stop in and ask for work at a few places and then go to *Birdy*, which she had missed the first time out. "To see it is to fly." Instead of looking for work she stopped for a slice on the way.

"To see it is to get bummed out" was Karen's assessment. A shell-shocked guy who thought he was a bird and his buddy whose face had been blown half away. A few months back she had promised herself that she wouldn't go to any more films on the following subjects: Vietnam, drugs, the Holocaust. *Birdy* had gotten her there on false pretenses.

She wandered down the avenue awhile. The day had turned raw while she was in the theater. As she waited for a light, she felt the scrutiny of a grizzled little woman carrying a worn khaki backpack slung over one bent shoulder. The sides of her filthy sneakers had been cut away to make room for ace bandages and bunions. Karen had made the mistake of meeting her gaze. This upstate habit she couldn't shake, looking at people when they looked at you.

"You and me," chirped the woman, in holy recognition, "two lone eagles."

Karen smiled wanly at her. Speaking of birds.

WALK flashed on. The woman walked, or hobbled. Karen didn't. Karen stayed where she was, on the corner where the curb slopes down for wheelchair access. Pedestrians brushed her as they passed. Her right eyelid began to quiver. Oh, I didn't need that, thought Karen. A lone eagle. How had the woman spotted her? What was there about her person that had given her away to this grim Spirit of February Future? Shaken, Karen ducked into the nearest store to collect herself, to protect herself from the assessments of other presumptuous street biddies. It wasn't the eagleness so much as the loneness. It was the loneness, absolutely. She would have to shake it off before she hit the street again.

Vinnie's Viddies was where she ducked. RENTALS.

SALES. REPAIRS. CHARTER MEMBERSHIPS AVAILABLE.
$29.95. Rows of racks displayed bright boxes decorated
with the likes of Gérard Depardieu, Bette Midler,
Claudette Colbert, and Woody Woodpecker. Karen was
drawn in even as she tried to maintain her misery for a
while longer. There were sections. FOREIGN. X. CHIL-
DREN. COMEDY. OLDIES. Like she died and went to movie
heaven. More movies than ever she had seen. And it
came to her there in the aisle that this was a video store,
where people could just rent movies and take them
home. Or, maybe to the Arcadia!

There were people doing just that. Checking the
racks. Chatting amiably with Vinnie. A briefcased man
in double-breasted gray was making inquiries. "So,
Vinnie, what about *Sexsations*?"

"It's out," said Vinnie.

"*Talk Dirty to Me*?"

"Out."

"Oh, well. Give me whatever fuck movie you think
is good."

"*Up and Coming* is supposed to be good."

"Great. I'll take it."

"It's Two-for-One Night," Vinnie advised him.

The man hesitated briefly. "In that case I'll take
Annie Hall, too."

You could take *Annie Hall* home! But it occurred to
her that you needed things to do this. You needed
money. You needed a machine. She remembered now,
Mark had a machine. Mark had rented a machine.
Maybe she could rent a machine!

"Can you rent a machine here?" she asked.

Vinnie pumped iron, you could tell. A tight white
undershirt displayed a case of *bicepses gigantis* to disad-
vantage. He also wore a black leather vest, matching

studded bracelet, one earring, two chains, and a moussed-up brush cut softening to nape tendrils. "Hey . . . you can rent me, if you want."

Karen didn't want. She put his comment in the memory hole and forged on, straight-faced. "So, how much?"

"I'm cheap. The machines are more expensive."

"You're forcing me to hurt your feelings," Karen smiled. "I pick the machine."

"That's what they all tell me." He was a baby-faced bodybuilder with actual rosy cheeks.

"How much?"

"The VCR is thirty-two ninety-five per month, minimum rental three months. I deliver," he added lasciviously.

"Um . . . can you charge on Visa?"

"Yeah, yeah. We give you a contract, you tell us everything about yourself, and then we let you charge."

"And can I charge my membership, too?" She thought of her remaining asset, the Visa card. Here was an investment worth the last few hundred. The only reason she still had that much was that she found it difficult to charge groceries and Scotch. But if she could start charging movies, one major drain on her cash flow would cease.

"Sure, lady . . . what else you wanna charge?"

"The tapes. Can I rent them on Visa?"

He lowered his voice and leaned toward her over the counter. "You wanna charge when you rent the tapes? But it only costs two ninety-nine to rent a tape and we can't take charges under ten dollars. Look, wait a second, willya? I gotta take care of these people. Rush hour . . . people comin' from work."

Karen accepted this because he seemed to be earnest, not trying to put her off. People *were* coming home from work. This was evident. She didn't take it personally. She knew it wasn't that Vinnie thought that people coming from work were superior to her. But they should get good service, people who worked all day. A short line had formed behind her of folks with briefcases and white bags of food, maybe tortellini salad from Pie in the Sky. They had put in their day and were going home. Don't idealize them, Karen told herself. They're working folk. They work at things that you probably wouldn't want to do. Still, the fact was that they had gone out someplace today, and talked to other people at that place, maybe joked around a little, and earned enough at that place to rent a tape and buy a half-pound of chic chicken salad. And this: they were going home to their VCRs.

She picked up a list of the tapes available. Hundreds of tapes—*Dracula 1931, Dracula 1979, Dressed to Kill, The Dresser* . . . She lost herself in a reverie of film titles, savoring, remembering, anticipating: Which tape would be the first one she'd rent? How could you make a decision?

"OK," said Vinnie at length, "now I can talk to ya. Things are a little tight right now, huh?" He eyed her sympathetically. She didn't want his sympathy. "Look, as long as Visa approves you, here's what we can do. You join the club, you rent the VCR, and I'll let you run up a tab. Everytime you hit twenty dollars, we'll work up a Visa slip, got it?"

"Thanks, yeah. But I don't want to inconvenience you."

"Hey, no problem. I still get the business, right?

And besides, I like to help. I'm only here because I'm working off my karmic debt."

He had meant for her to pick up on this last, an opener, Karen could tell, but when you've got a cloistered nun in the immediate family, and your mother is speeding her way to Simtra, you give zealots short shrift. Karen yawned. "I wish my only debt were karmic."

She felt like a charity case—he was only being nice because of his karmic debt. Still, she did want the VCR. She signed up for delivery on Thursday night. Vinnie only delivered at night because there was no one to mind the store.

"It'll be quick. I just come in, hook it up to your TV, and boom, you're at the movies."

"Oh, yeah . . . a TV! I need a TV, right?"

"Christ, yes, you need a TV! That's so you can see the pictures when they go past, get it?" Even Karen laughed. "You don't got a TV?"

Karen shook her head. Now he knew she was a rock-bottom P.

He comported himself well, she had to give him that. "No problem. I'll rent you one of those, too—we'll charge it on Visa. A package deal. Fifty-three ninety-five a month, a seventy-dollar deposit. Minimum three months. Sign here."

She signed and went home to 742, to find it well occupied.

"This is my roommate Karen. Karen, meet Michele and Brenda." Brenda and Michele were on Karen's bed and remained there, merely nodding as Martha introduced her. Brenda's boots were on Karen's bed, too, and Michele was smoking.

So it would not be just Martha but Martha and her friends. Nip it in the bud, thought Karen. Let 'em know right away they're not dealing with any ordinary pathetic. "Hi. Good evening. You mind, ladies? I need the bed." She put her hand on her forehead and shook her head. "It's been one of those days." She forced a smile in Michele's direction. "And could I ask you not to smoke? Allergies. You can smoke in the lounge." Maybe they'd take the hint, however subtle.

They didn't. "There are evening services in the lounge now," said Martha. "We sat and talked and talked in the dining hall till they locked us out, so we all just came up here." The women laughed in pleasure at their bonfemie.

Brenda stood up then, revealing herself to be a good six feet tall. Karen had not seen her before. Must be a new Corps recruit. She was young, in her early twenties, with straight hair that hung below her waist, a sixties throwback. She was wearing dungarees and a faded plaid flannel shirt with the collar and most of the buttons tucked under, exposing a fair amount of flat chest. It was such a surprising adaptation of the faded flannel look that Karen was sure it was meant to be provocative. The mixed-message mode of dress. She was large and angry, with eyes that flashed dark behind granny glasses.

Michele was a light-skinned black woman, with a close-cropped Afro that accented her fine features, her large eyes. Delicate of psyche as well as bone, Karen thought. She had seen her a few times in Ralph's. Always smoking, always drinking, always moving— hands, eyes, head, something. The play of a stirring stick in a glass, sharp short takes of cigarettes, the tapping of a lighter, the nervous smoothing of an eyebrow. The eyes had it here: intelligent, questioning, penetrating. Karen had been made uncomfortable by those eyes before, though in relative darkness and down the long bar of Ralph's. Now she was to experience them close up and in her own room.

Brenda and Michele reluctantly relocated to a place on the shag, at the foot of the straight chair where Martha was sitting.

"So you work at a nursery school near here?" Martha said to Brenda. Pointedly, Karen thought. Making some statement about Slow Girls. Was Brenda one?

"I think I'll take a bath," Karen announced, and stripped down to her underwear, using her dirty clothes to stake a claim to her bed. They'll be gone when I get out of the tub, she told herself. She bent to grab a towel from under the bed, and, as she straightened herself, noticed Brenda noticing her, her eyes on Karen's breasts, then quickly averted.

They were talking about their mothers when she got out. Karen sat on her bed and combed wet hair. It was cold in the room, bitter outside—the airshaft wild with wind.

Michele was saying how, as a child, she had found a sachet she had given her mother for Mother's Day in the garbage on Mother's Eve. She had made the sachet in her third-grade class, tie-dyed material, sewed it, stuffed it with potpourri, wrapped it in tissue, and her mother threw it out. "I think Mom meant for me to see it in the garbage."

Get over it, Michele, thought Karen, and her anger surprised her. There's life after Mother's Day. Karen climbed into bed and grabbed a magazine from the floor. *New York*. Five months old. She had taken it from the lounge a few days ago and read it. She had read it five months ago as well. She gave every sign of being absorbed in it now.

Martha sounded like the moderator. "Do you ever spend days shopping for just the right present for your mother? Why is that so important, I wonder?"

"God, I get in a sweat shopping for her!" said Michele. "Last year I pawned my wedding rings and got her a microwave. I mean, what did I need the rings for, anyway?"

"She liked that, right?" asked Brenda.

"*Oh, yeah*," said Michele, rolling her eyes as she sucked deeply on her cigarette. "She said I was trying to kill her. She said the radiation would get into every-thing, into all the food she ate. She said I wanted her to glow in the dark. She said it was bad enough that I got her the special bacon attachment, which meant I wanted her to eat nitrates, too. She didn't want it in the house, even unplugged and in the box. She put in out on the balcony in the snow until I left, then gave it to me to take back to Macy's."

"What are you gonna get her this year?" asked Martha.

"How 'bout a year's supply of PCBs?" said Brenda, but the joke seemed lame.

Martha told of the time her mother had asked for a belt for Christmas. It hadn't seemed like enough, just a belt, so Martha went out and got her an expensive knit dress. "What's this? I wanted a belt," said Clem Spinelli.

"I would have given her a belt!" said Brenda, at the same time Martha was saying, "She's dead now, my mother."

The women fell silent for a moment. Karen thought

155

of the vase from Bendel's, and how her mother had thought of it and been hurt every time in two years that she had seen it on the bookshelf, and of how she couldn't understand why Karen had chosen it.

Where were her mother and Sue spending the night tonight? Had they run into any bad weather?

Was this really what it was supposed to come down to, Karen wondered, being alone in the Arcadia instead of in a real life somewhere? All because you couldn't give your mother anything that was acceptable to her? Because you had nothing to offer that she would really love, that would make her whisper, "This is it. You knew exactly. This is what I had been secretly hoping for."

"It works two ways," Brenda was saying. "When my mother came back from a trip to Rome, I went back home to see her. My friend was with me. 'Brenda is going to hate the present I got her,' my mother whispers to my friend, like she's really excited about this present I'm gonna hate!" Brenda was speaking fast, high-pitched. "She was right. She knows I'm not religious and she got me a glow-in-the-dark, blessed-by-the-pope, statue of the Assumption of the Blessed Virgin."

"Christ, why don't you lay off mothers?" said a voice from behind *New York*. The others turned, surprised. Karen, confused and furious at herself, was tempted to sink lower behind the magazine, but then didn't. She had wanted to stay apart. "Well. Why *is* it always the mothers? How come fathers never get shit on in these sessions? I mean, even *successful* daughters bitch about their mothers, right? They always give credit to the fathers. I read one of these studies of women executives where they say, 'He treated me like the son he didn't have . . . He was supportive . . . He challenged me . . . He made me climb this really tall tree even though I was terrified . . .' that kind of bullshit. Christ! There isn't any hope in the world for a mother and a daughter, that's what you're saying, isn't it?"

The women looked at her, startled. Karen was enraged at her own outburst. Why couldn't she have kept her mouth shut? She didn't *want* to be involved with them! She didn't want to know about their mothers or their lives. She didn't want to see them.

It was Martha who was doing this, dragging them all out like this. It was something like a guy who goes to a party and right away orders a double bourbon. Everybody else might have stayed with wine spritzers, but they see him and they order the hard stuff, too, and the party really gets roaring. It was this guy, giving them all permission to drink, letting them all get dangerous. But in order for him to pull it off, he has to be OK, someone with a modicum of dignity, not an alcoholic, a known fool or pederast.

Martha had dignity. Karen had to give her that. She was older and soft-spoken and smart. Karen had to give her that, too: smart. And there was some inner hold she had on herself that maybe was the essence of dignity. Karen could see in her quick takes from behind *New York* the attention that Martha paid to the other women's words, the questions she asked, like she thought what was being said in this room right now was the most important thing happening in Manhattan. Karen could see how their eyes kept returning to Martha. She made them tell stories that they had been holding in their loneliness.

Karen put down *New York*. "Hey, ladies, services

have got to be over now. Could you please go to the lounge? I need to get some sleep."

"It's only eight-thirty," protested Michele, but she followed Martha out.

Chapter
9

Karen sat in the dining room over tepid morning coffee. She had come down late, and there were only a few women left at the tables—one studying on the second level, two in conversation at a small side table, another holding art transparencies from a blue plastic box up to the light and scanning them. Karen hadn't seen Mark for a week. He hadn't called. Only Annie had called. She had inquired several times of Mrs. Sergeant Major. No messages. She'd get over it. She was used to men not calling, and had decided over the years that it had something to do with men and who they were and little to do with her worth. She thought there had been men who didn't call because they cared for her overmuch.

Her first kiss, conferred upon Fred McFee in the mud room on Congress Street after an evening spent painting posters for his Student Council campaign: they had spent the evening in her basement, laughing and leaning on each other as they painted. MCFEE FOR ME, she had painted, in primitive calligraphy, over and over, until she had begun to think so. "Don't you have anything for me?" he asked before he left, his hands in his pockets, a hip thrust forward. He was three years older. She stepped toward him and kissed him in the direction of his lips, which, she realized in terror, were parted. She thought that meant they were going steady.

She had been thrilled, and lay about all weekend until she would see him again on Monday. She printed his name out below hers and crossed out the letters their names shared, then chanted "love, hate, friendship, marriage," touching a remaining letter for each word she said. It came out "hate." She added her middle initial to her name—T. It came out "love" that time. She did it again, printing both names, leaving the "T." in hers. She scratched out "Mrs. Fred McFee" in flowery script on the rough gray cover of her looseleaf. Monday came. Fred McFee barely nodded in her direction, though she stayed two hours after school mounting his posters. She had misunderstood.

And years later, there was Maury O'Neill, a student at Albany Law who had embraced her most enthusiastically in bed and said, "You are filled with life!" The first time she had given her body, she had given it to Maury O'Neill. He was slim and assured and wore pink oxford shirts from Brooks Brothers in New York City. He was richer than God, he had told her. His father was one of *the* lawyers for IBM, he said. He wanted to ravish her, he told her. And: *"You are filled with life!"* Indeed, in those days she had been. She knew he would call her. How could he not? He had seen her spirit along with her body. She found out later he was engaged to a girl from Rhode Island.

Maury and Fred were but early misunderstandings, to be followed by many others. The man she met a couple of New Year's Eves ago at Annie's party. They couldn't keep their hands off each other. They held

160

each other through dances fast and slow. "I didn't know you knew Howie!" Annie said, astonished. But Karen had just met Howie. She never heard from Howie all the New Year long. There was Ken, the photographer she had known only two days before he urgently pressed her to go to Barbados with him—a shoot that he was doing. He worked in the morning when the light was good, then came back to the hotel room and lay with her until there was no light at all. When they came back to New York, she left three messages on his machine before resuming life as she had known it.

She had loved all of these men, and she refused to believe that they had loved her less, unless men really were a different breed. This was not to say that all men loved her, but these men had. She *knew* they had! She was accustomed now to waiting out the pain until it passed, and it always did. What scared her was reading the poets in old age—Yeats' yearnings, or Thomas Hardy's—just yearning away in wasted bodies. So these stirrings just went on and on. It was too humiliating! Why couldn't you leave them back in adolescence with acne and training bras and the sweet lost taste of Fred McFee's mouth?

Karen had lived with two men. Lovely, crazy Phil was one.

The other, before Phil, when she was in Albany State at night and working days at the Department of Motor Vehicles, was an assemblyman who came to Albany when the legislature was on, then went back to his district for spring and summer. Karen had met him in a bar on State Street and had been impressed with his position (she had been very young at the time . . .), had not known until later that he had a pregnant wife and two children living among his constituents on the Pennsylvania border (. . . and stupid: she only realized when she was moved in and he told her she was *never* to answer the phone . . .) and had really liked the idea that he had a lovely apartment which he would vacate for half the year, leaving her with a housekeeper who came in a half-day each week to do dishes and wash whether they needed doing or not (. . . and not a little opportunistic). It meant she could leave the rodent-ridden ex-frat house she had shared with six other girls. It meant she had the quiet she needed for study after night classes, after days at Motor Vehicles. It wasn't all that admirable, this arrangement, but Karen could look back on it now and forgive herself. He was cute, her assemblyman, sort of, and somewhat witty. His place had given her a certain peace at a time when she needed it. He was an assemblyman of convenience, not passion.

But Phil she had loved, bird-beaked beer-drinking artist-boy, shining with Mylar and goodness, shattered by sorrow. She saw his back again, hurrying away from her at the Van Gogh exhibition.

And now this Mark Pitofsky. Weird and smart in the same way. Just maybe not as crazy. Please, not as crazy! No, she didn't think he was at all crazy. She nibbled idly at a rubbery English muffin. He was her fourteenth man, of the men she had actually had in her life, body to body. She wasn't counting souls. She wasn't even counting intercourse, because with a couple of them nothing had happened. But she had held fourteen men to her. She had held them close to her, chest by breast, cock by cunt. She wanted to hold Mark again. You couldn't say that Mark was convenient. You couldn't say he was the sort that called. She knew he wouldn't call if he hadn't called by now.

She was thinking about him too often! Like now, thinking of how she had lain on top of him one week ago, and pointed her feet so she could reach his toes, while all the time he scratched light circles around her angelbones. And, when she thought of him, like now over her empty cup, she felt adhesive tape wrapped tight around her heart. It was funny about the heart, that ugly bloody little pumper, mere hunk of muscle stuck in rib cage, that it should be the seat of her desire. Shit! Why couldn't she get a pacemaker installed that would regulate her impulses?

As she stood, she considered that there was another seat of desire and it was dictating right now. That tug she felt in the nethers was plenty physical. Heartfelt . . . cuntfelt. Wasn't her *brain* the organ that was supposed to take charge in these matters, so she could get a little healthy duality working, mind over body, alla that? Why was her brain so damn recessive in matters men?

Also, she knew it was this place, and the fact that she had never felt so alone before that made her frightened of riding out the customary pain of another man gone. She could find herself in a room like this when she was Martha's age! Did she want a life with a man? Did she want a child, ever? If she were thinking at all along these lines, there were certain preliminaries. If she wanted a man, she had to find a man. If she wanted a kid, she needed a man. And, the times being what they were, she would have to go get a man. The times being what they were, men were the new sex objects, to be pursued and courted and coaxed.

And so it was no mistake that after breakfast, Karen

went direct to the pay phone in the lobby with a quarter in her pocket and his number in her head. She rounded the last 0, humming "Love Hath No Pride." She counted the rings. Three.

"Karen," said his pleasant tenor. "What's doing?"

He sounded surprised to hear her voice, distant, as though he had never made contact with her angel-bones.

"So . . . hi," she said, affecting lightness and breeze. "How are you? Didja sell any swine stomachs yet this morning?" But she couldn't speak without her voice going high. You held me naked to you, she thought. We spoke in tongues, touching tongues. Your finger traced my lips, again and again.

She cleared her throat, then said, "I thought you were gonna call."

"But it's only been a few days," he said.

"Oh," said Karen, "but it was nice. I mean, wasn't it? I mean, I thought maybe there should be some kind of . . . *acknowledgment* of it . . . you know, that it was nice."

"Well . . . um . . . do you think maybe I should've written a thank-you note?"

She was silent.

"I'm sorry. Karen? . . . Did I hurt your feelings?"

"Yeah. Yeah, you did, actually."

"I don't know why I said that. A defense, I guess."

He needed a defense. A good sign.

The operator intervened.

"Give me your number," he said.

This time there was no one waiting behind her, so she gave him the number and hung up. She let it ring four times.

"To tell the truth, I was thinking about things," he said. "It's been a long time since I've been with a woman. You know, whether I should."

"Whether you should *what?*" Her heart dropped to the left of her bellybutton. Why was he throwing the scruples around? She remembered how hesitant he had been at first, when they were on his couch.

"I don't know you all that well." Silence. She decided not to make it easy for him by breaking it. "I mean, what you have in mind," he said finally.

Was it possible that *he* had something in mind? "You mean, are my intentions honorable?" she asked, smiling into the phone. A typewriter had started up. She covered her left ear with her hand and turned in the direction of the front desk. Mrs. Sergeant Major, working at her accounts in her uniformed shirtsleeves, nodded, too briskly, indicating to Karen that she had been paying close attention. She raised her voice a little. "You mean you think I only want you for your body?"

She heard his laugh, a little nervous, she thought. "You love sex," he said. Karen felt a movement in the nether lands as he said this. Also to know he was saying this at work. Karen knew what paltry privacy brokerage firms afforded. She only had Mrs. Sergeant Major listening in. There had to be three other brokers and a sales assistant at his elbow. Was it possible that he wasn't going for shock value, that the man was just himself? "You've been thinking about it?" he asked.

"Yes," Karen admitted. She was feeling quite weak.

"Which, me or it?"

"Hey, you're not supposed to have an ego, remember?" They laughed. "You and it," she said then.

"Good . . . that's probably good. We should see each other. Shall we meet? In five minutes? Lunch? Tonight?"

Karen was for meeting in his bed, but then he insisted on a bit of prebed sublimation, a viewing of *Stolen Kisses* at the Bleecker Street Cinema's Truffaut Retrospective that evening.

"So," he inquired, "how will you make the time pass between now and when you see me?"

"I'm going to get a job and an apartment!" said Karen with all the certainty she didn't feel.

"Wonderful! A day well spent. What are you looking for?" he asked.

But she knew he was getting into small talk, now that the arrangements were made. He was milking their conversation, stalling, to avoid little-old-widow cold calls. She had to ease him off the phone and back to brokering.

Martha's friend Michele was talking to Mrs. Sergeant Major now, leaning over the counter toward her. "Can I pay sixty now and more in a week? It's my last semester coming up and I have books to get. I can get an emergency loan, but even that takes time." Mrs. Sergeant Major said something about a waiting list. Karen heard but didn't hear as she passed on the way to the elevator.

She was thinking about Mark, wondering whether it was possible to see him clearly from Room 742 of the Arcadia.

She threw water on her face, and a little makeup. Martha's underwear was drying all over the bathroom. Karen never could tolerate a woman who washed handwashables by hand, and on a regular basis. Martha was one of these, Karen knew, even though she hadn't been there long enough to bear the regular-basis accusation. You could always pick a handwasher. Karen would never stoop to a hand job; it was one of her hang-ups.

Could Martha ever go for Karen's Save-the-Wash method? Karen thought with satisfaction that she was still a week away from laundry. She was wearing some old jeans and so still had several unders, one pair of skinny black pants folded neatly, and at least five T-shirts.

The funny thing was that, though Martha was compulsive about cleanliness, she never looked all that neat. Always like she just grabbed her crazy hair back in a rubber band, or a sweater too tight. She had a nice body, Martha, for someone her age, for someone any age, actually. Karen thought of the disaster coffee bean beads Martha chose to accent a pink turtleneck as she left this morning. It was different with Karen. She wasn't all that clean, but she looked hip. It was a natural quality with her. She was born hip and she would die hip. Indigent, dirty, wielding bags, but hip.

Karen picked up Martha's clipboard, sat on her own bed, and painfully calligraphed a sign on typing paper:

ME AND THE BOLL WEEVIL, LOOKIN' FOR A HOME!
BE IT EVER SO HUMBLE, WE'LL TAKE IT,
AS LONG AS OUR INCOME CAN MAKE IT.
REWARD

There was no real reward, since Karen had no money. The promise of one involved what her mother had always called a "mental reservation"—not a lie, just an omission.

("Ma! You didn't pay the phone company! How come you told them you did?"

"I didn't say I did, Karen. What I *said* was, 'The check is in the mail' *to you*. The woman at the phone company didn't hear me say *to you* because I said it to myself. I made a mental reservation. It's not a sin, Karen. You're just keeping something aside, on reserve. A mental reservation is *not* a lie!")

The words omitted on Karen's sign came after the word "REWARD." They were "IN HEAVEN." A celestial finder's fee. But then Karen felt guilty—truth in advertising and all. She ripped it up and calligraphed another sign:

REWARD
I'LL MAKE YOU A LASAGNE IF YOU FIND ME A KITCHEN
IT DOESN'T HAVE TO BE EAT-IN
(OR MAYBE YOU'D RATHER HAVE EGGPLANT PARMESAN?)

Karen's name and the Arcadia's number were written vertically ten times each at the bottom of the page. She would make a hundred copies, then clip a fringe at the bottom for an easy rip-off. A hundred copies meant that she'd have to go to Exec-Career for its primitive copy machine. The coast was clear, Annie had told her. H. Hank and Virginia Stubbs, the P who had replaced her, were in Palm Springs feeling around for franchise possibilities.

So. Back into the headhunter–job-hunter dress and pantyhose. She threw on her jacket and opened the door to be startled by Michele, who was startled in return.

"Hi . . . Martha's not here?" said Michele, alcohol on her breath. She looked down at the floor, trying to get control. "I'm sorry . . . excuse me. I was . . . uh . . . Martha's not around anywhere, is she?"

"No . . . she went out early today. I'm not sure where." She doesn't have to make it so obvious what a drag it is to see me instead of Martha, Karen thought, and then was irked that she should even care.

"She said to stop by. I'm sorry to disturb you." She reached in her bag for a cigarette.

Karen looked at her. She was in a bad way, even by Arcadia standards. Her hands were trembling, fumbling with the lighter, and her eyes were welling as she looked up. She was embarrassed by Karen's gaze and turned quickly. "I'll stop back again."

"I was going for a cup of coffee," Karen lied. "Would you like to join me?"

Michele lifted an open hand in front of her face and waved it quickly. "No . . . it's OK. I'll be fine." And then: "If you do see her, tell her to come to 516. No . . . I'm gonna have to go to the library. I'll check back later." She hesitated. "Do you think I should leave her a note?"

So urgent and needy, Karen thought, a little hurt, if she had admitted it, that Michele had turned her down, but wanted Martha so much. Karen motioned her in. "Go ahead, if you want, sure." She stood aside to admit Michele, then left. Karen got as far as the elevator and decided: Good. She didn't want to have coffee with Michele. She had just offered because she seemed so sad. Anyway, it would never be just coffee with someone like Michele. You'd get pulled down along with her. You'll never get out of this if you start fraternizing with the inmates, Carmody.

Karen stopped at likely places all the way up to Exec-Career inquiring about work, employment that would start immediately. An art gallery owner said he was between shows now and he'd get back to her. A school principal said she could do substitute teaching ad hoc, but that her teachers seemed to be enjoying good health right now. A waiter in a plate-glass restaurant said they were still serving lunch and that she should come back at five to meet the manager. McDonald's was looking for someone who took a size eight. That was the uniform they had when their last girl quit. They'd be reordering and would have twelves, maybe in two weeks. Could she come back then? A pasta store wanted someone with experience on the pasta machine. She could cook, she told the pastry chef at a large hotel, but then had to admit she'd never done a brioche and further demonstrated her ignorance by staring in mute astonishment at the huge whipped cream vat.

Annie answered the door and hugged her friend. Karen dragged in, dejected in the late afternoon. Annie was alone. "Stick with me for another half hour and we can cut out. Things are real quiet. All hell broke loose on Wall Street today. Ain't nobody thinking of changing jobs in the middle of this shit. Even though they all want to."

Annie was wearing her black turtleneck and her black skirt with the slit, and a pair of very high, very expensive-looking black patent sling-backs that Karen had never seen. Michael was out snagging out-of-town brokers at a "Dare to be Rich" seminar at the New York Hilton. Karen stuffed her Persian lamb into the broom closet for old time's sake, and sat at her old desk, Virginia Stubbs' new desk. Virginia Stubbs had a new desk blotter, pink, held in a frame of white fleurs-de-lis on pink leather. Karen took off her headhunter pumps, which had been pinching her feet after the combat boots, and put them on top of Virginia Stubbs' papers, next to a vase of yellowing baby's breath. She glanced at Virginia Stubbs' heart-shaped box of candy.

"My, my . . . another Valentine's Day has long since come and gone! Goodness! How *did* it slip my mind? Ah suppose my suitors couldn't *find* me at the Arcadia. Ah expect they are all just *in-con-solable*." Dead-on Blanche DuBois. She inspected the box. "What kind of a woman would be able to keep a filled box of candy on her desk for two weeks, even if they are soft fillings?" She stuck her index finger in one, then in two more. "All cherry liqueur." She screwed her face in disgust. She stuck her finger in one more to make certain, then closed the box. She wiped this finger, carefully, back and front, on Virginia Stubbs' new blotter. She looked up at Annie, who had been watching, amused.

"You are looking at a P," Karen said, and began to cry.

"Karen, don't you dare! You're being very hard on yourself, turning your anger at circumstances inward. Things happen to people, that's all. They should *never* be internalized. I thought you were doing so well, acting out on the cherry liqueurs." Annie's minor had been psychology, a discipline whose tenets she found herself calling upon daily, since there were plenty of head trips in headhunting. She came behind Karen and began massaging her neck and her shoulders. "Breathe deeply . . . God, I can feel the tension! Your neck is one big knot, poor baby."

This kindness made Karen cry harder. "My mother is on her way to the desert!"

"What about some tea?" asked Annie, and then, with forced brightness, "How's that guy, you know, that kept bugging me for your phone number?"

Karen wiped snot and tears away with the back of her hand, and wiped the back of her hand on the blotter. "I slept with him."

"Oh, shit!" Annie grimaced delightedly. "So?"

"I like him a lot, but I think he's reluctant." She lifted a strand of top hair.

"The nature of the beast," said Annie, shrugging. "Is he married?"

"No. Was. Now he lives with a valet." Annie raised her eyebrows quizzically. "You know, the wooden kind."

"He's neat, then," Annie said approvingly. A whistle from the kitchenette. She left to silence it.

"Actually, it's just a *show* of neatness." Karen stood and followed her to the doorway, her elbow resting on the handle of the broom/coat closet. "Anyway, I *really* like him, Annie. When you talk to him, he keeps saying things like, 'Just how do you mean that?' It's not enough that I say something, we have to backtrack over it, run it by him again while he *analyzes* it." She watched as Annie took the tea bags from their paper envelopes and put them in the cups.

"Enthusiasm doesn't become you, Karen." They laughed. Annie danced, squeezed, and discarded her tea bag, then shot in fake lemon. Karen took hers straight.

"Sorry to be so perverse." Karen stared at the "Teatime Thought" on the box, then held it up to Annie:

Hearts may fail, and Strength outwear, and Purpose turn
to Loathing
But the everyday affair of business, meals, and clothing,
Builds a bulkhead 'twixt Despair and the Edge of Nothing.

—Kipling

"Arrgh! What kind of Teatime Thought is that? How do you think an existentialist ever got hired as the Teatime Thought coordinator?"

But Annie disagreed. "I think it's a really good Teatime Thought. I mean, isn't making tea a perfect example of the bulkhead?"

"You've given this Thought some thought, I see," said Karen.

Annie nodded and shrugged. "Yeah, well . . . I make a lot of tea. Here, sit." She placed Karen's tea next to Karen's shoes. They sat down. "So . . .?"

"So?"

"So you got laid, sweetie?"

"Yeah." Karen pressed her tea bag on the blotter with her thumb and dragged it a few inches. It broke open, setting free its wet leaves.

"And?" Annie prompted.

"So did he."

"Great. We're making progress."

"Yeah, but then he didn't call for a week! I had to call him." Her words came out in a torrent, and she felt the hurt again as she said them.

"Aha! The emotional pullback," said Annie.

"Would you care to explain this phenomenon?"

"He liked you, darling. Too close, eh? He had to pull back. Otherwise, who knows?"

"Is this Freud or Annie?"

173

"Me . . . mine, formed after much trial and error."
She sipped most world-weariedly, holding her cup with
both hands.

"Sounds right." Karen told Annie about Maury
O'Neill, who told her she was filled with life and never
called.

"Well, *exactly*. 'Filled with life! *You are filled with
life!*' I love it! Well, we are, aren't we? Women are—
literally, right? And that's what scares them, eh?"

"What?"

Annie seemed exasperated that Karen couldn't see
it. "Possibility . . . children. All the stuff hooking up
with one of us means. Joy . . . pain . . . responsibility.
Life. It's part of nature. The female elephant has to
wrestle the male to the ground to get him to mate with
her."

"Oh, that must be a vision!" It reminded Karen of a
joke. "What did the elephant say to the naked man?"

"What?"

"How do you eat with that thing?"

"Shut up, Karen." They laughed. "Look," said
Annie, "I didn't tell you, you're so taken up with your
shit . . . there's this guy I met Sunday when my smoke
alarm went off. My battery was dying, and you know
the warning noise it makes . . ."

Karen launched into hysterics at this. She put her
head in her hand, upsetting her cup and sloshing the
remaining tea on the blotter.

"Jesus, willya listen? So, anyway, I'm taking it to
Radio Shack 'cause I can't get the battery out and it
keeps going off: this real high-pitched unearthly *bleet,
bleet, bleet!* Surreal, y'know? So this guy on the street
volunteers to take it out. He's lovely! He lives in the

building across the street. I'd seen him before at the bus stop. So, we had a drink. His name is Ed—one of those charismatic Irish types. I told him he was Special Ed. It was great. We went out Sunday night and then again on Monday. We went to this little Spanish restaurant in the village. His ex-wife is Cuban and they used to go there all the time. She's in Miami now, so he's free to use it. Anyway, we got looped on margaritas and just talked, you know? So I see him on the street this morning and *he barely nods at me*. He's terrified of me, is the point. This is actually a wonderful sign, is it not? This means he *adores* me. This means we had too much fun." She smiled broadly. "Oh, we had such a great time! I'm not going to give up on him."

"What are you gonna do?"

Annie spoke with considered emphasis. "I am going to lie in wait for a while, then wrestle him to the ground! It *is* a terrific sign, right? I'm *danger*, right? I mean, it's for his sake. I would feel too sorry for him if I didn't go after him. He shouldn't have to give me up when I'm so full of life!"

"Remember the old 'Let him go, let him tarry' song? Remember the 'plenty-more-pebbles-on-the-beach' line? Did your mother give that to you?" Margaret Carmody had always sung it. No man was good enough for her daughters, anyway.

Annie nodded and laughed. "What happens when you find a pebble you like?"

"That's right." Karen liked this particular pebble she had found. It was such a peculiar pebble, very bright and oddly formed—the way it caught the light and bounced it back again. "Even my mother now realizes that there aren't all that many pebbles on the beach. I'm no chicken, she told me when I was there last weekend. No chicken."

"It's what you need a mother for, to tell you things like that," said Annie.

"Mother-knocker," Karen accused. "Well, it's just so screwed up, eh? So many women . . . And all these gorgeous men who are gay, besides. Do you think it's nature's way of dealing with overpopulation?"

"I wouldn't put it past him," said Annie. "He's like that."

"I mean, think of all the women our age who won't have kids. At the Arcadia there are all these women going into their forties without children. *Barren.* Christ, what a word that is! Barren . . . so biblical and awful. You ever think about it?"

"Fuck it!" said Annie with feeling. "Fuck barren-ness and fuck the U.S. Census Bureau. What about just getting laid in this world? Isn't that the point? Lying with someone sweet?"

"If you can."

"If you can," Annie agreed. "For as long as you can."

"We're no chickens, Annie."

"Christ, Carmody, we need to stop sipping tea and get ourselves a drink!"

"Sounds wonderful. Oh, jeeze, just let me copy my fliers!"

"I'll go pee."

And so, since Annie was impecunious because of her new slingbacks, and Karen just naturally so, they decided to case the area for the bar offering the best free hor d'oeuvres at Happy Hour. They found a good one. It had Buffalo chicken wings *and* little hot dogs!

Chapter
10

Karen left Annie around nine and returned to the Arcadia to find Vinnie of Vinnie's Viddies in conference with the Sergeants Major. The Thursday night delivery!

"Yo! C'mere." He leaned toward her confidentially. "They think I'm some kinda crazed radical terrorist rapist or somethin', perpetrating upon all these women. They must think I got a bomb in here."

"No," Karen whispered. "They think you're a man."

"Oh," Vinnie mouthed.

"Miss Carmody," said the Sergeant Major, "this man says he's acquainted with you. He says he's got to go to your room to hook up a VCR. Men are not allowed in the rooms."

"Neither are VCRs," said Mrs. Sergeant Major. She and her man were in civvies tonight. Must be stepping out, thought Karen. They should stick to uniforms and keep their taste a secret. He was wearing waffle weave slacks, high pockets, the better to cover his small firm pot, and a button-down shirt with short sleeves that flapped over his skinny arms as he gesticulated. The missus was demure in a cerise bell-bottom pantsuit with a matching Ban-Lon mock turtleneck. Uniforms were more flattering to their forms.

Vinnie, himself in black, with a swath of black lace tied around his neck, was sizing them up, too. Then he looked meaningfully at Karen, the meaning being: "Let's take 'em!" She saw that he meant to take them by charm. Karen would sooner have chosen force. Vituperations, certainly. Vitriol even. All things came easier to her than charm in a fight.

He was concentrating on Mrs. Rawlins. It was done with an earnestness of blue eye and softness of manner that belied all of his punk musculature. He came easy to charm. "Hey, lady . . . I know this woman here. She's only gonna rent uplifting-type films, don' worry. I guarantee I won't rent her no X-rateds. She's gonna look at *opera* on this thing." He winked at Mrs. Sergeant Major. Karen wondered when Mrs. Rawlins had last been on the receiving end of a wink. "You oughta stop by my place and see some of the stuff we have. *Citizen Kane* . . . *Wuthering Heights* . . . *Charlotte's Web*. Good stuff, you'd be amazed."

"I didn't see anything in the bylaws about VCRs, Mrs. Rawlins," Karen said sweetly, trying. "I thought it would be all right. I already gave Vinnie my deposit."

"Aw, it's cool about the deposit if they say you really can't have it. I mean I'm just starting out in this business and all, and I like to make a little money, but I ain't gonna stick you for no deposit. That's not Vinnie."

They were conning Mrs. Sergeant Major the way she and Bill had always conned their mother. They were smooth in tandem, she and this Vinnie guy. He riffed, she played backup.

The Sergeants Major were quiet. Mention of the

bylaws had stumped them. They had taken time in the preparation of the bylaws, trying to cover all bases: drink, sex, rollaway cots, security deposits, activity fees, air raids, incontinence . . . They had printed and collated a thousand copies of the bylaws, eight pages each. It had been one heck of a lot of work! But they had not considered this new thing called VCR.

"I was planning to share it," said Karen. "There are a couple of women here who are in film studies at NYU. I thought they could use it for research."

"It'd be good for the morale of the place," Vinnie interjected, checking out the hallway, the shabby parlor.

"The morale of the Arcadia is just fine," huffed the Sergeant Major.

Mrs. Sergeant Major took a skinny arm and drew him aside. "Maybe we could permit it, Earl," Karen heard her whisper, ". . . could be a way of the Arcadia coming into the future."

"It could be a moral use of technology," Karen suggested as they came back.

"Exactly," said Vinnie. "That's how I look at it. I mean, I couldn't face each new day if that wasn't how I saw my business. You can't just do anything for a living when you know this isn't your only life. You gotta make it mean something when you want to move on to a higher plane."

What a beautiful son-of-a-gun bullshit artist this guy is, thought Karen. He was a lesson.

The Sergeants Major conferred briefly in their office behind the front desk and agreed to let Karen have her VCR, provided that she pay ten dollars more a month for the extra electricity. Karen agreed. She knew she'd be out of here in another month. She'd certainly have a job then. And besides, what was ten more bucks when you didn't have anything?

Nothing would do, then, but that Mrs. Sergeant Major would accompany Vinnie to Room 742 for the installation. If a man had to go to upstairs, it would be with her.

Going up in the elevator, Karen knew she was eviction bait. She hadn't been expecting Mrs. Sergeant Major. The Dewar's had been left out. She knew the room to be in a state of disgrace—newspapers, résumés, magazines, Tampax, shoes, and clothes strewn on the floor. Heavy New York City soot on the window sills. Martha's underwear hanging high. No doubt the condoms were still prominently displayed on her fake Ethan Allen dresser. There was no reason to suppose that they had thoughtfully hidden themselves away in a drawer. It was what had told her as a child that life was miserably real and unmagic. Things stayed where you left them. It was a principle of metaphysics. A lost object stayed lost no matter how much you desired it or prayed to St. Anthony to find it. An incriminating object would stay there to incriminate you no matter how mightily you wished it away.

Christ.

Her date with Mark!

It was nine-fifteen. She was supposed to have met him at the Bleecker Street at six.

Carmody, you fuck up! She wished she could wish this away. Wish it into one of those anxiety dreams and out of reality. She wished, at least, that she could wish Mrs. Sergeant Major and Vinnie away so that she could call him or go to him, or just lie on her bed and repent in dust and ashes. She would call him as soon as she was rid of them.

"Man on the floor, man on the floor," Mrs. S. M. was saying, unable to contain her excitement. Vinnie was suppressing a grin, enjoying it immensely, probably keeping an eye out for women in states of undress. For their part, the women refrained from throwing open their doors to catch a glimpse of the alien.

Karen turned the key, but Martha had used the chain lock. She was either asleep or in the shower. They knocked a few times, but no answer. Karen thought she heard movement, something drop behind the door, but still no Martha. Mrs. Sergeant Major opened it as far as the chain would permit and inserted her mouth in the aperture. "Oh, Miss Leonard, Miss Leonard," she sang.

"I got a cool way to get chains off doors," said Vinnie, deadpan. "It's a piece of cake, really, if you've done it a coupla times. All you need is a number-two pencil." Karen and Mrs. Sergeant Major exchanged an involuntary glance, and Karen decided he had been a sacker of towns in one of his previous lives.

After another full minute of knocking and waiting, Karen was wondering if Mrs. S. M. would ever go for the number-two pencil. Which was when they heard Martha coming toward the door. "We have a man out here," Mrs. Sergeant Major warned breathlessly as Martha closed the door to take off the chain.

Martha looked even more distracted than usual. Her hair was down and Karen realized, startled, that it was no longer the crazy red it had been, but faded now and streaked with gray, short fine new hairs of white wisping around her forehead. She was wearing the worn terry bathrobe Karen had become accustomed to.

And, because she was barefoot, and Karen was wearing her headhunter heels, Martha seemed small and vulnerable. She was quite agitated. The white of her hair seemed to catch the light in a kind of delicate aureole effect. She seemed almost radiant to Karen compared with the morning Martha, who had gone out into the winter day with some grimness of purpose, wearing strung-up coffee beans and her sober down jacket. Karen looked at Mrs. S. M., who was beaming into the doorway at Martha with immense approval.

"I'm so sorry, I was in the shower," Martha said. But there was not a bit of wet upon her. She flushed, and Karen saw how pretty she was.

Here goes, Karen thought grimly, as the missus entered the room. Welcome to the shithouse, Mrs. Sergeant Major. She cast a cold eye in the direction of her Dewar's bottle. But it wasn't there. Nor was the Ramses box in its place of honor on the bureau. In fact, nothing was on the bureau but the little lamp and the Corps-issued dresser doily. And, *mirabile dictu,* her bed was made! Martha's bed was a bit rumpled, but other wise their room was pristine. Martha had cleaned. She had insured Karen's continued stay at the Arcadia. For, as much as Karen bitched about the place, it would have been the pits to move. And to where? Karen flashed her a look of uncut gratitude, but Martha's eyes would not meet hers.

Vinnie deftly hooked up in the corner at the foot of Karen's bed. Mrs. S. M. asked him what he had meant by moving on to a higher plane.

"Well, it stands to reason, doesn't it? You've had past lives, you're gonna have future lives."

Karen, relieved at her reprieve, turned miserably to thoughts of Mark. Had he tried to call? Why had she forgotten? Her morning of résumés, her afternoon nap, her evening with Annie—which of these had been so consuming that it forced him out of her head, who had been in said head since their night together? She had talked to him only this morning, and things that seemed possible in her daydreams this morning had turned inconceivable. Things like children, maybe. Why not children? A child, anyway? Inconceivable.

It was inconceivable precisely because conception of them—children, life with a gentle smart man, some ease and, yes, even, fun—had already taken form in Karen's mind. Uh-uh-uh-uh . . . ! The Behemoth Self-Destruct, which rode on her back, didn't like that. The monster's vibrissae were all aquiver at the presence of positive thinking. Its very death force threatened; it did what it had to do. It kicked in. Hard. It was this behemoth and not Karen who had stood Mark Pitofsky up. Try telling that to Mark Pitofsky!

Christ! Why couldn't she carry Jiminy Cricket around on her shoulder instead?

"We are *here*," Vinnie was saying as he stooped to trail the cord to the outlet under Karen's bed. "Think about it. Isn't that *astounding*, that we're here, in this room in the late 1980s when alla those pharaohs are dead, and Thomas Jefferson and the Incas are dead . . . how come we're not dead? Did you ever think *you* are Thomas Jefferson?"

Mrs. Sergeant Major was standing above him, entranced. "But how do you know about all your past lives?" she asked. Martha was pacing between the beds. The amaryllis had shot up in the last day, Karen noticed through her gloom. Its firm bud stood a good six inches above the peanut butter container.

"Hey . . . I've been there." Vinnie stood up from his work and pointed both thumbs at his chest. "I've regressed into four of my previous lives."

"Really? *How?*" asked Mrs. Sergeant Major, fascinated.

Go away, please, everyone, Karen thought.

Vinnie shrugged. "You need a past life regressor to help, or sometimes a discarnate tells me about them, and you sorta go into this kind of trance . . ."

"What's a discarnate?"

"Oh, you know, a disembodied spirit. They get all their data from the Akashik records, you know what they are? Where the vibrations of every event that has occurred since the universe began are stored."

"But weren't you afraid?" Mrs. Sergeant Major asked.

Karen sighed, brushed past the pacing Martha and flopped back on her pillow. She sat back up and took the amaryllis bud, strong yet velvet-soft between her fingers. She closed her eyes. She had really blown it this time.

"Yeah, a course it's scary sometimes. In one of my past lives I was in shackles, and now *that* was really frightening. But I was with good guides, you know . . . I trusted them. And it's OK to be scared." Vinnie stood up. "Hey, miss, uh . . . Karen . . ." She started. "Everything's ready, just that you're gonna need to get an extension cord."

"Can you get *The Sound of Music* on this?" Mrs. S. M. asked.

"Sure!" replied Vinnie generously. Was he thinking of an untapped market of two hundred lonely women living in his area? Was he considering future installations?

Vinnie started to give Karen some instructions, but she couldn't concentrate. "Look, uh . . . you got anything written? Can I come by the shop tomorrow?"

"Sure," he responded largely, ebulliently. "Until tomorrow."

He went to the door followed by his guide. "Bye-bye," said Mrs. Sergeant Major chummily, and gave a little half-wave to Karen and Martha. Was it possible? Had Karen heard her giggle?

Karen sat up, picked up her bag, and began rummaging through, looking for a quarter to call Mark. "Thanks for cleaning. You sure did it fast," she said, absently, because Martha was standing silently by, and the moment seemed to call for someone to say something. "You saved my life."

Martha didn't speak, but waved her hand as though it were nothing.

"You got a quarter?" Karen asked her, and when Martha didn't reply, looked up, about to repeat her request. But it was apparent that Martha was greatly disturbed by something. She began to file her nails, standing at her dresser. She put down the file and shuffled through the shag to the window. Karen stuck her wallet back into her bag. Maybe it's the electricity she's generating with all that shuffling that's shooting the tension all over the room, mused Karen. Martha put her hands on the sill and leaned forward on straightened arms, her brow against the pane. She stared down at the Square park, then went into the bathroom and, for a moment, Karen actually thought she heard her talking to herself behind the closed door. She emerged and sat on her bed, and began to read the paper. Karen's own nervous system had begun to shoot out staccato impulses in sync with Martha's. Time to make a break. She would get change from someone in the lobby. Karen stood up. But then Martha jumped up and, still holding the paper, came toward her.

"What is the matter?" Karen asked finally.

"Maybe you can save mine . . . my life. Soon."

"What can I do?"

"I . . . uh . . . was hoping you'd be out tonight."

Yeah, Karen thought, I wish. He might not be home yet anyway. Maybe he stopped somewhere after he gave up on her, or maybe he saw the movie. She forgot what they were planning to see. How long had he waited for her? "What is it? I have to go downstairs for just a minute . . ."

Martha reached for Karen's wrist. She gave a little laugh.

"*What?*" Karen asked.

"We're roommates, right? We're thrown together here, sort of like on *The Bridge of San Luis Rey.*"

So far, Karen agreed. They were roommates, it was true, and there was no denying the arbitrariness of Room 742, This Life, the Arcadia. She hadn't read *San Luis Rey* since ninth grade, but she got the picture. What was Martha getting at? Skip the lead-ins, for Christ's sake. Hit me with it.

Martha did. "There's somebody here . . . he's in the bathroom."

Karen's reaction would have done Mrs. Sergeant Major proud. She was on her feet immediately.

"What?!" Had she shrieked it? "You're kidding." She was amazed at Martha's relative calm. Martha was nervous, all right, but she didn't seem to be terrified.

Karen whispered weakly, "Does he have a gun?" She felt her adrenalin seep out the pores of her great toe. Paralysis set in just when she most needed to move.

Martha gave another laugh. "I'm sorry. I didn't mean to scare you. I invited him."

"*Who* is *him?*" This woman worked fast . . . a week in New York, nearly fifty, and she has a man, against all odds! Karen leaned toward Martha and spoke softly and slowly, as one would to a naughty child. "Martha. Men aren't allowed."

"He's a boy."

"Boys aren't allowed."

"Neither is liquor," Martha said simply. "He doesn't have any place to go."

Karen ceased her protest for a moment because she was interested in the logistics of smuggling males into the Arcadia. "What, you just walked him right in and on up in the elevator?"

"I brought him up the back stairs from the basement. There's a door there that opens on the alley. It's a bolt lock, from the inside. He just waited out there till I got it open. It was a little rusted, so it was kind of tough. Then I let him in and went ahead on each flight to make sure the coast was clear. But nobody uses those stairs anyway."

"But who *is* he?"

"A kid without a home. I met him at Port Authority Bus Terminal."

"Port Authority . . . no place to go," Karen repeated dully, holding her eyelid. "Martha, he's got to go someplace!"

"But he can't. It's cold. It's *February*. He spent last night at Port Authority. You've been there, right? He said before Port Authority he had spent a night in an armory with four hundred other people. You had to lift up the bed and put each of your shoes under a bedpost so no one would steal them. He said it was like some weird cartoon, all these beds wearing shoes, like they were gonna do a dance together or something. You'd trip over them if you walked through the aisle to the bathroom. He said he was so afraid of being robbed or molested he didn't sleep all night."

They were silent for a moment. "Look, Martha, you're from Ohio, right? In Ohio people have places to go. But you gotta understand something. In New York there are plenty of people that don't have places to go. There are maybe"—Karen hesitated; she had seen a statistic somewhere—"a *hundred thousand* people that don't have places to go. So what are you gonna do, invite them all?"

"Just him."

"Who is he? What makes him so special?"

"He's a kid, that's all."

But Karen thought that she was lying. She thought of the boy in the glossies she had found. It was a setup. He wasn't just any kid.

"He can't stay here," Karen said as though it were final. "If they find out, we're out on our asses. If they find out, *we* won't have a place to go."

"He has to. I'm sorry to involve you, but he has to."

"Would you like to tell me how long you're thinking of? I mean, how long do you think we could stand it? How long do you think you could pull it off without getting caught? I mean, are you planning to enroll him in school? Shit, Martha!" Couldn't she make her understand? *He couldn't stay!* And where was Karen supposed to go? There was no other room in the Arcadia. No vacancy, and even if there were, she didn't think they'd let her make a change.

"Maybe a few days . . . until I can find him somewhere decent."

"If you find somewhere decent, let me know. We've got nothing *ourselves*. It's not like we're the Rockefellers at Pocantico Hills that we have room to take in derelicts and put them in our guest houses."

"But the Rockefellers *don't*, is the point, and he isn't."

"Isn't what?"

"A derelict."

"What is he?"

"A child who needs help."

"And you found him at Port Authority."

"Yes. He asked me for change."

He asks her for change and she takes him home! It was so outlandish that Karen was beginning to believe her. "Don't you think you're overdoing the Christian bit?" Even the mystics, nuns, and Social Freethinkers she knew didn't drag people home.

"I'm not Christian. I'm not anything. I was just brought up funny, I guess."

Karen heard a sneeze from the bathroom. "Where's he gonna sleep? On this filthy shag? Or are you gonna order him up a rollaway cot from Mrs. Sergeant Major and have him sign the guest directory and join us in the dining hall for breakfast?"

"Here. Look, we move my dresser over by my bed, and he can have the alcove by the bathroom."

She wanted Karen to help her move the dresser! "We'll have to step over him to get to the john, and how you gonna open your dresser drawers?"

"They'll open enough." Martha sat down and began undoing one of the balls on the chenille bedspread, waiting for Karen's response. "I think Brenda will lend us her exercise mat."

"You're gonna tell *Brenda* about this?"

"Certain people, yes, that I trust. Maybe they could help us cover for him."

"You trust me?"

"Well, I have to, don't I?" Martha laughed. "But I do, actually."

Karen had been raging at this woman, laying this intrusion on her and putting them both on the line like this. Suddenly she managed an ironic laugh at the absurdity of it, this crazy lady from Ohio taking in kids. But Karen knew this, too: she was good—more good than most.

"He can stay one night," Karen said. "Let him out of solitary."

He was young. Probably one wet dream past pubescence. But was he the boy in the picture? Blond like the boy in the picture. Ethereal blondness of hair and lightness of bone. Newness of bone also, bones still knitting from growth. Young and long. It was hair which would leave him early. The fineness of it and its peculiar white-gold did not stay long on a man. Bones so fragile as to cause a mother worry. He was wearing Karen's dirty sweat pants and her ancient Shetland sweater, a fact that did not escape Karen's notice, or her heart. They fit him, but for an extra inch of ankle showing above bare feet. "I hope you don't mind," said Martha. "His clothes were filthy . . . I threw them down the chute. He was taking a shower when everyone came to the door. Your stuff was on the hook in the bathroom, so he just grabbed it."

She had to hand it to Martha. If you were gonna take home a derelict, this was the kind you should pick. Sweet-faced, innocent, young. Martha had definitely saved him from the claws of the chickenhawks in Times Square. Karen hastened to remind herself that she was a lone eagle, not a chicken hawk.

His name was Terry. No last name was offered, probably so she couldn't get the truant officer after him. "I'm sorry to bother you," he mumbled, awkwardly shifting his weight from one bare foot to the other, staring alternately at the shag and at the ceiling. He licked his lower lip nervously.

"Oh, that's OK," said Karen. She appreciated understatement.

She realized that she, too, had been staring, not at him, merely, but at Martha. She had been staring at Martha staring at him. Martha was thrilled by him. It was with some effort that she removed her eyes from him to speak to Karen. "Terry had things hard, family trouble, you know?" Martha started to tell Karen his story.

"No, look . . . not right now. I'll be back in a minute, OK? I have to make a phone call."

Chapter
11

Karen tried Mark several times. Busy. She ducked out to the coffee shop to kill time . . . better than going to her room right now. She ordered a cup of soup and let it get cold while she tried him three times there, and then twice more when she got back to the Arcadia's lobby. Busy. He probably had his phone off the hook. She considered going to see him, then considered how obsessive that might seem.

She reluctantly returned to her room. The boy was sound asleep on the floor, covered by one of Martha's blankets.

Martha was already in bed, but sat up when Karen entered. "Terry was exhausted," said Martha. "Listen, thanks a lot. I promise you that things will be OK. I'm going to be so careful. Earlier, when I was in the bathroom, he picked up the phone, but there was no one on it . . . probably a wrong number. Anyway, I told him not to do that again under *any* circumstances, that no one can know there's a boy in here . . ."

"Somebody called and *he* picked up the phone?!"

"He didn't understand . . . it was a reflex reaction. He'd just come in the room after sneaking up the back stairs, and I was in the john and the phone rang and he picked it up. Don't worry, it wasn't the Sergeants Major. They would've been up here in a shot!"

"What time was it?"

"I don't know . . . about seven maybe . . . an hour or so before you came up with that fellow who installed your machine."

"Fuck!" said Karen. "Did he say anything?"

Martha was mystified. "Just 'hello,' that's all . . ."

"I mean the guy on the other end!"

"No. I said . . . whoever it was just hung up. I'm sure it was a wrong number."

"I'm not at all sure." Karen exhaled audibly, then went into the bathroom, taking care not to step on the sleeping boy.

*H*e was not really sleeping. It wasn't the floor. He had slept in plenty of worse places. It was just that he was a little bit nervous. He was exhausted, as Martha had said. He would sleep soon, just not yet. Still, he thought it best to pretend to be asleep. It was one of the easier things he had done this week. He lay still and let all the thoughts come, the way they do when you can't sleep.

He thought of his mother, as he always did at night. She had died young, of Hodgkin's disease. He never knew his father, but he had loved his mother. He was from Egg Harbor City, New Jersey, originally, and, after his mother died, Atlantic City, where he had been a ward in three different foster homes. He would not go to school. He went to the three foster homes because he would not go to school. It didn't matter. He still wouldn't go to school. In fact, he skipped school more every time they moved him to a new foster home. He was sixteen now, too old to be placed in a foster home, even if one wanted him. He should be in his junior year, but he had not really attended since ninth grade. The high school was too large, with hundreds of students knowing when their classes changed and what their homework had been and what to wear and what to say to their friends. He had gone back a few times in September, but he was in with young kids, junior high. Also, the place was too hot. When he sat in class, he started to sweat, and got the feeling he would hyperventilate. He had heard that if you were feeling claustrophobic you would hyperventilate. He never did hyperventilate because he always got out.

He had gotten into a couple of fights at school, once about his crummy sneakers, once because some kid said his mother had abandoned him, once because a guy had been getting weird with a girl a few lockers down from his. Fights were part of what he was afraid of, and the feelings that he got. There had been a couple of times in fights when he really felt like he wanted to kill somebody, really punch someone bloody. That scared him bad. He wanted to stay away from people if that's how they made you feel. People could be really nasty. He wanted to control himself. He had read about a basketball player who said discipline was important. You had to do things, keep busy.

He hung out on the streets for a while, went to the mall sometimes, or sometimes hitched along the Garden State Parkway up to Tuckerton, where he could work for the day in Clover Hill Farm and Country Store. That was what he liked. It was like country there, just a little ways from the exit. The women who owned it were sisters. They paid OK and didn't ask him anything. The day before yesterday, though, when he was hitching, he got a ride from a salesman who was coming to the city for the day. Only two and a half hours away, the salesman said—why not? He sold paper cups for water coolers. Terry thought it was funny that you could make your living selling just a little thing like cone-shaped cups. They stopped at the service area and he bought Terry a roast beef sandwich. Terry stayed in the car past Tuckerton and Toms River and Asbury Park, for the ride, for the hell of it. He had never been to the city, though he had lived so close for all of his life. What else could he do? Return to a foster home that didn't want him, didn't know what to do with him, to people who in fact had already told the social worker that he had to go. He couldn't blame them, that they didn't know what to do with him, since he didn't know what to do with himself.

He pulled the pillow over his face and lay still. The blond woman, Karen, was coming out of the bathroom. The place at the bottom of his spine jumped a little when she stepped over him, but other than that he was completely still, hardly breathing. He heard her undressing. If he turned, he could probably see her naked in the light from the window. That was all he would need, her catching him spying on her! She was furious enough with him already. He heard her bed creak a few times, heard her sigh, and then after a while there was quiet, only breathing in the room.

He moved a little then. It was safe. How long could he stay here? What would he do? He thought maybe he could get a job in the city. Or maybe get his equivalency, just take the test. Would they let you take the test in New York State if you were only sixteen? He was good in English and OK in math, at least he had been. It was exciting, driving in with the salesman, to see the buildings in the distance. The buildings, the city, had always, really, been so close. It was better to see it from far away, he knew now.

Coming in he had hummed that song his mother used to sing—"Oh, what a beautiful city, beautiful city, hal-le-lu"—he hummed it quietly, to himself, as they were driving along. But being here he saw things close-up—drug addicts nodding out, the poor scraggy prostitutes, some of them real young, some old women, out selling themselves in freezing weather in clothes that hardly covered them. Guys sleeping curled around empty bottles, their frozen spitty breath the only thing that showed they weren't dead. It was a mean city! He hated it. It made him nearly puke, what he saw. It made him cry, once, but then he caught himself. It seemed a long time ago that he was in the paper cup salesman's car, a long time since he was excited.

It was freezing outside and a beggar told him to go to Port Authority to get warm, told him where it was, only a few blocks away. He sat around there for hours the first day, and then the cops picked him up, made him go to the armory. "There's a bed there with your name on it!" one of them said. But the armory had been so crowded and scary he didn't sleep, and then in the morning the workers gave you a bag breakfast and you had to get up and out. He came back to Port Authority. He wanted to get out, but didn't know where to go. He didn't know whether to go to a cop for help, or to hide when the cops came along so they wouldn't take him anyplace bad. But wasn't anyplace better than Port

Authority, with all the weird things going on? Guys using the cold-water sinks to take baths and digging around in the garbage for half-eaten bagels, crowds of people, some going someplace—black people in line for a bus to Wilmington, Marines in line for Newport News—but lots of people going nowhere, just staying right there in the bus terminal.

He hadn't slept in two days, and now he still couldn't sleep! In Port Authority you had to act like you were going somewhere, even if the cops knew you weren't. If you slept, the cops would definitely wake you and question you and maybe try to take you to this halfway house a skinny red-haired kid there had told him about, or worse, back to the armory. He sat up across from Gate 319, New Jersey Transit, where the sign said ATLANTIC CITY. It made him feel a little better to sit across from its sign, that was all.

The red-haired kid said he was from the Island. Terry asked him what island. Long. He told Terry that Trailways would send you home free. Anywhere Trailways went, it would send a runaway kid to, *if* it were the kid's home. Terry didn't think Trailways went to Atlantic City. How did you prove what was your home to Trailways? Could you lie and tell Trailways that your home was Los Angeles or San Antonio and would Trailways take you there? Somewhere warm.

He had heard of all these buses that gave you free fare to Atlantic City just so you would go there and gamble. But he didn't think he could get it, being underage. And anyone could see he had no money for gambling or anything else. Besides, it wasn't far. He could hitch back if he wanted to. He could always hitch back to what he left. But then he thought, no, you can't.

Be real. What's there? So he sat on the wooden bench across from Gate 319. Should he scrounge money and go somewhere? He thought how funny the word "home" sounded for any of the places he'd been since his mother died. He just stared at the metal doors, the headlights of buses moving slowly through the terminal beyond the plate-glass windows, the bright shiny red of the brick wall, fake red, not dull like real brick.

And then there was this woman standing by him, looking at him. He decided to ask her for money, because he needed money and was going to have to start begging anyway, and because she seemed like a good one to start on. She was interested in him for some reason. She had smiled when he looked at her. She seemed bigger to him at first than she really was—maybe it was just the down jacket she was wearing, or maybe because she was standing and he was sitting there sort of small, asking for money. Her hair was tucked up under a wool hat, except for a few pieces of it wet from snow stuck against her cheek. She smiled at him, but her eyes seemed sad. She asked him how long he'd been there. Her name was Martha, she said. And then: "Do you need a place to stay?" She said it, then laughed a little. That really surprised him. He must've looked kind of hopeless for a strange woman to get pity in her heart for him. And then he wondered what kind of a person would want to bring home a kid. He stood up slowly, and started to walk away, real calm and easy. But she touched his shoulder and said. "I guess that was a little sudden, wasn't it?" He turned and she was smiling that smile. "Here, let me buy you lunch and we can talk a little."

What did she want, anyway?

Terry sat up in the dark room. He was thirsty now. Did he dare get up and get some water in the bathroom? Better not to. Karen might not be asleep yet. He rolled onto his back.

He and Martha had gone to a place called Walgreen's that was kind of like a drugstore, but there was this counter where they sat. She had some coffee and he ordered a cheeseburger. He was afraid that he would start salivating and drool, maybe, or that his stomach would make weird noises or that his hands might start to shake when he picked up the burger. He hadn't eaten anything much since the roast beef sandwich with the salesman—the breakfast bag at the armory yesterday morning and a half slice of pizza the red-haired kid gave him last night. Luckily, nothing embarrassing happened. He was able to eat as normally and casually as the man sitting on his right, reading from a folded newspaper and chomping a hot dog. He got the impression that this lady wouldn't care what embarrassing sounds his body made. She ordered him another burger and another glass of milk. He had eaten very quietly, trying to check her out in sideways glances. Her hair had dried and was curling. It had looked dark when it was wet, but now there seemed to be a lot of gray in it.

"How 'bout some apple pie and cheese?" she asked him after he ate the burgers. "I mean, it's a bus stop, after all. You gotta have apple pie at a bus stop."

"Yeah, really," he said, and groaned. "Some bus stop."

"Some apple pie," said Martha when it came. It did look sick. Maybe three hunks of apple, a ton of gluey stuff, and definitely store-bought crust. It tasted great. She had more coffee.

He knew he liked her then, though he couldn't get over it, some woman spending her money on him and inviting him to her house! Was she the stranger that he wasn't supposed to take apple pie from? But when you thought about it, wasn't he the stranger? Was she just another crazy who hung out at this place, like the woman who was really a guy who stuck her face near his and said "Darling" in a real deep voice last night? But her smile looked OK, not crazy. Pretty, sort of. She was clean. Her clothes were clean and nice. You could always tell by the shoes people wore. She was wearing boots, not ripped or anything. And, she had enough money to buy some food. Also, the thing was, she really looked like she knew what she was doing, like maybe she could help a kid.

Her Walgreen's cup had had tiny cracks along the rim. He couldn't stand to drink from a cup like that. All the germs festering. Maybe you could get AIDS drinking from a cup like that. His biology teacher had said no like he was sure, but how did he know? Anyway, the cracks against your lip felt disgusting. Real scuzzy.

"It's not good to drink from a cup like that," he had said. She looked at him. "You could get germs. Especially in a place like Port Authority."

"This may be true, but you don't know the things I would do for a cup of coffee! You know that Patricia Neal ad? . . . Her voice dropped low: 'I *like* . . . a . . . good . . . cup . . . of . . . coffee.'" He looked at her then. What was she talking about? "Well, I guess you're a little young for Patricia Neal." She took a quick sip, put her napkin in the little brown puddle that had formed in her saucer, then carefully set the cup down. That was when she turned her face toward him, and spoke, real serious. "Look, I mean, I don't have a real home yet, but I will."

So that was the punch line. Very funny, except that his chest went so tight right then it was hard to breathe, and his fingers ate his napkin into a ball and held it hard against his thigh. So funny I forgot to laugh. He decided to pretend it was all a joke. "Uh . . . you want to take me home but you don't have a home? I don't think I get it."

"Yeah, I know, sounds crazy, right? But it's clean where I am, and you'll be warm and fed, and you'll have a place to sleep. Come and have a look."

He remembered sitting quietly then, staring across the counter and through the greasy window at the crowd of commuters and derelicts. He thought of a lot of things, his night in the armory, and his last twenty-four hours in the bus terminal, and of the things he had seen since he had come to the city. He remembered the old woman he had seen the day before, who had stood in the corner near the escalator that was out of order. She had such a weird and struggling look on her face, which just kept getting redder and redder. He couldn't figure out what she was doing until he saw the shiny turd she left on the floor in the corner after she limped away with her skirts and her blankets. He was furious at her, and so embarrassed that he had been watching her! Why did she have to go *right there?* Then he realized that she probably was so dirty they wouldn't allow her in the bathrooms. After that he just felt sad.

So this afternoon he finished his pie and thought of the junkies he had seen outside the huge bus station the one time he had gone out to Eighth Avenue, guys nodding and slobbering and weaving. One guy had his pants around his thighs, holding them up with one hand and his penis with the other, grinning and waving it in the February night. Terry had gone directly back inside then, and up on the escalator to the bright yellow 319. Junkies were disgusting. Drugs were a sickness. He wanted to stay clean.

He lay back down again and rolled on his right side. Even though he was lying on an old rug without being able to sleep; even though he was thirsty, he was *so* warm! He wasn't hungry. He wasn't afraid. He closed his eyes and had a flash of the junkie wearing a tank top that said NONSMOKERS DO IT WITHOUT HUFFING AND PUFFING who had approached him as he sat at 319, and, like he was a magician about to do a great trick, waved his hand and pulled a knife from his waist. It was a switchblade, Terry knew. He flashed it around, while Terry's fingernails dug through wads of old chewing gum to the hard wood of the bench bottom. It was only a minute, then the man laughed crazy and took his trick somewhere else.

The kid from the Island knew about the magician with the tank top. He also warned Terry about some Rican with three braids who came around offering jobs. He promised high pay, but really what it was was a housework business using runaway kids like slaves. The kid from the Island had been told all this by the Pakistani at the newsstand near Greyhound.

So, no wonder he had decided to come away with the lady with the nice smile and dark eyes, the white-red hair pulled up under her hat. He believed her. He saw that she would help him. He saw this, too: that there was no one else who wanted him.

"Why do you want to help me?" he had asked her at the counter in Walgreen's.

"Because you're not lost yet."

He had blinked tight, then, as he picked at a particle of dishwasher-hard food stuck on his unused spoon. He knew she meant he was OK, that he could make it out of all this. It made him so happy, hearing her say that! He had thought for sure he was lost. After a certain point you couldn't feel more alone. You could feel hungrier and dirtier, after a while, it was true. You could be sicker or more exhausted, you could lose all caring about what you did with yourself, or let your mind go so you wouldn't have to think. But as far as lost goes, or lonely, he had felt as lost as anyone could feel, as lost as the poor old woman who had to shit on the floor.

He got up and got a drink of water.

Karen knew it wouldn't be just one day. The first two days he had been so exhausted, there could be no question of turning him out. He slept through the first night and first morning on the rug. He awakened around noon and ate the food Martha brought him from the dining hall—a slab of meatloaf between white bread, cartons of milk, an apple. He used the bathroom, looked listlessly at the paper, then slept again until the short day began darkening. Karen watched him sleeping that first afternoon, and was affected by his slumber, so deep and necessary and forgetful. His young body had claimed rest so urgently that Karen decided Martha was absolutely right to take him in. And she decided to award herself a few points in altruism for agreeing to it, however grudgingly. Another woman would have reported Martha—though Michele and Brenda had not reported her.

Still, he could not stay. His body was restored now with sleep and nourishment and warmth. But the atmosphere of 742 had deteriorated as Terry had improved. He would have to go. Easy for Michele and Brenda to be sympathetic. He wasn't in their room. He was here, where she had to step over him to get to the bathroom. He was here, taking up the little bit of space she had rented in this world. The women were more than sympathetic, Karen could see. They were downright enthusiastic, bringing in blankets, an exercise mat for him to sleep on, food from the dining hall, lending a Walkman and tapes. It was as though this unknown kid had brought them something they had been missing. Maybe part of it was the pleasure at flouting authority, duping the Sergeants Major. But it was something more, she knew—a hope for themselves, if they could help a boy.

Karen, too, had brought him things: a banana ("Potassium," he had said, and nodded, by way of thanks), small cartons of milk, a peanut butter sandwich from the dining hall, a Big Mac and a shake. She brought him food, but she wanted him out.

It was now Monday morning, the beginning of Terry's fourth day in the room. Terry was reading on the exercise mat, his head propped up on one arm. Karen was still in bed, waiting for Martha to get out of the bathroom so she could shower. The shower was their demilitarized zone, their isolation tank, their only place of solitude. It was a great shower, besides— generous of flow and steady of temperature, the one luxury the Arcadia afforded its tenants. Someone was always in it or going into it. At least body odor was no problem in 742.

Karen tried, as much as possible, to be out these days. Where? Anywhere. She posted her flier, checked out terrible apartments she could ill afford, and half-heartedly looked for work. She visited Annie, George at Ralph's, museums, art galleries. She did not, in her wanderings, go to Mark Pitofsky. She had tried to call him, but he never answered when she called his home, and at work a sales assistant took two messages which he never returned. (Still, there were times she could not suppress the memory of his hands upon her body.) She had even considered going to Phoenix to see her mother, but she had no money, her mother had no money, her mother wouldn't even be settled yet, and the days of idleness in the sun would bring her no further from her problems. (But she thought, *I want you so much, Mom. Mommy. Mama.* The pretty mother on the front porch, smiling and waving good-bye. *I want you so.*)

Anyway, why did she have to leave when it was her room?

But sooner or later each day she had to return to Room 742, and when that time came, she would first stop at Vinnie's Viddies for some tapes. *Mildred Pierce* on Friday, *On the Waterfront* Saturday, *The Way We Were* last night. She had acquired a set of earphones, so when she arrived back at the room, she would take a long shower, don her flannel nightgown, sit on her bed, and plug in. At the movies. What *will* I choose tonight? she mused, as Martha emerged in her bathrobe. Karen passed her in tense silence and stepped over the boy's knees.

She turned the shower on hard and hot. The water pounded her back. She closed her eyes and breathed in deeply, turning her head in small circles to relax her neck. She couldn't stay in long, though, because she wanted to catch Martha before she left for the day. She got out, dried herself, wiped the steam from the mirror and combed her hair. She dressed quickly in the clothes she had carried into the bathroom with her. All their dressing was now done in the bathroom. She pulled down a turtleneck, and zipped up a job-search skirt. Damn, of course she had forgotten to bring in underpants! She pulled on her pantyhose anyway, and went back to the room as Martha was putting on her jacket and saying good-bye to Terry.

"He has *got* to go!" she told Martha, catching her in the hallway, actually grabbing her by her down-filled elbow. Martha was leaving as she did each morning and would be gone several hours. Karen didn't know where she went, didn't give a damn either, except that she left her alone with the boy.

"I need some more time, just a few days," said Martha soothingly. "I'm trying to work things out."

"*I don't have more time*! I want him out now, you hear me? You bring some . . . waif in off the street to my room and then you act like *I'm* being so damn unreasonable. You're unreasonable, Martha, not me! And don't think I don't know that you're trying to manipulate me with that controlled tone of voice. I mean, it's just so fucking condescending! You're making me play the heavy, trying to get him out, when all I want to do is get my life back together." Karen's hands were trembling. Her eyes were stinging. She was aware that she was speaking too loudly and angrily, aware of Martha's efforts to quiet her, Martha's fear that someone, another woman, would hear. Maybe Terry would hear. Well, Karen didn't give a damn! In fact, it pissed her off as much as anything else, another restraint upon her, like the boy in the room. She was *right*, that was the thing. She knew she was right and Martha was wrong. So why did she feel so crummy? "What do you mean 'work things out'?" she asked after a moment.

"Make arrangements"—Martha shrugged—"find a place . . ."

Karen remembered now the phone call from the House of Hope. What had that been about? But that was before Terry, anyway. "That could take weeks, getting him in a place." Karen knew about red tape from her state jobs. "He's got to go *now*. There's no other room I can go to here. No vacancy, I've already checked. I can't *think* with him in there."

Karen was silent for a moment, then blurted: "Besides, he's a thief!" She hadn't actually meant to say it, but there it was, and it was true. She wasn't sorry. Martha would have to get rid of him now.

"A *thief*?" said Martha in a hushed tone, genuinely surprised. "What did he take?"

"He took a diamond ring belonging to my mother!" Karen shouted. Her eyes were moist with righteousness. Her mouth quivered.

"How do you know this?"

"It's *gone*, that's how! I put it in the pocket of my

black sweat pants and it's gone! I've searched through all my stuff. It isn't anywhere. He was wearing those pants the first night he got here, remember?"

"I remember that he was wearing a pair of your pants. But don't you have a few pairs of black pants like that?"

"They're all black, but they're not alike. You have to know my pants. The ones he wore were my old ones. They had the ring."

Martha eyed her keenly. "You've checked everywhere."

Karen nodded. "All *my* stuff, yes."

"Karen, think how many people have been in the room besides him . . . Brenda, Michele, the fellow that hooked up your VCR, Mrs. Sergeant Major, someone on the housekeeping staff maybe . . . and me. Why not me? How can you say it's him?"

"He was wearing my pants," she said.

"I'll take your word for it that you had such a ring—I believe you. Even so, it could have been anyone. You might have put it anywhere. Why would you leave a diamond ring just lying around in a place like this? In fact, why didn't you put it in the safe downstairs? That's what the bylaws say to do with valuables."

"Please, don't *you* quote me the bylaws!" Karen was furious, mainly because Martha was right. "Also . . . he's been drinking my Scotch!" She had noticed this last night. She had a new bottle, with three missing inches she couldn't account for. She *knew* she hadn't drunk that much in one day.

At this Martha laughed. "*Terry*? Come on, Karen!

You can't be serious. You know what he thinks about liquor and drugs!"

"Well, someone has been drinking my Scotch!" Karen said, aware of sounding like Papa Bear.

"Look, about your ring . . . I don't know what to say. Just that, if you feel you have real grounds for suspecting him, you'll have to take whatever course you think best. If that means pressing charges . . ." Martha's voice trailed off.

Karen had not expected this suggestion. She was stopped, then said, "Press charges, Martha? That'd be wonderful for all of us, wouldn't it?" They were quiet in the shabby hallway. Karen spoke softly, fighting for control, "Martha, please—screw the ring, OK? My mother didn't even care about it. It's just that this situation is so . . . unbearable." There was nothing more to say. She started to reach for Martha's arm, then pulled her hand back. She turned to open the door.

There was a rustling sound inside, but when Karen entered, Terry was lying back on the mat, ostensibly absorbed in his reading. He appeared flushed, though, and sounded out of breath. He was licking his lower lip assiduously. He licked his lower lip a lot. Nerves. Concentration. It was why his chin was chapped raw. But right now his tongue was working furiously. He stole a quick glance at her, but their eyes met. He looked immediately back at his page. He had heard every word! Good, she thought, but then felt miserable. She wanted to speak to him, to try to explain. Instead, she went into the bathroom and dried her hair.

Karen had actually come to be impressed with Terry since he woke up. Mainly she was impressed with the way he spent his time, which could as easily have been idle. He had good reason to be idle. And yet he read indiscriminately, voraciously, from a stack of donated books and magazines the women brought him . . . some short stories, an Agatha Christie mystery, and now he was beginning a dogeared *Les Misérables*, abridged. Karen savored the irony of *Les Misérables* being read in this room. When he wasn't reading, he listened to the Walkman and quietly did what seemed to be thousands of sit-ups and push-ups on the mat. She saw that he took great stock in his physical well-being, keeping in shape. Was he preparing his body for an unknown ordeal ahead, being out on the streets again, Karen wondered, or, was the extreme discipline of strenuous workout a way of keeping order, of keeping his mind? He ate very well, too, considering it was mostly food from the dining hall. He requested fruits, vegetables, Grape Nuts. "Builds brain cells," he explained when Martha asked him why Grape Nuts, which could not be had in the dining hall.

Brenda had brought him a large Hershey's bar. And Michele, who, Karen had learned, was in her last year of law school, took time from her studies yesterday to make the him some chocolate chip cookies in the tiny kitchenette on three. "Therapy," she said, to explain away her kindness. Terry thanked them, but said sugar wasn't good, no more sweets, please. Karen wolfed down a good many of the cookies and privately marveled that anything more challenging than instant coffee had been made in the kitchenette.

She fingered gel through and coaxed her top hair higher. No, he was a very nice kid. He said very little, probably sensing even before this fight between her and

Martha (and how could he not?) that he was an intrusion, and not wishing to intrude further. Like Pitofsky, Karen thought, and laughed shortly, then hit the wall in frustration, loosening a cracked bath tile, which fell on her toes. "Ouch!" She applied some makeup and went back into the room.

"Can I get you anything while I'm out today?" Karen asked Terry, who was now reading at Martha's desk.

"Oh, no, it's OK. I'm fine, thank you very much." But when he looked at Karen, his expression was dark. She felt his accusation deeply, as she knew he had felt hers.

When Karen returned in late afternoon, still unemployed and armed with her video, Martha had just arrived, still in her jacket. They nodded curtly at each other. Karen looked at Terry, but he wouldn't look in her direction. Martha had three bags full: clothes for Terry from Hudson's Army-Navy—a parka, a sweater, some pants, and a couple of flannel shirts. Karen sat on her bed and watched them from behind the *Times,* saw how happy Martha was to be doing something for him, delighted that she had gotten the right size and style of jeans, delighted that he had been so pleased. He had been very pleased, touched, really, Karen could see. He had sucked in his breath when she handed him the first package, and smiled shyly. He went in the bathroom right away to try things on, probably eager to get out of the sweat clothes of Martha's that he was currently wearing. New jeans, stiff and dark and one hot wash away from the right length. He rolled them up while Martha made a good show of occupying herself at her work, opening mail, reading the paper, jotting a note, watching the boy. She had given him a drawer in her bureau. (Karen didn't like what his own drawer implied.) He removed the tags from each article, refolded it, smoothed it out, then placed it gingerly in the empty drawer.

"All dressed up and noplace to go," he said and laughed. His eyes met Karen's accidentally, then looked quickly away. He shrugged, embarrassed, before resuming his place on the mat. He picked up his book, the blond hair falling forward, the tongue working against the lower lip.

"Soon," said Martha. "You'll see, it won't be long."

Karen dumped her nighttime glass of water into the amaryllis and went to dinner.

Late that night Michele and Brenda came by. Karen was watching her movies, a double feature tonight. Once, rewinding a cassette, Karen looked beyond the television screen to the room. The women were playing Michigan Rummy with him, laughing, making wild plans for their evening's take of change, drinking sodas from the machine down the hall, eating popcorn Michele had made in the kitchenette. Michele looked up and, seeing Karen's gaze, offered her popcorn. Karen shook her head no. The too-short wire from her earphones pulled out with the motion. She leaned forward and plugged it back in, sticking in the cassette of *Notorious* at the same time. Someone had brought flowers to the room, she noticed. Daisies in February. Brenda had brought a fat candle which threw a flickering gold on their faces as they concentrated on their cards.

She saw how it was. These women needed Terry more than he needed them. They needed to be taking care, nurturing, like it was the only thing women were made for or something. Michele, who had seemed so despondent only a few days ago, was calmer. He was their cause, their child. He gave them purpose and hope. He made them women again. It made her sick. He was a false hope! Wasting their time playing Michigan Rummy with a kid wasn't going to accomplish anything for any of them. Not for him, either, because it wasn't a permanent arrangement. He would leave to nothing again, and they would be without him and the false purpose he brought. And yet, here they were on this dark winter night, ignorant, with smiles and glow on their faces.

Chapter
12

The next morning Karen was alone in the room. Terry had sought the sanctuary of the shower and Martha had gone out. Karen, who had been considering the situation anew, had decided for certain that Martha already knew him, that she had not found him in Port Authority. Not even Martha would bring home just anyone. House of Hope had called Martha even before he arrived. But there was another reason. Karen thought that she had seen his face before, that surface blond-and-blue combo, the child behind it. It was definitely the face on the eight-by-ten glossies. It hit Karen last night and she couldn't shake it. Now she had to know. If she could prove that Martha was connected to him somehow, that he wasn't an anonymous homeless boy, it would mean that Martha was doing this because it was her duty, and she could do it someplace else as well. If he had a mother, Karen would be less sorry for him, and less of an ogre.

She sat on Martha's bed and opened each drawer of Martha's bureau, looking for the manila envelope she had seen before. There was no manila envelope. She looked through all the drawers, through the drawer with Terry's new clothes, then bent awkwardly to look in the bottom drawer, which could only be partially opened in the cramped space. The envelope was gone. She gave a check to Martha's closet. No envelope, no pictures. It had to be, though. The real boy and the glossy boy had to be the same boy, and a good thing, too. It would be a connection. It would make sense, be safer, if he belonged to Martha and hadn't really been lifted from a bench in Port Authority.

He could be her son, though he didn't look like her. She was certainly old enough to have a sixteen-year-old. If he were her son, though, why were they here, instead of back in Cornwallis leading a normal life? How long did she intend to have him holed up here, and why?

There was lint on her knees from kneeling. She brushed it off, located her boots—one in the closet, one in the far corner by the exercise mat. She laced them up, donned her jacket, snapped last night's cassettes into their plastic cases, and left to return them to Vinnie. She was in the hallway when she heard the boy emerge from the bathroom. How would he make it through another day, the prisoner in 742? Besides everything else, it was a cruelty to him, lonely, boring, an insult to his youth and all the longings that went with it.

It was plenty cold. The day was as clear as it was freezing, stinging the nostrils and opening the eyes to others on the street who look at you knowing the same thing. It is exciting. It is fucking freezing. It is New York City, and you are in it, enduring, but not merely so: alive, too, and, even, rather young. Sometimes even Karen couldn't put it down, that feeling.

Sometimes it took something else.

Like here, this man lying on the sidewalk near Vinnie's. A man whose bodily fluids, it seemed to Karen, were seeping out and freezing to the dirty pavement: urine and semen, mucus and tears, snot and pus, and blood from the open sores on his swollen raw ankles. He would secrete himself most pitifully and slowly onto the frigid sidewalk, and when spring brought thaw and flowers, his reeking remains would merely melt away into the gutter, without trouble to anyone. Except about the smell. His head lay on a piece of corrugated cardboard. His bare feet were stuck into ripped, laceless, canvas high-top sneakers. He was without hat and gloves, only an ancient cloth coat of speckled tweed and filth. She did not know how he was still living in this cold, but as she bent low, she could see a bit of breath and hear the rasp within. He could have been any age, there was no telling. He would have been handsome in a different life.

"Come and help me!" she opened the thick glass door and yelled in to Vinnie. "We gotta get this man inside."

"It's OK," said Vinnie, coming from his counter to her, standing by a life-size display of De Niro and Streep: YOU'LL FALL IN LOVE WITH "FALLING IN LOVE." "I called the cops already. Twice. The second time I told them there were some kids that looked suspicious, that they looked like they might torch him."

"Torch him?" Karen was horrified. "There were?"

"Nah. But you want the cops to get here, right? You want him off the street?"

"What do you mean, off the street? Off the street for him, or off the street for me and you? Come out and help me, please! We've to get him inside."

216

"Inside? Like, you mean, in here? Hey, no way, Lady, uh . . . Miss Carmody . . . uh, Karen. I got a business to run here. Give me a break, huh?"

He was serious, she could tell. "What are you talking about? *Business?* This is called time out, understand? There is a man dying in front of your store." Furious, she returned to the sidewalk beside him. Vinnie had probably considered torching him, she thought. That's what had given him the idea of it to tell the cops. *Torch him!* She shivered, but not from cold. She began shaking the man's arm, trying to wake him. It would be easier if he could walk. She couldn't budge him. She squatted there by him and massaged his bare cracked hands. Four hands together, like that stupid children's game where hands pile up in order, then everything goes to hell.

Vinnie was next to her then. "Don't cry like that, please! I'll help ya, goddamn it!"

She looked at Vinnie blankly, then dragged her ratty fur cuff across her eyes.

Vinnie had been pumping iron at Workouts for almost seven months now. This guy was a piece of cake for him. Fireman carry. Except, Christ! he wanted to puke having him up against his white shirt, new, from Barney's. You had to dry-clean silk, and, even so, he didn't think it would ever look right again.

Karen raced ahead to get the door, using her hands to cushion the man's head from injury as they passed through.

"Yeah, so, uh, Mother Teresa, where do you want me to put him? You want me to prop him up in the window, or would he look nice behind the counter? You think I could dress him up in a security guard uniform? I can't afford a security guard and I got a lot of expensive stuff in here. Maybe someone will like him and take him home on Two-for-One Night." But as he talked, Karen noticed how gently he lowered the man onto the gray industrial carpeting and rested his head and shoulders in the corner. ALL OF ME said the poster above his head. A Steve Martin movie. "Why not take all of me?"

Assured that Vinnie would let him stay, at least momentarily, Karen went back out, to get him some coffee at the deli next door. She asked for sugar with the coffee. She never took sugar, but junkies like sugar. You're sick, she told herself. Does he have to be a junkie because he's on the skids? People have hard times. You should know that, Carmody. When she got back, she sat next to him on the floor, took out the coffee, ripped open the two packets of sugar and dumped them in. If he isn't a junkie, at least it's energy. He moved, then moaned a little. She held a cup to his lips. "I love N Y," the cup said. She focused dumbly on the logo, in wonderment at such a cheerful cup. She was annoyed, then, that she hadn't gotten him some broth instead of this cloying caffeine. Something nourishing.

He had a small scar over the bridge of his nose, though the nose was unbroken and fine. It had miraculously made it through the rest of his life. His thinning dun-colored hair was electric with the new warmth and took on a bizarre festive life of its own. Again, she thought, he's handsome, or was. If there were only some way to really rehab these guys . . . make them the clean-living husbands and boyfriends they were meant to be for me and Annie and all the other women out there . . . There could be these halfway houses where they got off drugs and got clean. Then they could be given what shots they needed and be tested free of disease and guaranteed a good sperm count. Women could come in, like at Bide-a-Wee, pick one out, and promise to give him a good home and try to get him a job . . . She laughed ironically. Sick-o, Carmody. But really, it was like losing men to war. This guy could have been Clint Eastwood with that nose, but instead, he was him.

He grunted, nodded, and took the cup from her. No, he couldn't be that old, her own age maybe, yet his cracked and shaking hands looked older than God's wrath. She wondered whether there were tracks up his arms, whether he had AIDS.

Vinnie stepped heavily past them and opened the door, motioning to the squad car pulling up outside. It double-parked, and two young cops emerged. The man by her stirred, knowing that they had come for him. The tags on their leather jackets read BURKE and SULLIVAN. Burke was wiry and blond; Sullivan black Irish and balding and merry. The man became agitated when they came through the door, and struggled to his feet. *"No!"* he shouted, *"No!"*

"Him," said Burke to Sullivan. "Hey, fella, remember us? You wanna come with us today? We'll take you over to the armory and they'll get you some food." He put his hand gingerly on the worn tweed. *"No!"* shouted the man. *"No!"* He pulled away from Burke and made for the door, grabbed the glass handle once, lost hold, then gripped it tightly and was on the street.

"He won't bother you folks again," said Sullivan, almost apologetically. "He knows to go someplace else for a while."

"But he'll freeze someplace else, too!" said Karen.

"He can go to the armory, if he wants, but we can't make him go to the armory," said Burke, and shrugged.

"But you can," said Karen.

"How, lady? How'm I gonna do that? Tell me how," said Burke, exasperated, then blew through closed lips.

"You have a gun, don't you?"

At this the three men laughed, and Sullivan said to Burke, "Jeeze, the *Post* would love that one, right? 'Cop Pulls Gun on Homeless Man.' "

This was not what Karen meant at all. They knew it. Though, really, getting someone in from the cold sounded like the best reason for police force and guns that she had ever considered.

"Karen," said Vinnie slowly, "you can't make them go if they don't want to. It's against the law." His condescending manner was reminiscent of something, but she couldn't think what.

"Whaddya gonna do?" asked Sullivan rhetorically, and shrugged. "He ain't hurting nobody, he's just . . ." Here he touched his index finger to his head three times in the international symbol for lunacy. "Most of the whackos at least knew enough to come in from the cold this week."

But Karen pushed past them and out the door. He hadn't gotten far. He probably knew from his unhappy experience that he would never be pursued if he moved on, that nobody cared, and so he had the luxury of moving on slowly. She saw that he limped in the ancient loose sneakers. "Wait!" she shouted, but when he stopped for her, she had nothing to tell him.

They were very close. She took off her black beret

and placed it on his head. She threw her scarf around his neck. "A duck goes quack," he mumbled, his cold breath bitter. She let him go.

It was what he had said, she was sure, but she didn't know what it meant. How could she? He probably didn't know himself. Maybe his mother, if she had been anywhere, would have known. A small child's ritual, maybe, something he said each night at the moment sleep took him.

She stood in the cold watching him, then stopped back in the deli and bought coffee for herself and Vinnie. A peace offering. Vinnie had helped her, after all. When she returned he had just plugged in the Picture of the Day, *That's Entertainment*. Musicals were only ninety-nine cents today. "I'm sorry," she said. "Temporary insanity. Frostbite." She touched her head three times with her index finger.

"Yeah, so how 'bout you just get out and we'll call it a day, OK?"

She stood still, holding the coffee bag.

"I'm serious. Go already. I don't need any crazies in the place. Not you, not him."

"You think I'm *him?*" Karen asked dumbly. She was starting to feel shaky.

Vinnie sighed. "All I know is, I'm starting a new business, I'm up above my eyeballs in work, and I got no time for this stuff. Here I'm trying to measure for new shelving an' all and you come in with this bleeding-heart crap. I got more tapes coming in all the time and I'm running out of space. Space is money, right? In Manhattan it's big money. The rent is gonna go so astronomical next time that *I* could be on the street. Understand?"

Karen nodded, took out the cups, and pushed one tentatively across the counter to him.

But Vinnie was off on a riff. "Meanwhile, I gotta work out some streamlined storage system or else come up with a way to put cassettes on microfiche." He laughed. "Now *that* is not a bad idea. It's gotta be the thing of the future, right?—and if I'm the one to do it, I retire! Shit, Tahiti is looking good right now." He looked at Karen. "You don't realize that I got problems, too. Only you got problems, right, and this guy you drag in, ruining my morning. The place is a madhouse in the afternoons, but it's quiet in the mornings. I need time in the morning, to alphabetize cassettes, organize the mailing list, select the Picture of the Day, look over new orders, think. I like my mornings. Usually."

"I'm sorry, Vinnie . . . really . . ."

"Look," he said, "You don't remember? . . . In *Midnight Cowboy*, when Jon Voigt comes in from out of town and sees the guy lying across the sidewalk and he just stands there looking at all the people walking past? You remember that?"

She nodded. "Of course I remember. It was a terrific scene."

"And he can't believe it, remember? So, when was that movie made? A long time ago, right? Check it out, almost *twenty years*. You think things change? You think you're gonna change things? I see it different from you, is all."

"But doesn't it bother you that there are so many people on the streets and nobody's doing anything about it?"

"It's their policy not to do anything about it."

"What do you mean, 'their policy'?"

222

"It's their policy, that's all."

"Whose?"

"*Whose?*" Vinnie rolled his eyes. "Koch's, Reagan's. The guys running the show. It's very simple, easier than wiping out Indians." Vinnie took the coffee and removed the plastic top. Karen thought that was a concession. "I call it 'Gentrified Genocide,'" he continued after a swallow. "You're right, that guy is dying. They're dying all over New York, all over this country, of exposure or AIDS or malnutrition. They wait until the last minute and then drag them into a hospital and then off to Potter's Field. Pretty soon they'll all be dead and the town will be left to the gentry. Because the other thing about Manhattan right now is that it's like a handyman's special, like the house my old man fixed and fixed because it was all he had. This is all the land they have, this island, and they're gonna fix it and fix it for the folks who can pay, who are dying to pay. So you've gotta clear out the other guys, see? You can't put 'em on a bus to Houston. Houston don't want 'em. So the only way of clearing them out, see, is to let 'em die. It works, but it's sorta nasty for a while. It's disturbing to people for a while, but then they'll be gone."

"You really think that's it?"

Vinnie nodded emphatically. "Believe it. It's what they're doing. What you're supposed to believe is that there are places for them and that they're just too nuts or lazy to take advantage of a good thing, or that they really love being so free. But there isn't anything much out there for them that's good. It's just this myth we're supposed to latch onto so we can walk by them on the street and carry on with our own lives."

"You look like you're doing a pretty good job

223

getting on with your own life," said Karen, surprised by her hostility. Why so sarcastic? Maybe because he *was*, in fact, getting on with things? Maybe because, more than anything, she wanted to get on with her life.

"Of course I am. What am I supposed to do? I mean, what do you want me to do? I could work with him, people like the guy you dragged in, I mean, if they would let me," Vinnie continued. "I have these healing crystals I use. But a guy like him, he won't let me. He's on too low an incarnation to accept help."

Healing crystals! Give me a break, thought Karen. "Oh, so that explains it all, right? That makes it easy. He's an untouchable and you're some kind of damn Brahmin. You get to dismiss misery that way."

"Hey, don't get hot." He sipped his coffee silently. "It's the only way I know how to figure things."

They stood in silence, elbows on the counter, while on the monitor next to them Debbie Reynolds, Donald O'Connor, and Gene Kelly danced joyously up a wall. Maybe he was serious, Karen thought. At least he's thinking about things. She had done a good job of dismissing human misery until recently. Until she landed at the Arcadia. Until Martha. She knew it was Martha, bringing the boy onto her turf and forcing him on her the way she had forced the derelict on Vinnie. But Vinnie had been thinking about it right along. So what if he had come to some conclusions that would let him live?

"I'm not an elitist," Vinnie said at length. "I'm on a pretty low level of incarnation, too. So are you. Face it. Anyone walking around on this planet musta really sloughed off in his past life."

"What makes you say that?" Karen asked, as an

intellectual exercise merely. Because, in fact, she could just see herself pissing away every single one of her past lives.

"What makes me say that? Can't you see it? Earth *sucks!* There are much better places to live."

"Oh," said Karen. She considered this while Debbie kissed Donald, then Gene, and all three flopped back on a loveseat, lifting their legs straight out and laughing. Karen looked around and, after some time, selected *Pennies from Heaven* for her evening viewing.

Chapter 13

It was early afternoon of the next day. It was just the nuclear family in 742, the good mother, the bad mother, and the boy. No Brenda or Michele yet. Karen observed Martha and the boy, plugged in as she was to *Pennies from Heaven*. Absorption was easily feigned. She did think Steve Martin was a genius. A madcap, banjo-picking, tap-dancing all-out and all-knowing fool. But now and again Karen would push the round foam pad on her left ear slightly back, the better to hear them talking. She could rerun Steve Martin later.

Terry was sitting on his mat, drawing, doodling, flipping through *Time*, doing math problems from a Regents prep book Martha had found for him. Martha was reading the paper on her bed, once in a while reading him a news item or asking about his work. On the way into the bathroom at one point, she leaned to adjust the collar of his new plaid shirt, another time urging an apple on him. Martha read, hemmed a skirt, and wrote on a legal pad, holding her pencil fiercely at the nub. But with all her activities Karen knew she was as aware of the boy's presence, made as content by it as a mother is the nearness of her sleeping babe; a new lover, her beloved.

He would leave her, whoever he was—did she really think he wouldn't? He will certainly leave her, Karen thought. What will hold him clothed? What would keep him in fair weather? Martha seemed absorbed in thought, her chin thrust back, absently running a forefinger up and down her neck. The wind in the air shaft blew bitter and Karen knew its cold. What will she do when he goes?

Food held him here, and shelter against a New York City winter. She shuddered as she thought again of the man who wore her beret, beyond hope of redemption. She thought of the corny corporal works of mercy: feed the hungry, clothe the naked, comfort the afflicted. You learned them, but it was embarrassing to take them as seriously as Martha did. Giving a beret and a scarf to a freezing man was one thing, but taking a boy in off the street was another. It was as extreme as Sarah getting her ass cloistered. Extreme, inordinate, excessive. Karen knew the type, all right: her mother, her sister, her brother. It was submerged in her genetic pool; it ran recessive in her. It scared the hell out of her.

Martha seemed never to be at rest, never once caught snatching a nap. What was she always writing, anyway? Heavy-duty correspondence was conducted upon Martha's clipboard. She was always getting mail: Karen had seen a few return addresses on her bed: House of Hope, West Side Project, Human Resources Administration. An occasional furtive phone conversation, quickly ended if Karen was in the room. Karen had answered a few times, hoping for Mark, hoping for something. Instead, official-sounding voices requesting

Ms. Leonard. Karen had taken a couple of messages, once from the Hudson Guild and another time from Saint Peter's Home. Probably looking for a social-work job, Karen figured. Why so damn secretive, especially when Karen had spilled her spotty employment history and hopes to Martha, and when pieces of Karen's life could be found everywhere? Pictures of people she loved were yellowing on her dresser, and the documents that made her official were in an unruly pile on the closet shelf. Even now a letter from her mother was on the bathroom floor in front of the toilet. Any unauthorized biographer could just walk into Room 742 and scoop up Karen's life in a handful of dust and papers. Not so with Martha.

Martha now leaned over the bed to her Adidas bag, and produced a package from the deli, setting out plastic containers of things and plastic spoons with which to eat these things. Terry heard the rustle and looked at her quizzically.

"Lunch. A change of pace from the dining-room takeouts."

"Gee, thanks, Mom!" he said lightly. He moved to the foot of the bed and they ate something that crunched. It looked like Greek salad. Karen could smell the onions.

"You want my anchovies?" Martha asked him. "I don't like their little hairs. Their little hairs give me the creeps." They sat on the bed together, crunching away and laughing.

Soon Martha was going out again. To the library, she said. Karen didn't want Martha to leave her with him. Like two children. What would they do here without her?

He asked Martha to get him some mysteries and some books about carpentry and flowers.

He wants books about flowers, Karen thought.

"I'll get you the algebra book, too."

"Thanks," he said. "Wait! Can you get me some bran tablets and some dried chick peas, too? No salt, OK?"

Martha paused as she opened the door and looked in Karen's direction, but Karen's eyes were fixed, straight ahead on Steve Martin dancing with Bernadette Peters, who was his love in real life, too.

*H*e was old for a boy, for sixteen. Things can make you old, can make you understand. The things that had happened to him made him patient now. But it was a funny kind of patience, because he wasn't really waiting *for* anything. The kind of patience a dying man has when the anger leaves him. It was this patience that let him accept this room and his place in it. Another sixteen-year-old might have thought that this room was like jail. He still wasn't sure whether to believe Martha when she said that there would be something now for his patience, that soon they would leave this room and have a home. But he decided to keep the promise ahead of him. And if it didn't happen, it wouldn't be the first time things didn't happen. So he held it out there, with the embellishments she had spun up for him with such delight: a home with MTV in it and a stereo and a separate room for him, a home with her in it, and friends allowed to visit and a dessert that she would make one night called fiendish fudge cake. He would go to the high school near this home, she told him, and he would not be afraid. A home that they would be in by spring, as soon as her settlement came.

Something else he knew from all his foster homes was about the other woman in the room, and how he should behave. He knew he had to go light. Very light. She was kind of pretty, this woman, but cold to him. Get back, she was telling him, and he read her, no mistake. She wanted him out. He was crowding her. She had accused him of being a thief!

After Martha left, Terry sat back on his mat, picked up a pencil, and tried to sketch from his memory the huge plexiglass box he had seen in the bus station, on the main floor by the escalators. Pool balls in perpetual motion through a maze of red grooves. A ball would travel along on its course, dropping down on the tight leather of a bongo drum, then down a xylophone in steps, to a cymbal and a series of bells and on to a steel drum, rolling around the perimeter of the steel drum several times before dropping through a hole in the bottom and on to the next sound. The ball traveled through water and caves, and funny red doors, uphill and down. Going downhill, it would gather exactly the amount of momentum it needed to make it up the next slope. There was a break in the groove at one point, and the ball made the leap across the chasm. Every time. Finally the ball would come to rest, but not before knocking the next ball into motion. The plexiglass box was where he went when he left his seat across from Gate 319. He would stand before it for a half-hour at a time, or walk around it, following one pool ball on its journey back to the beginning. Other people stopped and watched it, too. Sometimes people who were going on their own journeys, to work or from work, would stop and check it out, but mostly it was other people like him, people who were there, not going anywhere, killing time watching the pool balls make music. These people didn't look happy, but once in a while, through the plexiglass, he caught one smiling at the music of pool balls. It helped him a little, to pass the time. It let his mind go free to think about other stuff besides what he was going to do. It helped some of these other people, too, Terry knew. He wished he had thought of it. He wished he could have made it. It even gave him a good feeling to try to draw it. He liked it when he could get things on paper, all together and neat. Sometimes he could make things better than they really were. He was pretty good at drawing.

God, she had never noticed how flagrantly phallic an amaryllis stalk was. Standing strong and thick above its straplike leaves in the peanut butter container beside her bed, a seam running along its entire length. The full bud showing a shot of obscene red beneath the pale, veined covering. She grabbed onto the stalk and ran her fist up to the fat bud, then touched it gently between two fingers. She looked quickly at the boy, but he was turned away from her. It would open to two more buds, maybe four before it burst forth scarlet. Karen unplugged herself and fetched a glass of water from the bathroom for her plant. She would call it Marko. She returned her glass, closed the door, sat on the pot, and bent to pick up her mother's letter:

My lovely daughter:

Nous sommes içi, Sue and me!

One knows eternity in the desert. Did you realize
that a cactus doesn't even *grow an arm* until it's
seventy? I do not think they die. Except sometimes
boys shoot at them, and then they do. Bored, I guess,
the boys.

Simtra visited us yesterday as we were unpack-
ing. "Welcome," he said. "I am your host in this
place and your channel to Chiricahua in another
place." He was on his way to the pool. He was very
formal and polite, though Sue said she didn't expect
him to be wearing *that* kind of bathing suit. He looks
terrific in it, for eighty. No negative energies and
swimming every day, I guess. Also, trances eat
calories like crazy. Actually, there are men here who
are younger than Simtra. We met two men at the
commissary and they took us on this sightseeing tram
through a beautiful canyon. They said they've
reached bliss here many times and also they play
bridge. Sue says they're just a couple of plants, you
know, a kind of added attraction so that we'll like the
place and decide to stay. I said I don't care, I like the
place.

Chiricahua speaks on Saturday! Simtra says she
wants to welcome us herself. I am happy, Karen! I
feel positive ions all around me here. Sue says its
impossible since we are not near water. Also she has
an allergy to something.

Love, Mom

Karen folded the letter, and stuck it in her pocket.
She went back to her bed and closed her eyes, pretending to sleep. She heard Terry get up from the desk. In a

little while she sat up, put her earphones on, and turned on her machine. He was wired, too, to the Walkman Michele had lent him.

He was a cold fish, she thought, but at least he stayed where he belonged, on Martha's bed, or on the exercise mat. He probably hadn't taken the ring. She may have lost it or misplaced it through her own carelessness. She had lost things before. And the Scotch—was it Michele, or the housekeeper, or maybe Martha playing hostess at one of her at-homes?

Now he was neatening things, throwing out all the lunch containers, going into the bathroom and returning with a damp washcloth belonging to Martha, to wipe up a spill on the floor. A blouse of Martha's was on the bed. He inspected it, smoothed it out, then hung it up. He retrieved a small pile of underthings, socks— his? hers?—from the floor and stuffed them in Martha's laundry bag on the floor of the closet. He was smoothing out the bedspread when he realized Karen was watching. "Just call me the houseboy," he said too loudly, in order to be heard above earphones. It was the first time he had addressed her directly since he had overheard her in the hall.

Karen smiled and nodded to indicate she had heard. "OK, Mr. Clean," she said.

But then he was standing at the foot of her bed holding a bundle aloft. "Excuse me, these are yours, aren't they?"

Damn! Leave my shit alone. "It's not necessary," she said curtly. "I'll take care of my things." In the manner to which they've become accustomed, she thought.

He placed the bundle at the foot of the bed and

raised both his hands up. "OK, sorry. Just trying to help." He shrugged, then walked to his mat, awkwardly slapping his hands against his thighs.

It was possible that he was too young to know that Martha needed him. But Karen didn't think anyone could be too young. Babes in arms know their only weapon is their mother's need. He knew how he was strong. Love was need and neurosis. Love debilitated. One had only to look to Martha for proof. Rushing around on errands for unworthy youth. Proof.

This consideration of how neurosis seasons love brought her thoughts round again to Mark. She had called him a final time, got someone, another broker, maybe, gave her name, and was put on hold for a long minute, and then: "I'm sorry, he stepped away from his desk."

There was no point in pursuing things further, she knew. She was one of literally millions of women in this city. Probably half of them were prettier and smarter and funnier. Not that Mark Pitofsky deserved anyone prettier, smarter, and funnier than herself. It was just that they were all out there. He was a man, smart, single, and halfway handsome. He was most likely undiseased, too, given his heroin-free halfhearted hetero history. So, of these, say, million women in her age range who were prettier, smarter, and funnier, probably a quarter of a million would sleep with Mark Pitofsky if he asked them. She didn't see Mark actually out propositioning all these women, or they him, but on some level he had to be aware of his opportunities. In Mark's case, though, this awareness, rather than hurtling him into vaulting promiscuity, probably had the reverse effect, rendering him inert. Even so.

How did anyone ever get special to anyone else? How did people decide to stay with each other?

The boy on the floor had taken off his shirt and was now relentlessly doing sit-ups, tonguing tight lips furiously in concentration, a glisten of sweat lighting taut smooth muscle. She would go to Mark. She snapped Stop hard on the remote, went into the bathroom and splashed water on her face, then a glob of Nivea. She ripped a comb through her hair and touched it on her thick brows. A pert tube of Martha's lipstick stood at attention next to the new toothbrush holder on a corner of the old procelain. She took it up and made clown spots on her cheekbones. Laughing on the outside, crying on the inside. I'm just a clown who can't say no. She rubbed the spots into the natural look, then applied a slick to her lips.

Back in the room she retrieved her jacket from her chair, laced her boots, found one glove at the foot of the bed under the paper, its mate on her dresser top. No more beret. No scarf. "Ehhhh," breathed the boy from his exertions. She stepped over his ankles and said good-bye. "Yhhhhh," he said. She opened the door again and stepped over him again and went back to the dresser top. She rammed the Ramses in her pocket and stepped back over the boy.

She was off in search of Mark and sex in a state of highly honed horn. A man to make up for all the things that were missing. A little healing sex. Out looking for it, mad bitch in heat. And on this frozen day. That was it, merely: animus . . . animal.

She waved to Mrs. Sergeant Major, nodded to the security guard, and went outside. Burning up in a city that had turned to tundra. What upset her was the

235

knowledge that the boy on the mat had made his contribution to her condition, that sweat on bare young chest. If idle minds were the devil's workshop, try idle prone proximate bodies and you come up with the devil's promised land. She thought of the boy's thin fingers and remembered Mark's thicker fingers working her through the night she had been with him. The incessant flicks of the boy's tongue over his chapped lips were those of another tongue in the inny of her bellybutton, the cavity beneath her Adam's apple, the recesses between her toes, her wide-crying mouth.

Chapter
14

Mark Pitofsky was Broker of the Day. All day long. It was no honor, but rather a duty to be performed once a month by each broker in the office. He had been Broker of the Day once before. It was an inconvenience. You couldn't eat your fried egg on a roll when you were Broker of the Day. You couldn't read your *Times*. The Broker of the Day was on display, in the front desk just beyond the receptionist, fair game for anyone who called the office, anyone who walked in off the street and wanted a quote. Just window shopping, these folks, passing the time picking his brain. Slim pickin's.

"How's the market?" they'd ask.

"Up two points," he'd tell them. Just the facts, ma'am.

"How's General Telepathics looking?"

He'd check the Quotron. "Up one."

"Yeah, but what do you *think*?"

What did he think? He thought this was the last generation on earth, and yet he still found hope in his days. He thought "My Way" as sung by Frank Sinatra was one of the angriest songs he had ever heard, and that people who loved it had very rarely had things their way. Perhaps at Burger King. He thought the Roche sisters were raving talents, and he liked to think of the day they had signed his album at Tower Records, the only turn as a fan he had ever done. He always thought about women, and recently he had thought of one in particular. He thought light beer was an abomination and that W. S. Merwin's poems were haunting. He thought he'd stop by Tower Records tonight to see if he could find *The Best of the Dixie Hummingbirds*. He thought he might go to Morocco and sit with his friend David in David's cave next year when his first two weeks of vacation came due.

He did not think about General Telepathics.

"I'm afraid I have no opinion on General Telepathics. Some people do like it, however. On the other hand, there are those who think it's a dog."

He liked his own desk in the lower right hand corner of the huge room, secure and unseen behind the great square pillar, where he could do the crossword whilst gearing up for the little-old-widow cold calls he loathed. He always thought of his mom, and how confused a stonewall cold call would make her. Not that his mom was a little old widow, just preoccupied. "Take time to smell the daisies!" she would say. Not that she had to tell him that. He was her son.

She was kind of cute, actually, and quite young for someone who was his mother. "You should get a boyfriend," he would tell her.

There had been no man in her life since Mark was in third grade, since the day he came home from school and found her pounding a FOR SALE sign into their front yard. "We're moving!" she told her only child. Without Dad, as it happened. Without Dad, who on that May day in 1960, had allowed himself to be seen by his wife and her whole card party squeezing Mary Cuneen in his company car, thereby proving himself to be a real true philanderer instead of mere suspect philanderer.

They left their trees and porch in Flatbush and went to Bayside, where they lived in half a house owned by his mother's brother, Uncle Joe, who lived in the other half with Aunt Rita. His mother had no truck with men again. She had consigned herself to life alone. "Why don't you find a boyfriend, Mom? You don't have to marry him."

"I play for keeps," she would say, with an edge of old hate and wasteful pain. She was only fifty-seven. And 1960 was a whole lonely long time ago.

The funny thing was, even though he had been married and divorced in his twenties, he thought he played for keeps, too. He hadn't played very often, that was certain, and he had never looked for women the way some men did. The grounds for his divorce had been indecision. His. Sally said he couldn't make up his mind to leave the liquor store. But leaving the liquor store then had not been on his mind, only on hers. She said here he was, a college graduate. She couldn't stand to see a man waste his potential. She said he couldn't make up his mind about a child. She said he wasn't ambitious and she was certainly right. He was on hold. There was something stopped in him, a vision of things that somehow took in his mother pounding the FOR SALE sign into the Flatbush lawn.

He had not done well when Sally left. He had loved her a long time and believed she loved him. And though he knew her leaving him was right, even overdue, for the people that they both were, he had missed his marriage badly. He had gone a little crazy when she left him.

There had been other women since his divorce, women who had found him and called him from his quiet. But it wasn't until he met Karen at Burger Paradise that he began to think again of living with a woman, of something more than blind dates and new sex and the certainty of partings.

He had analyzed it often enough to know that it was not just Karen Carmody and the way her hazel eyes changed to almost gold when he had sex with her. And, though their bodies had not come at the same time, their smiles did not fail to. It was something new in the last year, this aching for life and an intimacy with a woman. The switch from the liquor store had not been accidental. Though he thought it at the time, he now wondered whether things like that were ever accidental. When he met Karen, he realized that he had been getting ready for something new. He was thirty-five years old.

And then she stood him up. He had waited like a fool too long in the lobby of the Bleecker Street Cinema. Like something Antoine Doinel would have done in *Stolen Kisses*, which he had seen three times before but didn't get to see this time. It was a comfort knowing that Truffaut, up there looking down on him, knew how women made fools of men.

They would have postponed their delights in movie dark, stopping after to linger tantalizingly over a cup of coffee before walking in the cold back to his bed. He had wanted her the whole time he waited, hating her in the lobby. He had even worried that something happened to her and called her room. He was so stunned when a man answered that it took him a few seconds to hang up. He had believed her when she said men weren't allowed in rooms. It was almost as though she had set him up—made the date, and then for a big laugh got her boyfriend in the room to answer when he called. You chump, Pitofsky!

Damn. He wanted her now as he played Broker of the Day. But he knew from his limited experience that the need lifted, and that he would find someone else. He was in a good position, he reminded himself, being a straight man in this city at this time. He probably could take out a SWM ad in *New York* if he wanted to and get—who knows?—maybe twenty responses. "Demographically Desirable: a sober man, going bald, given to introspection." Pity the New York woman, he thought, and laughed.

The phone rang again. He picked it up. "Up two points," he said. "You're welcome," he said. "Goodbye." Two women were sitting in the folding chairs reserved by Merrill Lynch for Broker of the Day petitioners. The first was a woman from the streets, in to get warm, hip enough to latch on to the Broker of the Day scam. He figured she probably stopped by every brokerage office in the area, glomming up fifteen minutes of warmth in each one. More power to her. Her face was red over a naturally dark complexion. Windburned. Weathered. On her way to skin cancer from exposure. Her hair was gray and turned under in a surprisingly neat page-boy, interrupted by a protruding ear on the right side. This attempt at neatness given her circumstances touched him deeply. He could see her making her humble toilet this morning in the frigid ladies' room at Grand Central. Had she even washed her hair in one of the sinks? She certainly looked clean, and though she wore drab clothing in many layers, and though she carried an old bag with someone else's initials, she carried it with dignity.

The woman in the second folding chair was Karen Carmody.

He started, then nodded as noncommitally as he could manage to them both, and motioned the older woman to the more comfortable chair by his desk. He decided to take a good amount of time with the bag lady and her financial worries. Karen Carmody would learn that personal concerns took a back seat with the Broker of the Day.

The woman was small and smiled tentatively at him. She was probably hungry, he realized, and then thought of the egg on roll wrapped and uneaten in his briefcase. He dug around for it and held it low, discreetly close to his desk, toward the woman, saying quietly, "Maybe you would like this."

"What is this?" she asked as she took it. She had an accent he couldn't place. Mark never could place an accent.

"Egg on roll."

"Egg on roll?" she asked, puzzled. "For you." She held it back to him. Opalescent spots of grease had formed on the white deli bag.

He leaned toward her and said confidentially, "I can't eat it at this desk. You take it. It's cold, I got it this morning, but it will still be good."

"No. No thank you. I been eating all ready. Thank you too much."

Pride, Mark thought as he stuck the bag back in his briefcase next to the *Times* and a short-story collection he had gotten at the library. Before he left today, he would tuck the book in his own desk for tomorrow's reading. Pride, man. Here she probably hadn't eaten since maybe a soup kitchen last night. He had tried to present it to her as casually as possible. He glanced quickly at Karen, who was fiercely intent on the glittering symbols of the tape that clattered mockingly across the side wall. He noted that Mullaney, the office manager, was passing his desk rather slowly. He had to show that business was usual for him.

"Can I help you in any way?" he asked the woman at his desk. That should be general enough.

"Yes, I wish to make the purchase of ten thousand shares of the IBM stock."

Christ, groaned Mark to himself. A comedian bag lady. He had made Karen wait long enough. Seeing her now, he knew he wanted to talk to her. Now what was he gonna do? He would have to go through the motions now that he had started them. "Do you have an account with us?" he asked her as something behind his forehead clicked to Off.

"No."

He took a buff-colored New Accounts Form. "Why have you come to Merrill Lynch?" It was the first question on the form.

"I am new to States. My family owns your building. I am Pahlavi. I wish to show to you and your business my gratitude. Many businesses fear to rent from Pahlavi."

This babe sure was an original. How had she come by the secret of their building? It was kept under wraps for obvious reasons. He hadn't found out until he had been working here two weeks and inquired about the vacant first floor. New York was in the middle of a real-estate boom and yet the entire first floor of their building was empty. *Nada.* The plate-glass windows were painted a tasteful green, with thin gold leaf bows in the center of each. On Fifth Avenue! On Fifth Avenue where Cartier and Tiffany's and Fred the Jeweler packed them in at lunch, and where this guy Bijan would only see customers in his boutique by appointment, and then only five customers a day! Ah, but Bijan told the *Times* that each customer dropped twenty-five thou per visit, which anybody could do if he spent four hundred bucks on a shirt. One guy bought ninety $400 shirts. Why did he need ninety shirts, Mark wondered, but then figured he wouldn't have to go to the Laundromat so often.

Anyway, with Bijan raking in that kind of dough in his little old storefront practically across the street, how come there were no takers for the street floor here?

The answer Mullaney had given him: people who worked on the ground floor at this particular corner of Fifth and Fifty-second were bomb fodder ever since the Iranian hostage crisis. Mucho threats and two real scares, Mullaney told him. "Any fuckin' ayatollah nut with a good arm could pitch one in, or, better, hop in a wired car and pretend the ground floor is a Drive-Thru. You're talking a lot of people," Mullaney said. It was only then that Mark realized that most office buildings didn't have metal detectors and stringent sign-in systems in their lobbies. Still, even the security didn't make Mark feel all that great about being an occupant of the second floor. "You gotta start somewhere. Someone had to be on two. They gave us a break on the rent,"

Mullaney had told him. "Anyway, when your number's up . . . all that."

The woman next to him was speaking. "I have been in London since exile and now I will live here with cousins."

"Mrs. . . . Ms.?" Mark continued, deadpan, but his forehead had clicked back in.

"Princess," said the little lady.

What the fuck, thought Mark, and suppressed a chuckle as he crossed out the more pedestrian choices and block-lettered her handle in. Mark believed in permitting people their preferred personae. But *princess!* Still, she said it with such dignity. The princess would have been a great diversion any other day, but today Karen was sitting there with her choppy blond hair and those clunky boots, waiting for him. Some days he went nearly catatonic from boredom, and today Karen and the princess arrive at the same time. Karen's eyes were still glued to the quotes on the wall. Too bad. If they ever did speak again, he'd want to rehash this scene with her.

"Princess Sherry Pahlavi," she said, and gave a Sutton Place address. "Was Sherazade, but Sherry to Americans." She was pretty funny, the princess, but not that funny. She could've said she was staying at the Sherry Netherland. He wondered if he should give her that line to use the next time she came in from the cold.

"OK, princess, ten thousand shares of IBM, eh?" He kicked it up on the Quotron. "At a hundred twenty-five and three-fourths . . . that's one million two hundred sixty-seven thousand five hundred dollars, plus commission." His pulse did double time as he saw on the screen what a commission on that would be: the grid worked out to $8208.63. Ah, if it were true, if it could be the first of many such trades and commissions! His fleeting, fervent, foolish wish was to confer royalty upon this wiseass street lady. He looked at Karen, but she would not meet his gaze.

"How do you intend to pay, Princess Sherry?" he asked, then added for his own amusement, "You can't use American Express."

She caught his wrist and laughed in a light trill, then opened the worn purse and took out a checkbook that didn't look like any checkbook Mark had ever seen, certainly not the red plastic one Citibank had issued him. And only now did he notice that the hand that had been on his wrist wore a ring in the shape of a frog, a ring that took up half her finger, encrusted with clear faceted stones, with two larger green stones for the frog's eyes. The frog's teeny flippers were splayed gold. Was it possible? But even if the whole thing were fake, it was still some kind of amazing ring. He wiped sweat from his forehead and twisted his Wallabees around the base of the swivel chair.

"Excuse me, Princess, we can't take personal checks, either. Certified checks only. And I'm afraid we need identification."

"Of course, yes. I shall be back with both. Please to write down the amount." This he did, on the back of his card.

"A visa will be all right for the identification?"

It took him a moment to realize she didn't mean the credit card. "Yes, certainly." He stood up and she handed him her hand and smiled. To his credit he didn't kiss the frog.

"You will be here?"

"Hey, Princess, I gotta be here . . . I'm Broker of the Day!"

"Thank you again for egg sandwich." Was it his imagination, or had she said it serenely? She walked past Karen, who seemed finally to be paying attention. By the reception desk a man in a dark suit carrying a bulky coat over his arm stood, nodded to her, and followed her out. Mark was beginning to feel giddy.

Karen had taken a seat at the Broker of the Day desk. "Who was that?"

Mark merely groaned. Would she be back?

She shook his arm. "Mark, I'm so sorry about the other night. Can you take a late lunch? I'm buying." She hesitated and laughed sheepishly. "You like peanut butter? I'll take you to Paley Park . . ."

Mark grabbed Karen's shoulder with one hand and put his brow in his other hand and began to laugh softly.

"Look, Mark . . . I'm a real shit-for-brains. I don't blame you if you want to stay back from me, but just let me take you to lunch, OK?

He rocked his head in his hand.

She took his hand from her shoulder and held it in hers. "I really like you so much."

"I like you, too, Karen," he said, and laughed again, then jumped from his chair. "Come here. Quick!" He motioned her to the window.

"What's doin', Pitofsky?" asked Yat Tsu, a broker who sat in the back next to Mark's real desk, on his way back after placing an order. Mark grabbed his sleeve and pulled him to the window.

"Look!" Mark commanded them urgently. A burgundy stretch limousine was parked in front of the building, a uniformed chauffeur standing beside it in the frigid sunshine.

"Ho-ly shit!" said Karen, who was putting two and two together.

"A limo," said Yat. "Very nice. Hey, yeah, Mark, baby, there are limos on Fifth Avenue. I bet you've seen one before. I gotta get back to my desk." He patted Mark's back and winked at Karen. "Maybe you oughta take a break, kid."

"*Look!*" It must here be reported that the Broker of the Day now lost all trace of his normal laid-backness. The Broker of the Day was jumping up and down. The princess, a fur thrown carelessly over her shoulders, was being hastily ushered from the building and into the limo. Mark first kissed Karen's eye, then Yat's lips.

"You wanna tell my why you're losin' it, Pitofsky?" Yat motioned Weinstein over and Mark flashed the new order form. He explained in bursts punctuated by jumps. " 'I am Pahlavi,' she goes! Fuckin' Pahlavi!" His voice cracked. He laughed madly and thrust the form at Weinstein.

Weinstein rolled his eyes at Yat and Karen. "Yeah, Pitofsky . . . I really think that you oughta do that order. Sure, baby. And if you do real good, I'm gonna call Monaco and line you up for the Grimaldis next week, dig?" He muttered, "Ten thousand shares of IBM," and chuckled. "Are you gonna tell him, Tsu, or shall I?"

"Pitofsky," said Yat kindly. "There's something Mullaney should have told you when he hired you. It's sorta cruel to have to tell you now. Weinstein's enjoying it because he got taken in so bad by Princess Sherry once." Mark's head turned violently from the window to Yat.

"She ain't gonna be back, Pitofsky," Yat said quietly. "Not for a while, and then to a new broker, not you. She really is Pahlavi, but she's also really whacked out. The exile did it to her. She's real lonely, so she comes in here and hits on somebody unsuspecting. The family gives her an allowance and the car, but no way has she got any control over investments. She feels like she can come and go in this building and so she does, comes in and chats up whoever's sitting at this desk. Her brother, the Satrap Herbie, will probably be around later to apologize to you, maybe give you free tickets to his Cinema 14. The Satrap is a cool guy; he'll be real gracious and apologetic and all, but it *is* a problem." Yat shrugged, then hit Mark's arm in a mock punch. "She's an embarrassment to the family, what can I say? Look at it as your initiation."

Mark looked out the window again and saw $8,208.63 in small bills, each with a dainty pair of hard-pumping wings, flying down Fifth in the wake of a burgundy limo. He laughed wryly. It was not to be. He would never be rich. It had been held out to him so mockingly, and now he was chagrined to realize that he had been swept away, as tempted as the next. Still, it had been only a moment and it had passed quickly enough, with only the briefest searing stroke through his entrails.

One thing he didn't understand. "Yeah, but then how come she was wearing those poverty-stricken clothes, all those dark rags?"

"Those weren't rags," said Karen, who had recently seen just such rags given prominent space in one of the *New York* magazines from the lounge. "They only look like rags. They're by that Japanese designer . . . you know."

She could see Mark had no idea. She had to laugh. It was part of his great oblivion, though every second woman on Fifth Avenue was dressed in loose dark clothes and coolie shoes like the princess. He probably thought they were all bag ladies. "Yohji . . ." Karen strained for the last name.

"Yamamoto," said Yat, who had recently acquired an item from Yamamoto Pour Homme. Yat had been in the training program with Mark, and was doing well. Karen noticed that he wore a tie of the softest silk. He threw a comforting arm around Mark. "Aw, Pitofsky, it's all anybody needs, right? A client like that," said Yat reverently. "Look at Orville."

But Orville wasn't there to look at. He was home. "Picking toe jam," said Weinstein. Orville had the one client he needed. The Island of Bermuda, which he came in to call every Monday morning whether it answered or not.

"Yeah, and think about the morality of taking shah money," said Karen as comfort. "I mean, we all know how they got it." She realized her error immediately.

The three brokers, Pitofsky, Weinstein, and Tsu, fell silent and looked at her incredulously. Then Weinstein spoke for the brokers. "All the more reason to take it from them." He squeezed Mark's arm and walked to the back with Yat.

The Broker of the Day phone had been ringing intermittently, hopelessly. Mark slouched his way back to the desk. He grabbed the phone. "Up two points," he barked into it, placed it back in its cradle, and turned to Karen, who had followed him from the window.

"You can't come to lunch with me?" she asked meekly after a moment of hoping he'd speak first. "I'd like to talk to you."

Only now, in the calm after the princess, did he remember waiting in the lobby for Karen. "It's probably not so good for me to talk to you." He looked at her face for the effect of his words and was gratified.

"Please," she said. "I'm really sorry. Can't I explain?" she asked, though she had no idea what form the explanation would take. Would he buy her theory of self-destruct? And what kind of an ad was that for herself, anyway?

"You're gonna explain? You're gonna explain the guy that answered that night when I called your room?"

"A *guy?*" Then: "Yes! . . . Yes, I can explain that guy! Do you have a half-hour to talk? Can you *please* come to lunch with me?"

"I'm Broker of the Day," was all he said. Was it possible she was being straight with him? He looked at her standing awkwardly at his desk—that moth-eaten fur jacket, her hands shoved in the pockets, her punk hair, the expanse of face, her lovely eyes. He thought how it had been to lie with her and hold her, how smooth her skin. She had come here, he knew, because she wanted to lie with him again, and though he was a SWM in this great city, she was the best offer he had had all day, the best in many seasons. "You hurt my feelings," he said, petulant, like a child. Like a charming child, he knew. "Sorry isn't good enough," he said.

"Huh?" Karen said.

He laughed. "My mother used to tell me that, and I would always say, 'Yes it is, it's good and pretty.' "

They laughed, then were quiet. Mark began digging in his pocket, a mysterious smile on his face. He pulled out his keys with a flourish, then dangled them before her, holding one between his thumb and forefinger. "Look, I don't want to hear explanations until you make reparation. Do you wish to make reparation?"

She nodded without speaking. Her throat had gone dry. She focused on the thick fingers holding the key.

"Very well, these are your instructions. Go to my apartment and take off all your clothes. Then sit on my bed and wait for me. You are not allowed to take a nap. You are not allowed to read or watch television. You are not allowed to eat the potato chips. If it gets chilly, you may get under the covers. But if it starts to get dark before I get there, you can't turn on a light. You're only allowed to sit on my bed and think of me." His face was distorted, almost a grimace. "Think of what we did the last time. I want to be here thinking of you thinking of it."

She swallowed hard and nodded again. She came closer to take the keys. He looked in her face and with his empty hand brushed her lightly between the legs. Casually, as if by accident, unmindful of the room of brokers, sales assistants, clients, clerks. She felt his touch through heavy clothes.

"You are not allowed to reach orgasm until I come to you. Is that clear?"

She emitted an assenting sound.

He affected indifference, though he felt something

like pain in his loins. "It's two-fifteen. I may not be there until six or seven. I can't be rushed, and maybe I won't even think about you. Who knows? Maybe I'll be late. I am Broker of the Day today. Do you understand?"

"Oh, yeah . . . one other thing." He broke into a grin, reached again in his pocket, then handed her a twenty. "Would you pick up some wine, and then stop at Tower Records and buy me *The Best of the Dixie Hummingbirds*?"

These things she did to make reparation.

Chapter
15

They sat on the floor of his apartment sharing a quart of beer and finishing off the pizza they had begun much earlier in the evening. It was midnight. Karen wore an old gray sweatshirt belonging to Mark. Mark wore a blanket.

He yanked her baby toe. "Something wrong?" he asked.

"No. Why?" In fact Karen thought things were fine.

"Those sounds you're making . . . almost like a sob."

Karen feigned great cool as she removed a wilted onion from the clotted cheese. But she was betrayed by three gasps in succession, quick but deep-felt, gasps that rose from her core. She absently put the rubbery slice back in the box, smiled at Mark, and shrugged. "Sex does that to me, right after. You know how some people smoke after sex? I gasp." She did again. A husky hiccup. She flushed. "When I think about it."

Which she always did. Whenever she considered how the man she had just lain with—this one sleeping heavy next to her, or that one in the shower, or this other one searching for his cigarettes and in a great rush to leave, or, this one now, this man right here in his faded blanket sitting beside her, smiling and salting his pizza—whenever she thought of the things so recently done to her body, the way a particular man had just tenderly brushed her breasts with his lips or passionately grasped a whole buttock in one hand—whenever she did an instant replay, she would gasp involuntarily. Was this phenomenon unique to her, she wondered? She always thought of asking Annie, but of course Annie was never there when it was happening, and Karen would forget the next time she saw Annie. "Do you gasp after sex?" Maybe Kinsey or Masters had a chapter entitled "The Postcoital Gasp."

Mark chewed thoughtfully on his crust, watching her. "These . . . er . . . sounds . . . would you say they're proportionate, in degree and in number, to the amount of satisfaction the act brings you?" He raised his chin and narrowed his eyes, affecting an exaggerated preen.

"Are you asking me this to feed the ego that you don't have? Yes." She looked directly at him, one corner of her mouth pulling upward. "The answer is yes. But there's this question I have. In my uh . . . limited experience, I've never once heard a man gasp afterward. What do you think? Does this mean men are less satisfied by sex than women?"

He laughed out loud. "You're serious, aren't you? How can you say that! How can you doubt when you heard me just before? Didn't I make a lot of noise? Doesn't that count for something?"

"It's true. Men's orgasms do *sound* good. Sometimes I get jealous . . . all that noise they make. Are they having more fun? What is it like for men?" She held her gaze and smiled broadly now. "Yours are particularly clamorous."

He laughed again, shaking his head and raising his eyes ceilingward. "God, woman! I'm not sure how I feel about your comparing my come cry with others you have known, even if mine does come out on top. So to speak." He put his face up against hers. "Permit me my illusions. I want to think I'm the only one who's ever fucked you."

She emitted four more gasps now as he said this, as she smelled herself on his face, as she recalled his face between her thighs, how his eyes had searched her eyes as his mouth and tongue worked hard into her. She had been propped up on his bed, her back against his wall, her knees bent, her leg wide apart to welcome him. For a moment as she sat there, she had been a-mused by how her pubic hair had become his facial hair, how he seemed to sport a thick curly mustache, but then she was drawn back by the need in his darken-ing eyes and had begun her helpless writhing against his face.

His face near her face. Her smell on him; his smell on her. She touched his cheek and thought idly how odd that he should be bald when the rest of his body was so thickly haired.

"So you like thinking about it." He moved his hand from toe to ankle and up the inside of a wet thigh. "Where I touched you, what we did. And you'll think about it when we're apart, too." A finger slid quickly inside her, then out, its tip dragging down, digging into her other thigh. It was more like a moan this time. Mark's face had gone to the grimace she had seen earlier. "The recollection in tranquillity of sex just past, eh? You love it so much it can do that to you, even after, eh?" He grabbed her shoulders and shook them lightly. "God, you are such a sensual woman. I *love* fucking you." He kissed her four fast, hard kisses. "Do you mind my saying that?"

She shook her head no, unable to speak. A half-gasp, the last of them. The sweatshirt moved up and down as he rubbed the small of her back.

"You have certain enthusiams, it seems," she said after a while.

"Oh, you noticed, did you? Yes, I do indeed. But I hadn't done . . . that . . . in quite a while. I've hardly done it at all, actually, but I'm good at it, eh?" He eyed her for a moment. "My wife never wanted it. She was raised repressed, Presbyterian variety. She got past a lot of their strictures, but she was stopped cold by sodomy. And after we divorced . . ." He laughed. "I assure you that wasn't the reason for the divorce . . . anyway, after, I never quite knew how to approach it with any other women, whether they'd be repelled, you know, whether I would. And it seemed to me there were enough other things to keep one busy in bed. But you certainly conveyed your preferences." He kicked aside the pizza box, knocking over the salt. "My wife said it was animal, all that sniffing around and licking. She said it was like dogs. I agreed, actually. It is rather canine, isn't it?"

"Arf," said Karen, nodding her assent.

"Grrrrr," Mark replied, with the best leer he could manage. It was this failed leer that convulsed them. They laughed giddily between gulps of beer.

Their physical cravings satisfied for the nonce, they brought the same hunger to talk that they had to pizza and sex. Everything was up for consideration, because everything was new. He held her and she asked the questions. There was a lot she didn't know about Mark Pitofsky.

They discussed wealth and how Mark had been a rich man for a moment that afternoon. "You don't care, though, right?" asked Karen. "I mean shah money . . . blood money . . . think about the hands that got chopped off, just for the measly cut you'd get of their bucks."

"Yeah, but isn't it like what Gina Lollabrigida said when she got caught with an endangered animal on her back: 'But dahling, the leopard was already killed and on a hanger when I first saw it.'"

Karen looked puzzled.

"I mean, the hands are already cut off, right? And they can't cut off any more hands 'cause they're in exile. That's what exile means." Karen was not amused. "So I see you're relieved. You think I need this"—he indicated his wooden valet and his mildewed fridge—" to stay pure. Pure and poor. But I think I'm really the kind of guy who could rise above riches. I'm happy to say I believe that about myself, though it doesn't appear that I'll ever be tested."

"What about God?" she asked.

"Yeah?"

"What's it to ya?"

"A lot. It's sort of basic to me. Either you do or you don't. I don't know . . . I don't think I could get very deep with a real religious type." She flushed. "I mean, you can take just about any issue, any discussion . . . the homeless, the bomb, population, environ-

258

ment, death . . . it all comes down to *God will provide* if you're real religious. The old lilies of the field biz. So how you gonna argue with that? You can't have a good argument with them because you know that in the end they'll pull out all the stops and hit you with God."

He laughed.

"But it's true, isn't it? Maybe I resent religion mainly because it's such a damn conversation stopper. I mean, there are some religious people I'm very fond of . . . some of my best friends and all that . . . but I don't share my men with God. It would be like . . . having sex with someone who voted for Reagan, you know, something so different." He laughed again. "So anyway . . ." she demanded, "God?"

"No. I don't. Believe or vote. The last time I did either was when I was twenty-one. Just sowing my wild oats, I guess. A wanton youth."

Satisfied with this response, his interrogatrix moved on to his lap and the next item. He leaned back against the couch. "Kids," she said, and draped her free arm around him.

"Yeah. What about 'em?"

"You want 'em?" she asked, then laughed. "In the abstract, of course." He was quiet for a moment. She thought she had gone too far, frightened him.

"You have a crooked nose, Karen Carmody," he said, touching it and smiling.

"Answer the question."

"What about you?" he asked. "Do you want children?"

"Yeah, I do. I want one. Yes. My shot against the

Void, I guess. But then, I don't know . . . having a kid when all these people are on the streets . . ." Her voice went a little high by the time it reached "streets."

He moved his hand up her back. "But maybe that's it," she continued. "You know, maybe that's exactly why you need your own kid."

"But isn't that just kind of creating a meaning for yourself?"

Karen looked at him, then shot back, "Hey, I got news . . . I don't think creating a meaning for myself is such a bad thing." She was startled by the fervor of her reply. She had a quick flash of Martha, and then of Vinnie. For a moment she stayed quiet in his arms.

"What would you tell a kid about God?" she asked then.

"If I had a kid?" he asked, and there seemed to be a hint of exasperation in his voice. "If I had a kid . . ." He paused. "I would sit her down when she turned seven and say, 'Jane, you have reached the age of reason now. There's something you should know. Your mother and I are atheists.' "

"Jane." Karen laughed softly. She liked the name Jane. "But you wouldn't hedge? You wouldn't at least say you were agnostic?"

"Never," he replied. "So, what else? You got a lotta questions for a girl from upstate. Did you know your eyes have these crazy dark spots on them? Listen, you keep the conversation going, all right? I have other things I must attend to." He removed his sweatshirt from her and took her left nipple lightly between his teeth.

As he went about these other things, she found herself telling him about Sarah being discalced, quoting her mother's latest letter in its entirety, telling him all about Simtra and his Apache maiden hype.

"Ummm," said Mark, turning her around to kiss the discs down her back. "I see," he murmured, and turned her around again to kiss her lips quiet.

He had brief success. She came up for air and another question. "What am I gonna do about the boy in my room?" She had explained who the "guy" was earlier. She thought there was something that Mark could say about the events in 742 that could cast light.

He sighed a special essence of annoyance and amusement. "Can we talk about the boy in your room in a little while? Concentrate on the man in this room." He spread her on his floor.

Later, lying spent upon him, but true to her obsessive nature, Karen continued her canvas interruptus. "The boy in my room."

"The boy in your womb?" Mark mumbled, confused, as what was left of him in her took limp leave. "Oh, yeah . . . so . . . How's it going?"

"Wonderful . . . great. All I do is zombie out in front of the VCR." Another problem, which she wouldn't lay on Mark: Vinnie had told her that her Visa card had declined the pleasure of doing business with her. She owed Vinnie two hundred and forty-three dollars.

"The kid's name is Terry, right? Does he do anything?"

"Sit-ups. He does a lot of sit-ups. He reads about flowers, he cleans. He studies algebra." She told him how Michele would come by and monitor his algebra while she read her briefs, eschewing smoke now during her visits. Terry did not approve of smoke. Michele

261

didn't seem to miss her cigarettes as she worked with the boy. Karen told Mark how Martha was in and out, on errands for the boy, about whatever other business she had. She described how she watched her movies, and how she watched her roommates as though they were in another movie, "a kind of *très long cinéma vérité avec beaucoup d'ennui.*"

"Sounds like even in that situation he's got some sense of purpose and accomplishment."

Karen took this as a rebuke. "And I don't, right?"

"Christ, woman! That's not what I said. You're working things out." He was quiet for a minute. "You like this kid, right? You want to help him?"

She wasn't sure. He seemed grateful and deferential to Martha. He seemed willing and bright, and his movements in the room were precise and unobtrusive. It was just that he was there without end. "Does it matter if I like him? Martha likes him. Yeah, he's OK, I suppose, but . . ."

Mark came up from under her and shrugged. "It's up to you. If you want to or not."

"I don't *not* want to help him . . ."

"Then you probably have to let him stay awhile. It's cold out, you know."

"Easy for you to say," she snapped. "I notice you're living a life without any entangling alliances, uncommitted to anything much." She was immediately sorry.

"Hey! How come so hostile?"

"Look, I don't know. I'm sorry. Maybe I envy you, being alone."

He scratched at his ankle. "Of course it's easy for

me to say. Don't attack my life for what you don't want to do. My life is empty. So? I know it. Some days I think I can change it, some days I accept it. But this woman Martha *is* doing something for her life. Whatever inconvenience it causes you, it's fulfilling to her. You've got to decide how you really feel about it. You're not obliged to do anything for this boy. You'd be within your rights to report his presence. It's up to you." He wrapped her in his blanket, then slouched nude to his bed to grab another. Like a bear, she thought, lean in early spring.

"Fidelity," she said, to change the subject, when he returned and wrapped them together.

"Huh?" he asked.

"What about it? What do you think?"

"I think it's becoming more appealing these days, don't you? Apart from considerations of disease, however, I don't care," he replied, "but if a woman did—care about it—she'd have a good one in me. I don't send out signals to women. Too lazy, I guess. No. Too afraid of rejection. That's it. Any woman who wanted me would have to ferret me out." He laughed. "Not many do, you know."

"But you don't care? You wouldn't care if . . . if your woman slept with other men?"

"As I said, I want my illusions. But if I didn't know, no. In fact, I find this idea of a secret life kind of enticing."

"Where did you come from?" she asked. "What would happen if you knew? This is theoretical, of course."

"Of course. If I knew, I assure you, I would carry

on in the manner of the best Sicilian out there." He gave a histrionic southern Italian eyeball roll. They laughed, but not as much as at his leer.

He licked her mouth lightly. "Sometimes I think marriage is this device invented by Jerry Falwell's forebears to keep people from screwing like rabbits and fucking up the lines of inheritance. Except now AIDS makes Falwell redundant."

"Oh," said Karen.

"Still, knowing this, I think one day I will suspend disbelief and marry again."

"God, what a romantic!"

"What about you?"

"No . . . Maybe . . . I don't know."

"Why not?" He asked softly as he drew his index finger back and forth across her lower lip.

She shrugged. "Vows for life, I guess. I'm not even all that great for the short haul." She sighed and her eyes filled. "Look, if you want to know the truth, I'm too busy working things out to take on another person."

"But you're not so bad off," he said, his voice a sweet mix of irony and tenderness. "You had the good instincts to ferret me out, didn't you?"

"There's a comfort," said Karen solemnly, and they laughed again.

Chapter
16

They spent the night to-
gether. In the morning he told her he couldn't have a
child. Offhand. Mere mention of a technicality. She had
been collecting her things, snatching up underwear
from the floor, her jacket and pants from the valet
where he had hung them, scarecrowlike, in jest. "Here,
I'll leave you my rubbers for a housegift," she said,
laughing, proffering the box. "But you have to promise
only to use them when I stop by."

He was already dressed for work, in shirtsleeves
and tie, studying her from the couch. He didn't smile.
"Thanks, but I don't need them," he said.

"What?" she asked absently. She was still nude,
and shivering, rushing to get her clothes on. They had
made love again when the alarm rang, and she stayed
under the blankets until it was her turn in the
bathroom. "Oh," she said, "look, of course you don't
have AIDS, but my diaphragm is a relic and right now I
can't afford to go to the gyno—"

"I don't need them," he said quietly. "I don't need
anything." It was snowing lightly outside. "I'm fixed,"
he said.

"You're fixed," she repeated dumbly. She had one
sock on.

"I had a vasectomy seven years ago."

Seven years ago. She stared at him, his face so youthful. She began figuring back. "But you were *twenty-eight*."

"Yes. It was after my divorce." He bent his head and patted the hair combed neatly and sparely back. "It was probably in reaction to my divorce. We had kicked the subject of children around so often. I just wanted it decided for me."

"But you had no children," she said. "You have no children." She held out her clothes and looked at them helplessly. It seemed impossible that she would ever get them on. And now she had begun to cry. He came to her and took her things from her. He smoothed out her shirt and carefully draped it over her arms, bending to button it. Crouching before her, he moved his hands down to rest on her hips and leaned in to kiss her. She whacked his face away. He lost his balance and fell to the floor, from which he stared at her, startled.

"*Why?*" She moved to the couch and sat there, crying softly, her clothes between her legs.

"I don't regret it," he said very quickly. "I didn't want children . . . I still don't. I have no hope for children, not the way things are." He remained on the floor, leaning back on his arms.

"What was all that bullshit about what you would tell Jane?" She knew she was taking it too personally, as though he had been leading her on with Jane, as though they had said more than they had to each other. As though he had promised her something.

"Jane?" he was puzzled.

"*Last night* . . . what you would tell her about God . . . I mean, about no God."

"Oh, Karen," he said, and then, very softly, "I'm sorry . . . It was hypothetical, wasn't it? I meant, *if* I had kids."

She thought: If you had Jane, you mean. You jerk! That was what she was thinking. She stood and pulled on her pants. "I'm overreacting. It's your decision, of course. I'm sure it's right for you." Clipped and efficient. Cool.

She also thought: You asshole! Were you getting laid so damn much in those days that you had to take *surgical* measures? Wasn't a rubber good enough? How much sex were you having that contraception became this really *major* inconvenience? She did not say these things.

But then, as she put on her jacket, she said, "It was after your divorce. I think you were angry. You were trying to cut things off."

"Symbolic castration, you mean?" He rose from the floor. He was working to control an incipient smile. It was a nervous smile. He wasn't annoyed. If anything, he had been moved by the strength of her reaction.

"Not *it* off. People. People you could be with and kids you could have. Some weird way it was gonna make you untouchable, right? There wouldn't be all this . . . I don't know . . ." Her hand waved between their faces. *You are filled with life!* She looked blankly at the ceiling and exhaled audibly. "Possibility," she said then, and waved the word away as though it were smoke.

He grasped her wrist and looked deep into her. "There are possibilities without children. And there aren't many possibilities for all the children that people keep on having so mindlessly. I didn't want to add to it.

It was that simple. I believe that strongly, no matter what psychological implications you read into it. Anyway, why should you care so much?" And, he wondered, why did he care if she cared?

Why indeed? She pulled away and grabbed her stuff. "I'm going, all right? Look, I'm really sorry I made this scene and all, you know. Really. It's your business."

A dusting of snow covered the gray of Avenue A. She scuffed her way toward First Avenue. She was thirty-three. If she had a child named Jane, Jane would be walking beside her sticking her tongue out to catch the snow. She could love a child named Jane too much. Jane kicking at her from inside, Jane at the breast, drinking from her, Karen. Nourishment from her. Bald Baby Jane doing rumpy bumps with her father, her hilarity, riding up and down on his ankles, the way Karen and Sarah and Bill had with her father. R-r-r-r-umpy *bump!* She could see a man on his back, you couldn't make out the face, but the baby's dark eyes flashed light with laughing above him, the blur of movement. It was too disorienting, the blur— she couldn't see the floor, what rug they were on or what room they were in. She couldn't tell whether it was city or country. What room, where? Mark's bare floor, or the shag rug of the Arcadia, or the worn dark flowers from the varnished floor of Congress Street? A futile fantasy. It was impossible, they were impossible, she and Mark. But there were these things you could do if you had a kid. You could sing "Petit Chat Noir" to her. You could read her *Good Night, Moon*. You could show her the surprise of an egg cracked from its shell, and how it changed when it got scrambled.

"Don't step on the grate!"

Karen looked up, startled. An old black man wrapped in a filthy blanket was standing vigilant in front of a Laundromat. Cheekbones so prominent and cheeks so sunken that Karen saw straight to the sorrow of his skull. He was pointing in urgent jabs at her feet.

She looked down where she stood, upon a grate, small dark rectangles outlined by snow. She was standing in a cloud of cold white smoke. The man pointed his fierce stabs. He wanted her off the grate. She shivered and obliged him by taking a giant step sideways to sidewalk. "The devil walks beneath," he said, mollified. In the Laundromat behind him a child was ramming a wire cart into a soap machine as his mother measured bleach into a paper cup. Karen was no lover of a Laundromat, but this one now seemed a scene of such serenity, light, and warmth! "Thank you," she said to the wraith and continued, mindful of her tread, wondering what it was that caused those cold clouds. She had lived in New York for nine years and did not know what lay below.

She stopped in Palermo's and picked up a bulky bag of anisette toast and next door, at Di Bella's, for some cheese. Treats for the folks in 742. She stopped in a discount drug place for shampoo to replace what she had used of Martha's. Back on First, she stood trying to consolidate her purchases into the largest bag before continuing. The bag, wet from the snow, gave. Shit, thought Karen, and stooped to collect the disparate items. She was still blocks from the Arcadia. She found a balance, however, and continued on with her armload.

"Reefer?" said a whisper next to her. A youth with EMILIO stitched in white on a kelly green pull-down Jets cap stood shifting sneakers in the snow. Karen walked apace. "Sens?" he inquired, alongside her, or had he said "Sex?" She ignored him and struggled to keep her burden. "You need some help?" But he remained at the corner when she crossed, not daring to go beyond his turf. Con artists could be as provincial as the next guy, Karen decided, as she caught the descending shampoo between her thighs.

Vinnie's Viddies! She'd get a bag there and warm up. Then she remembered her recalcitrant Visa card. Visa declines. Visa sends regrets. Visa does not approve! Dear Customer, No Longer Valued: Kindly take your arrearages and shove them. Though she dreaded it, she must speak to Vinnie. She needed more tapes. To face her room, to avoid her life.

His back was to the counter, head down, intent, his pencil moving slowly down one side of a printout, his lips moving silently. "Heya, how's it goin'?" he asked, when he turned and saw her. Karen relaxed. The man had a warmth that transcended the vicissitudes of Visa. She took a brief bask in his smile.

"Look, I'm sorry I screwed up on the Visa, Vinnie. I know I had credit with them, but they probably closed it when they found I didn't hunt heads anymore. The only reason I got it in the first place was that I had that job with Exec-Career. A week after I got the job, it came in the mail. Unsolicited."

"Ah," said Vinnie. "Visa giveth and Visa taketh

away. Visa is all-knowing. Visa abideth." He removed the plastic cap from his coffee, poured half into a dirty mug, and handed Karen the paper cup. "You like black?" he asked.

"I like you," she said, and drank in the warmth. "Listen, Vinnie, can I pay you twenty-five a week, plus interest, and pay as I go on any other tapes I take out?" She looked at him again and blurted, "Hey, let me work for you, why don't you? I can *work* it off!" She laughed then, surprised. She could have thought of it before. It actually sounded like a good idea!

It sounded like a very good idea.

She talked fast then, selling him on it, as though she had considered it before. "What about three fifty a week, two seventy-five until I work off what I owe? Look, you're the only video store for two blocks in any direction. You're going crazy without help, trying to do the installations and deliveries and having to be here ten hours a day, besides keeping up with the orders and billings and new offerings and having your new shelves put in—"

"Karen—"

"I've seen this place around five-thirty. It's like the corner of Sixtieth and Third if Cinema 3 premiered *Return of Return of the Jedi* the same night Cinema 2 opened a Rambo Revival. Am I right?"

"Look, uh—"

"Make it three seventy-five a week. I'll pay off what I owe you, and I'll stay the ten hours instead of eight. That's minimum what I'd need to live."

"OK," he said. "OK, we'll try it out. I was actually gonna advertise. But why are you doing it? The money will be zip. It's not what you made before."

271

"It's more than I make now. And it will give me time to think."

"Yeah, well, I think you'd be good. You know movies. We'd get along."

"I would. I do. We would," Karen said, and laughed. "When do I start?"

"I got stuff I gotta do right now. You come back at two, I can train you a little before all hell breaks loose."

"Later!" She guzzled the rest of her coffee and was out the door empty-handed. Vinnie opened the forgotten Palermo's bag, when he discovered it, shrugged, removed a piece of anisette toast and dunked it, with no small satisfaction, into his mug. In another moment he collected Karen's leavings from the counter and returned to his printout.

*I*t was snowing harder when she left Vinnie's. Mark had said he did not intrude. If you died without a child, you could not be said to have intruded, not really. That's what got her most, what made her feel so bad for him. Didn't Mark think he was worth it? If you didn't have a kid, you didn't leave anything of yourself that would take up space. And if you didn't, then you didn't owe anything either. You could go through without debt and with as little pain as possible. Karen felt suddenly that she wanted to intrude most violently and carelessly upon the world. She wanted to suffer it and take what joy it had, then one day die in debt, owing everything. How depressing to be paid up. How lacking in trust.

Or was it bravery on Mark's part? I have seen the future and it's a mess. Take me alone without any

272

support. I do not believe in you, world, and I will not perpetuate the folly.

Karen saw both sides quite plainly. She saw perfectly well how Mark could have gone out and gotten it done. But she also saw what he would be missing.

And, she saw now, clearly etched by Mark's choice, how much she wanted a child. It's want she might have been hoping for, lying with him this bleak morning. Some hope beyond sex and the moment, something she couldn't say, had been giving it light, and she thought now that part of it was this hope, because she had been so dashed by his announcement.

Those operations weren't reversible. In some cases, maybe. Mostly not, though. She had read it in one of the ladies' mags in the lounge. She forgot what the statistics were, but Mark was comparatively young, so maybe the odds would be for him if they were for anyone. If he wanted to, but she was certain he wouldn't. A woman might take up with Mark Pitofsky for one of several reasons: brain, humor, skewed vision, sex, dimple, chest hair, the things he chose to read and view, his angelbone massages. Good reasons. But he was not a breeder. No. He wasn't to be used that way. If you decided to love him, you would have to do it purely. Just him.

She thought of the biological clock relentlessly flashing its sinister numbers on her dark screen. Karen's was digital, all the more threatening. It was a gods-are-laughing kind of joke: wanting a kid, finding a man and thinking maybe, and this man being Mark, all fixed for years now.

Was that what women wanted, after all, she and all the other women who were single in this city? A stud?

And marriage just a stud farm? But after, wouldn't there be this steady steed, this good helpmeet work-horse yoked together with you? And sometimes, wouldn't you stop to horse around a little, get your field plowed by the beast who knew it best?

The people who had purpose were walking briskly along with it. Karen envied them. She shouldn't feel this way. She had a job now, too. True, it wasn't a great job, and she still didn't have a place of her own, but she knew, despite Mark Pitofsky, that things were finally lifting for her.

But life hadn't changed for everyone. There were still drifters in this snow, a man drinking wine, a wizened bewildered old woman with only a frayed and filthy ski vest over a ragged cotton skirt. Karen noted that several of the buildings she passed had facades which sported newly installed pronglike fixtures be-neath their plate-glass windows. Prongs jutting out from brick at back level, if one were sitting on the sidewalk, at intervals so frequent that a human back could not fit between them and rest against the building. The buildings were thus protected from the homeless resting against them. Karen thought with repellence of the entrepreneurial fiend who had con-ceived of such a consummately contemptible business opportunity as prong installation in the city of New York. May he know the feel of those prongs on his back before he dies. May he sit long hours in freezing rain against those prongs as the poor and the abandoned of this city pass in procession before him, stopping to insert small sharp things under his fingernails and under the toenails of his discalced frostbitten feet.

She turned the corner, refining her curse against the Prong King, when a leaflet affixed to the lamppost caught her eye. Your basic missing person leaflet, the standard picture and sad bill of particulars, the number to call.

HAVE YOU SEEN THIS PERSON?

Yes. Karen had.

The tight sinews of young arms, the close-set eyes, the chipped front tooth, the detachment. All there. It was black and white, and cheaply copied, but even without the blue of the eyes and the gold of tan, it was apparent that it was boy in the Kodacolor glossies in Martha's drawer. And something more. Maybe it was the starkness of black and white that reduced it to its common denominator, or the fact that Karen had grown so accustomed to Martha's face. Whatever it was, Karen saw it now. Plain. Nothing physical, but something of the spirit that belonged to Martha. "James Leonard, Jr." So it was—it could only be her son. The Arcadia's phone number. "Contact M. Leonard." Her son, and she had lost him.

Not Terry, after all.

Standing in the snow looking at this boy from a gone summer day, Karen felt some of his mother's despair at his loss. Martha didn't have a shot at finding him, didn't she know that? "DOB"—weird how DOB sounded like DOA—"DOB: 1/14/65." But that would make him twenty-three now. The boy in the picture was maybe sixteen, like Terry.

Like Terry! Karen began to cry. "Last seen: Astor Place, 12/03/81." She counted back. Six years ago! Why was Martha just looking for him now? And why bother now? Another kid long since sucked up in the great backwash of apathy and loss, drugs and poverty and violence. Just another beautiful young face to stick on a milk carton. And now, even if she found him, he would

275

not want her. He was a man now if he was at all, and men can come home if they want to. He would be on junk, if she found him now, or wasted on alcohol. He would be beyond.

How would a picture of a boy help you find a man?

People loved Martha. Even Karen, who resisted her because she had to, saw her warmth. The way she was with the boy Terry. How could someone like Martha lose a child? How could anyone have a child if Martha could lose one? And, having one, and losing one, what let you go on?

Mark was right. Not having one could be smart. She touched the hopeless flier once and continued on.

As she went the last two blocks, she counted back again. Counting back days this time, not years. An effort to find why she was crying so hard when she had so recently thought herself to be happy. It had to be hormones. She had to be premenstrual. But she wasn't. Ten more days to go.

The thing was, any happiness she found now would always be cut by what she knew. You take your basic blissful scenario—take your pick, there are about ten of them in the world—and follow it through to its logical conclusion. Just see how long bliss gets to sustain itself. The situation Karen thought of as she trudged into the Arcadia was the basic one of Meeting Your Lover.

Meeting Your Lover

You are going to your lover who is handsome and wise and crazy for you, as well he should be, because he is, after all, your lover, and because you are pretty and witty and still kind of young. You

276

could be meeting him at Windows on the World and you could be wearing your black silk skirt and the top your grandmother crocheted light years ago. And New York will be pink before twilight, and you know when you get up there that the harbor will be still and the boats will seem unmoving and your lover will have already ordered you a Stolichnaya on the rocks with a twist. But the trick is getting there. If you go by subway, you'll find yourself wondering whether the man at the far end of the train, abandoned by all others and by you, who are crowded in a pack at this end, whether this man knows that he has been left because he is befouled, and if he does, does it bother him—that he is befouled and humiliated and abandoned at one end of the car? And if you take a cab, you step out onto Church Street and see this old man with two canes making dignified but tortured progress from Vesey Street to Chambers, and you see the holes in his clean hard-pressed pants, and you know that you will be inside and up on the elevator, you will have checked your coat and kissed your lover and sipped your Stolichnaya before he arrives at the next corner.

It could start you thinking about the waiting lover and the boats going nowhere and the fact that the very building you are speeding up in is oft-cited as the epicenter of the bomb that would certainly fall upon you and your lover (or the next one); thinking about the man below on the street, and the derelict in the subway below him, stinking and alone, hurtling to the end of the line.

Then what was the point of taking on a man or a new job or a child when you knew what you knew? Mark would probably say: You're right, no point. He would be wrong. You better fucking believe there was a point, was the point. You would take what you could get and hold it all the closer for the fearful knowledge that you had. You had to do it yourself. Maybe all of them—Vinnie with reincarnation, Martha with the boy in the room, Bill and her mother and discalced Sarah— maybe they all had the right idea. Maybe what you had to do first was decide you were worth the meaning you created. Suspension of disbelief, Mark had said. But Bette Midler was the one who really put her finger on it on an interview show Karen had seen in the lounge, before she got the VCR.

BARBARA WALTERS (with sincere furrowed brow): Bette, are you a ten? On a scale of one to ten, where would you want yourself, Bette?

BETTE: Lessee . . . one to ten, eh? I give myself five hundred.

BARBARA: Weally?

BETTE: Honey, if I didn't think I was a happenin' lady, I wouldn't even get up in the morning.

Barbara didn't understand Bette, you could tell, and you could tell Barbara definitely didn't think Bette was a five hundred. Karen did, though. Take Barbara Walters! There was a prime example. If there was ever anyone to suspend disbelief about herself and carry on with created meaning, wasn't it Barbara Walters? And she did OK, didn't she?

"Hello, Karen." A strange male voice. Karen looked up. It was Joe from Uganda, his thin Army jacket buttoned high.

"How are you?" Karen asked.

"Not bad. I have a job now, as a messenger, and I get a place with the cousin in Jackson Heights in March. So then I leave the AA and this neighborhood and you are sad to see me no more. How are you?"

"I've been better . . . I'm getting better." She smiled. "Are you gonna be one of those killer bike messengers?"

"I promise you, no. I work for a gentlewoman who runs a good character business. Superior high-class act, you see. Mopeds. She pay us good, not by delivery, not fly-by-night. You want coffee with me?"

"Another time," said Karen, and shook his hand.

Karen walked past Mrs. Sergeant Major, went up on the elevator and through the dim hall to 742. She rummaged in her purse for her key and opened her door to find Martha and the boy in bed. Together. She stood transfixed at the door. And then she slammed it closed and stood in the hall in a rage.

There could be no mistaking their purpose.

Karen leaned against the wall and drew a deep breath. Martha's fingers had been dug into bare boy buttocks, high and tight and small above smooth slim thighs, the sinews of his back knitting together with each movement.

She heard movement within, and then Martha was at the door in her bathrobe. "Karen . . . I'm so sorry."

"Shut the fuck up," said Karen, and walked past her.

The boy was wrapped in a sheet and stood, dazed,

closing his dresser drawer, his hair gold as summer. He looked beyond them to the window light, then took himself soundlessly into the bathroom. Soon Karen heard the frying sound of shower.

Karen sat limply on the edge of Martha's bed, suddenly exhausted. It was eleven-fifteen in the morning. She sat, facing away from Martha, crying between her fingers. Martha lay beside her.

"Oh, Karen . . ." said Martha. "Listen," she said, "I am so sorry." She rolled over and smiled pleadingly, her body in a loose curve beside Karen, her elbow on the bed, a hand supporting her head.

Karen stared out the window, then at the amaryllis on the small table between their beds. She stared at it until it came into focus, until she realized that the bud had opened and dropped four smaller bullet buds. Like some bad joke. She had seen enough cocks for one day. Yessir, she had just about had it with cocks, no matter if they were mere metaphor, no matter if they just shot blanks or belonged to boys. "Jeeze, look at that damn thing," she muttered, and thwacked a bursting bud hard with her middle finger.

"What?" asked Martha.

"I know what you're doing," said Karen softly then, looking directly at Martha.

"What?" asked Martha without challenge, returning her gaze. "I guess I'd like it if someone could tell me what I'm doing."

"I saw your flier."

"You did," said Martha quietly. A statement, not a question.

"It's your son."

"Yes."

"Why did he leave?"

Martha opened her mouth, then waved speech away with her free hand. Her breasts jostled softly.

"He looks sort of like Terry," Karen said. "He's older than Terry."

"Yes," said Martha. "But I can't see him now. Only when he left."

"Martha, don't you understand what's happening here?" Karen flashed a mix of frustration and fury across the small space. She spoke very slowly. "I mean, you take in the kid like you're altruistic. At least, I guess I wanted to think so . . . that you were perfect, you know, that someone or something was . . . like you're some . . . goddamn . . . Mother Teresa! *Shit!* And then . . . Jesus, it's all so clear! You've lost your own son . . ." Here Karen's voice cracked. She put down a sob with a swallow, but still, her body shook. "You've lost your son . . ." Her voice broke again.

Martha sat up now, and went to put a tentative hand on Karen's shoulder, then pulled it back to safety. She had lost Jimmy, and years ago, and now a stranger was weeping for him when her own tears had nearly dried.

". . . and so I come in and see you *in bed* with Terry, and he even looks like him a little . . . it's sorta shot through with your basic Freudian implications, wouldn't you say?"

"I guess I never paid that much attention to Freud. But he's not . . . my son!"

Karen grabbed the pillow, put it in her lap, halved it with her arm, and folded it over. "Did you have to have sex with him?"

"He was upset, worried about what was going to

happen to him. I only wanted to comfort him. I went over to him and put my arm around him. He put his head down on my breast. It happened, that's all. Sex just happens sometimes." Martha focused at the wall. "It's been a while for me. Maybe we both needed to, who knows? You get sick of being so damn vigilant."

Chapter
17

Karen stood and realized she was still wearing her jacket. Good, because she was leaving. She really must be going. She walked to the door, opened it, then closed it again. Someone was on the other side of it, a fist raised, about to knock. No escape! Karen leaned against the door. Well then, she would stay. It was her room, after all. She was exhausted. She would pull blankets over her head, and take a nap.

Knock-knock. Who's there? Karen knew who. She sighed, opened the door once more, and faced Audrey. Audrey was wearing a reversible plaid pleated skirt and a dingy yellow mohair sweater, a hole where it had begun unraveling held together by a rhinestone brooch in the shape of an arrow. She was holding two reams of paper.

"Hi," she said to Karen. "You said you were an English major, right?"

Karen nodded dumbly.

"So, I was wondering . . . I have to do a talk for the Society . . . I wondered if you would read these? Actually I wrote a few, but I think these two are the best. One's on the acting company that Jane Austen and her sister Cassandra were in in Steventon, you know, and how that influenced the dramatic sense in her writing. Each of her scenes is like a little one-act play, don't you agree? Or, maybe, do you think I should read the one on the period between 1801 and 1805, when her father retired from his parish and they went to Bath, where they went schlepping around from one temporary lodging to another, and lived with relatives a lot . . . You know, discuss how hard it must have been for her to get anything done . . .''

The second one, Karen decided but was unable to say as she stood in the doorway looking at Audrey, then at the papers in Audrey's hand, then back at Audrey. The period from 1801 to 1805 intrigued her, the schlepping around to lodgings . . . Martha was dressing. Terry was still in the shower. At least I have a job, Karen thought. I have to go to Vinnie's soon! "Uh . . . Audrey, do you think you could come back later?''

*B*ecause Terry was in the bathroom, Martha dressed without washing—sweat, sperm, sex smell still upon her, her own juices still flowing, fresh underpants immediately drenched through. I will walk out dripping, she thought. It will run down my legs and dry to crust in the cold. She thought this and was not displeased. She sat on her bed and rifled through her drawer until she found the earrings that dangled bananas. She screwed them in. She was terrified of piercing. Martha brushed her hair. After holding the boy, all she wanted, really, was to be alone, to walk someplace, along the East River maybe. She would go out and be pelted with wind and pierced through by cold.

Also, she knew Terry needed to be alone now. He had been a virgin. He told her, but of course she knew. He had come very quickly and was embarrassed. She had not come. He could not know yet what to do for a woman. Still, she loved the feel of him in her, the sweet strength and hard urgency of his first thrustings against her, through her, in her. She would go out and leave him alone, with new thoughts.

But there was Karen, all dressed for the elements, but instead sprawled facedown on her bed, one leg dangling off the side. So angry and troubled and bright. So afraid of hope, Martha thought, as she herself had once been. The way Karen was lying there was the exact way Leslie would fling herself down in her childhood griefs and piques: that foot off the side, the way the arms encircled the head without touching it; the way she would find Leslie when she came upstairs to comfort her. Martha set down her brush and picked up her lipstick. "Would you like to go out with me, Karen?" she asked softly. "Have a drink, maybe? At . . . what's the name of that place on the corner?"

Karen didn't answer. But she couldn't be asleep! Martha was surprised by the disappointment she felt.

And then Karen sat up, her right cheek dotted red by impressions of chenille balls. "Ralph's," she said shortly, holding her pillow. But she was secretly glad to go, glad of decision, and glad to get a drink.

Martha led the way to a table in the back. "Hey, Karen," said George when they entered, and Karen waved. They ordered beers from the waitress. Karen threw her jacket on an empty chair and went directly into the ladies' room, since she had been unable to use the bathroom at the Arcadia. Martha closed her eyes for a moment. Billy Joel was on the Muzak when Karen returned: "I Love You Just the Way You Are."

"Isn't this the most *peculiar* love song?" Martha said, too brightly, for conversation. Karen looked at her. "I mean, saying, 'I love you, you imbecile, even though you're not clever and I'm lazy.'"

"I guess I never took it that seriously," said Karen, amused.

"Well, I suppose there aren't that many men who want to work that hard, actually, in a relationship."

Karen shrugged. She hated the word "relationship" and had remembered that she was still angry at Martha.

"No more changes," intoned Billy Joel, joyfully, rhapsodically. "That's my problem, I guess," said Martha, "I like change."

A couple came in and sat two tables away. "I can't believe I'm having an affair!" they heard the woman say, then laugh, high-pitched. The man laughed, too, and said something, but Martha couldn't hear. The waitress brought the beers.

Martha took a sip. "When I was twelve, my father checked himself into the county mental hospital," said Martha. "He stayed there two days. He had tests done. *He is obsessed with sex!* my mother told me."

"Your mother told you *that* and you were twelve?" Karen asked.

"Yes, well, I was an only child. My parents always told me things they shouldn't, whatever frightened them or shocked them. They wanted me to help them, tell them what they should do."

"That must have been weird."

"Well, it was funny. I saw how they sought my opinion. They were like babies. I came out of it with this strange confidence in myself, and at the same time this terrible doubt because there was this awful fear that grownups, and now myself, were frauds, real fools."

"So your father—did he stay in the mental hospital for his . . . obsession?"

"Oh, no! It was a voluntary admission, so he just walked out. But after, I would always look at him and wonder: Is he thinking of it now?" Her father lying on the couch scanning the paper, coins spilled from his suit pockets onto the couch, his small, squarish, brown Supp-Hosed feet crossed and raised against varicose veins on the gold velveteen upholstery. A spectacled, balding, quiet man.

Obsessed with sex!

Her own father!

"It was horrifying. From the moment I heard the diagnosis . . . so intriguing, this malady." She added, darkly, dramatically, "Would I have it, too?"

Here Karen cleared her throat. "No comment."

"Well, at least it's not terminal. At least then it wasn't. He died years after of something else." They both laughed.

"How did they find out what was wrong with him? Did they shoot him with some truth serum to make him tell?"

"Yes, that's what I always wondered. Or maybe they showed him a film filled with subliminal breasts, and maybe he didn't miss a one? Or maybe they gave him a battery of Rorschach blots that all turned up vaginas . . ."

"Yeah, but you know they *always* look like vaginas."

"But he turned himself in, so maybe he just told them. If he knew. But what made him think his thoughts were so different from other people's thoughts? Were they? What was his first clue? What made him check in to find out? I would always look at the fathers of my friends for signs. In those days, of course, I never thought of looking at their mothers."

Their food came—french fried zucchini and burgers. Karen bit into a zucchini. It seared the roof of her mouth. She quickly quaffed some beer. They ate in easy silence.

"What happened to your son?" Karen ventured at length.

So Martha told her story, the story she had recounted so often in the last few weeks. She had told her story in so many churches, in synagogues and missions, in hospitals and morgues, to cops on corners, hookers, drug dealers and doers, people on the street themselves, to anyone who might know him or might be him, anyone who would listen. They heard her through and, no matter what their mouths would tell her, their eyes would always say the same thing: "No hope in hell for finding your kid, lady. Give it up and go home." She knew there was no hope. She would give up eventually, but not yet. She told her story to Karen now, dry-eyed, all the tellings having taken her tears.

"People have been wonderful and people have been indifferent. What surprised me was how incredulous some people were. That I could be looking for one person in this city, that one person mattered when so many were lost. I spoke to people that no one has ever looked for. They knew it and they certainly let me know it. Also, that I'm looking for him now, when he's been gone for years. That made people very angry. One of the people I spoke to was a man at the Bowery Men's Shelter. The psychologist there thought it would be OK. He was smart, and at first he was cooperative. But then he became very agitated when I showed him Jimmy's picture. 'You have no right' he said. and grabbed my arm. I knew I had to speak very calmly.

"I have no right?' I asked him.

"'To make one special. To have false gods.' He said that. 'You must take me because you have been given me in this moment.' The psychologist settled him down and took me away, but the thing was, I agreed with him in a way, you know?—that maybe you take who you're given."

"*I*t's Two-for-One Day," Vinnie warned when Karen reported for duty. "It'll get crazy, so just take it cool."

Karen's first job was sorting out the returns of the day and straightening the shelves. Karen and Vinnie were talking about genius, and who was. Vinnie said Fellini. Since this was a task that required only one-fortieth of her nongenius mind (even after the beers she had had with Martha), it left the other thirty-nine fortieths free to engage in all manner of inquiry with her new boss.

"Didja every see that early one of his, where Giulietta Masina plays a hooker? It's such a beautiful thing that Fellini's stayed with Giulietta after all these years and his fame."

"Hey, why not?" Karen shot back. "She is Giulietta, isn't she? And, like you say, the guy's no dummy. Did you ever think that she was the genius and he was the hanger-on? You probably think it was all Federico, the auteur, who got those expressions out of her, that she had nothing to do with it."

Vinnie chuckled about the idea of Fellini as hanger-on as he cracked change tubes into the cash register and watched the dark cubicles shine with nickels, dimes, quarters. "So you don't go with the idea of the actor as a vacuum, waiting for a personality to be poured into him? You know, a vessel?"

"Yeah, well if they're vessels, Giulietta is a Grecian urn. A damn Ming vase." At the moment she held in her hand a new starlet's exercise cassette. She waved it at Vinnie. "As compared to Fiona here, who's a Tupperware pop-lid pitcher."

Vinnie laughed. It was probably going to be OK with Karen. "But I just think Fellini must've worked really hard in a previous life to attain this level of genius. People think genius just happens, but it's what went before."

This observation put Karen in mind of some saccharine song from *The Sound of Music*. She adapted it and sang it, falsetto, forthwith: "Somewhere in my youth or past life, I must have done something good."

"Mockery. Dontcha' know we reincarnationists thrive on it? We play to it. We know it's all part of the karmic shit we have to eat toward a really transcendent transmigration." They laughed. Vinnie applied a vigor of Lysol and paper towel to the glass counter. He spoke again, seriously. "I can understand, though. People are afraid of us and our truth, especially people with real psychic power. They're afraid to get in touch with it because they might have been burned at the stake for it in a previous life. Maybe that's what happened to you, Karen." He looked at her meaningfully. "That would explain a lot of things."

"Hey, you know, that's what kills me about alla you subscribers to zeal! It's always *my* failing that I don't go along with whatever cozy little scheme you work out for yourselves. My fear! That makes me laugh! Did you ever stop and think that *I'm* the courageous one?" It did, it really pissed her off, but once she got it off her chest, she softened enough to say, "You think I have psychic power, Vinnie?" Actually she was flattered.

Also, though she lost no opportunity to kid about karma, she was going soft. Her rigid attitude had gone to lassitude. So much so, she was beginning to think Vinnie made sense. Could she convert to reincarnation this late in life? She would come back as a work ox in Bangladesh, but, ah! she would have such a radiant work-ox soul. The Ferdinand the Bull of work-oxdom. But she would impart these insurgent ideas to no one. They were her dark side.

"Psychic power?" Vinnie asked. "Yeah, but you oughta practice it more."

Karen laughed. "So, what's the afternoon feature on the demo, Vinnie?"

"Go ahead, you choose. It's your first day."

"*Under the Volcano*," said Karen without hesitation. It was in her hand and she had always wanted to see it.

"I don't think Jacqueline Bisset shows any tit in that," Vinnie complained.

"Vinnie, you're an ass. Jacqueline Bisset never shows any tit. She *suggests* tit, but she never shows it. She's too big a star. You only show tit if you have to in this world."

"Oh," said Vinnie.

Karen decided that work here passed most of her tests for the ideal job:

1. The first of them being time, and whether it passed for her. The day was flying by at Vinnie's.

2. She believed in it. She was providing a needed service. People needed movies. Fantasy might not be meat and drink, but it was right up there. It was the alternative to television's miniseries, which were only make-believe fantasies. She and Vinnie brought folks the real thing, and, in the case of mothers of small children, the infirm or the aged, and lovers who could not leave their beds, the fantasy was delivered. Free.

3. It was always new. There would be new tapes all the time on the demo monitor. Old ones she had not seen. A challenge to keep up with the new, a delight to run by old movies again. She could always be at the movies!

4. There was a feeling of camaraderie in the place—with Vinnie, with the customers— and what passed for intelligent conversation.

5. It was around the corner from what passed for home. Karen had traveled to get to work in the past and resented it deeply.

6. She got to wear her black sweat pants.

Sure, she could have gone for more money, but Karen was an intrinsically motivated employee. A fringe person without fringe benefits. Take preventive medicine—internals, breast exams, Paps, the whole schmear—well, Karen didn't have the price of admission to the foyer of any gynecologist's office in all of Manhattan. It worried her, but she would have to lean on her relative youth and basic good health for the nonce.

"Is that *really* Albert Finney?" cried a plaintive voice. Karen looked around her shelf to see a corpulent, fair-complexioned woman at the counter.

"Hi, Julia," said Vinnie. He introduced Karen. "Julia's a freelance writer—you know what that means—they got nothin' to do, which is why she can always show up here on Two-for-One, 99 Cent Comedy, 99 Cent Musical—whatever."

Julia laughed good-naturedly, then shrieked, "I can't believe that's Albert Finney! You remember him in *Two for the Road*, don't you?" She appealed to first Vinnie, then to Karen (seated on the floor, the better to sort), to anyone who would tell her that this man on the monitor was not Albert Finney.

Neither Karen nor Vinnie was old enough to have seen *Two for the Road* when it was first released, but each had seen it a few times since.

"He was so beautiful in *Two for the Road*!" said the mournful Julia.

Karen agreed. He was dashing and gorgeous and a perfect heel in *Two for the Road*. "But he's playing a role here. He's *supposed* to be dissolute and decadent and all . . ."

There was no comfort in it for Julia. "But look at

those bags under his eyes and the jowls! Look at his stomach!" she wailed disconsolately. "All those wrinkles can't be makeup! That's him! You can't do all that with makeup."

A man Vinnie introduced as Lieutenant DePasquale, from Community Relations at the nearby Police Academy, had come in and was now looking over Julia's shoulders. He was big, blue-eyed, benign. "That's the flaw in the movie, I think," said Lieutenant De, who had by chance taken it out last week. Karen wasn't sure Julia was in any frame of mind to concentrate on Lieutenant De's assessment. "I mean," he went on, "here's this guy that's gone to pot, and here's Jacqueline Bisset exquisite an' all, and *she's* supposed to be so crazy about him, traveling all that way and actually going to bed with him? 'I don't believe this garbage for one second,' I go to myself."

"But if you read the book," Vinnie interjected, "I think you'll see the charisma and brilliance of the guy Finney plays. Lowry really puts it over in the book. Actually I think Finney does a remarkable job with the part."

"I didn't read the book," said Lieutenant De in a kind of nah-nah-nah-nah singsong as he simultaneously dragged the backs of his fingers up his neck and under his chin, thrusting them suddenly out at Vinnie. "In a good movie you shouldn't hafta read the book!" He emphasized each word.

"He's right," said Karen.

"Right?" Lieutenant De said, open-palmed and high-eyebrowed, grateful for Karen's support. Vinnie conceded the point.

"Lieutenant De comes here instead of his video

store on Staten Island because he likes the conversation," Vinnie explained to Karen. "Ain't that right, De?"

De laughed. "I'm gonna miss you guys when the Academy moves to Harlem."

"Is it going to happen?" asked Karen.

"It's gotta happen," said De sadly. "Harlem needs us more somehow." He brightened, "Hey, can you see the movies? *Police Academy Goes to Harlem I, II, III!*"

Karen and Vinnie groaned at the prospect.

"What's weird," Julia was saying, "is that *Two for the Road* was where Jacqueline Bisset got discovered by Truffaut. Remember, she had a bit part—she was the one who got the chicken pox, so Audrey Hepburn got picked to drive off with Albert Finney instead? And, right, Truffaut said later he became obsessed with the actress who got the chicken pox? Which was why he starred her in *Day for Night.* Remember?"

Of course they remembered. They all did.

"So how come *she's* still beautiful?" Julia was off again in her elegy *pour les temps perdu*. "How many years ago was it? How old do you think he is? How old does that make me? Not to mention Truffaut and how long he's been dead. Oh, I cannot tell you how depressing this all is. Oh, Jesus, *look* at the time! I'm supposed to meet Rupert for lunch uptown. Can you get me *Das Boot* and *The Karate Kid*? Are they both in? Great!"

Karen stood up and stretched expansively. She had found a certain happiness at Vinnie's Viddies.

Chapter
18

Karen stopped by Annie's when she got off work.

Annie told her things hadn't been working out with Special Ed, so she was considering the possibility of walking through the Wall Street area during lunch hour with a deliberately defective smoke detector. What did Karen think? And how did you get a battery to do that before its time?

"Pathetic," Karen pronounced. "Definite P."

Annie though it was "well . . . kind of interesting" about Martha and Terry.

"It's sick, is what it is," Karen said. "And you're depraved, Annie."

"On accounta I'm deprived, maybe."

Annie said Vinnie sounded "sorta winsome and endearing." Or was Karen interested?

"No," Karen said. She wasn't interested. She liked him a lot so far, but she wasn't interested.

"It's his nape tendril, then."

"No, no." Annie knew her better than to think she could be daunted by something as trivial as a nape tendril.

"So, then, when do I get to meet him?"

"It depends on when you're available . . . this life or next?"

But Karen did not bring up Mark Pitofsky, and only shrugged noncomittally when Annie asked about him, a shrug which maddened Annie, causing her to pursue the question of Mark all the more. Still, Karen said nothing. She wanted to discuss Mark with Annie, but she also didn't want to. Not now. She wanted more to think of him herself.

It was nearly eleven when Karen came in to 742 from the harsh and sleeting night.

Martha was there. Michele was there. They were sitting cross-legged at opposite ends of Martha's bed. Karen's Scotch was on the table next to the amaryllis and they were drinking it. They had drunk a good bit of it, Karen could not help but note. Not only Michele, whom Karen already suspected of dipsing drams of her Dewar's, but Martha was drinking, too. They greeted her dispiritedly. Terry was not there. The bathroom door was open and he was not there. The shower was not going. He wasn't drawing or reading or doing sit-ups on the mat.

"He's gone," said Michele.

"Why?" asked Karen. "Where? Gone where?" Good, she thought, feeling an immediate relief. But then she looked at their faces and knew it could not be good. He had nowhere to go. "Where did he go?"

So stupid to ask. You want them to tell you that his mother rose from the dead and came for him. That his unknown father had arrived, recovered and repentant, and begged in tears for his boy.

"He left his stuff," said Michele, maudlin, her eyes

297

red-rimmed and tearing. Though she had been pretty good about the booze of late, Michele was definitely gone tonight. Karen knew how affected she had been by Terry, and knew from Martha the pressures she was under with law school and money problems. Terry was a kind of focus and now he was gone. "He left everything that Martha bought for him," she said mournfully.

No use talking to Michele. Karen turned to Martha. "What happened?" She sat on her bed and began unlacing her boots. Her feet were wet and cold even through the thick soles. It was hideous out there, sleeting and freezing, the whine of wind in the airshaft.

"He left, that's all," said Martha, affecting indifference.

"He left because of you," Michele interjected, looking darkly at Karen.

"That's ridiculous," said Martha hastily. "Why even say that?"

Karen laughed nervously. "He left because of me?" She sat up, pulled her head back, and looked directly at Michele. She held her mouth straight and sardonic as she pulled at the wet toes of her socks.

"Of course not!" said Martha quickly.

"But you know it's true! What about the note?" She turned to Karen as she grabbed up a tiny piece of lined paper ripped from a small memo book. She thrust it across the narrow space at Karen, who accepted it reluctantly. She smoothed it absently on her thigh before looking down. He had printed it, fast, tall, angular letters leaning left. She had not really seen his writing before.

Dear Martha,

I can't blame Karen for being mad at me. I know I have to go so that you won't get into trouble. Thank you for everything. You were good to me. Don't worry, I'll be OK. I'm strong, like you said.

Yours truly,
Terry

Karen folded down the top edge of the paper, evening it off where it had been ripped from the ring binder. She breathed deeply and massaged her toes slowly before reaching for the Scotch. There was a plastic glass on the table, with two parallel cracks running halfway down it. Karen took it up, inspected it, pulled out the strip between the cracks, popped it back in place, and poured two inches, just to where the cracks began. "Sorry, Michele, you can't lay this on me."

Michele began crying softly. "We looked *all over* for him! And now Martha has to go, too. All we needed was a few more days! It won't work out now will it, Martha? I know everything will get screwed up!"

Martha stood and spoke to Michele kindly but emphatically. "You are going to bed immediately. All your studying and then coming back to chase all over the city with me . . . I should never have let you. To bed! Now." She scooped up Michele's coat and bag and pulled gently on her arm. She rubbed her back tenderly as she ushered her across the room and out the door. But going out, Michele stumbled and nearly fell on something. It was Martha's Vision Realty bag, Karen realized, and it was packed.

Karen went in the bathroom, brushed her teeth, splashed water on her face, then held the towel against it for a long moment. She got into bed. She had brought home a Woody Allen movie but was too tired to watch it. Besides, she wasn't sure she was in the mood to see a glitzy Manhattan. The room was chaotic with Martha's packing. Also, Terry's things were thrown about, as though they had been searching his drawer for a clue to his departure.

There was a knock on the door and Audrey's head tentatively appeared, to be followed by the rest of Audrey in a pink sateen robe. It was a puffy robe, quilted into machine-stitched flowers. "Martha's not here? Oh, I feel just terrible!"

"Why? What is it?" Karen wondered if Audrey had discovered some new sadness that Jane had endured.

Audrey seemed surprised. "You didn't hear what happened? I was quite startled . . . it was so unexpected, you know. I just started screaming. I suppose I lost control. May I have some of that?" She indicated the Scotch. Karen nodded and poured her a shot into Michele's cup. Audrey sat on Martha's bed. Her face glistened with fresh moisturizer. "I came by to see you again, like you said to . . . oh, about three or so . . . and this . . . young man was coming out your door! He darted away when he saw me, down the back stairs. I realize now that he was probably frantic, but so was I. I've had some difficulties lately, and I had just heard about a liquor store murder near here and . . . Well, anyway, there I was absolutely frozen to the spot, just screaming." Audrey paused, took a slow sip, and stared absently at the Aztec-patterned drape.

Karen pulled a feather from her poor pillow. "So, what happened?"

"Oh! So Mrs. Sergeant Major and the guard were there in no time. The guard went chasing him, but he got away. The secretary said he just burst through the lobby and out the front door. Apparently he tried the basement and it was locked. By then a few people were after him . . ." Audrey stopped and coughed. She touched her throat, indicating that the Scotch had gone down the wrong way. She coughed a few more times and raised her index finger. A moment. She'd get back to her story in a moment.

Karen felt a wave of sadness. How frightened he must have been, poor kid! All these people screaming and chasing after him, and not even having a place to go to from here. Where was he tonight, this frigid wet night on the far edge of winter?

Audrey had gotten control over her larynx. "The guard came back then and unlocked the door. I was so afraid to go in with them, what we would see . . . I know it's my nerves lately. But I did go in after Mrs. Sergeant Major said it was OK. And then we realized that he had been living there. His clothes . . . the mat, drawings that he had signed . . .

"Right away Mrs. Sergeant Major thought it was you, that you had been keeping him in here. She said you had been flying in the face of her authority all along. That was the expression she used. But then Martha walked in on us and seemed so distressed to hear what happened, and that now we all knew about it. She said you had nothing to do with it, that she had insisted that he stay. She said that right away. She was

301

really quite emphatic about that, that you had nothing whatever to do with it. Mrs. Sergeant Major said that Martha could stay tonight, but then she would have to leave in the morning, that they couldn't have people flouting the rules like that here. Oh, it was so sad about the boy. I felt terrible, especially when she told us."

"Told you what?"

"Oh! That he was her son."

Karen bolted up. What had awakened her? A nightmare? Or a noise from Martha, who was up and dressing in the dark, now putting on her down coat? Karen stretched for her watch, sleepily squinting at it as she held its face toward the dim light from the bathroom. Two-thirteen. She exhaled and flopped back heavily on her pillow. She had been in a dead sleep. She rolled into the fetal position, the better to get back. She was shivering . . . so cold . . . no blankets. Where were her blankets? But then she remembered something and felt a waking sadness. Terry was gone. And Martha . . . Martha must be going someplace, standing there in the dark, wrapping her scarf around her upturned collar.

"You're not leaving now, are you?" Karen asked, and Martha jumped, startled.

"Oh, Karen! I woke you. I'm sorry! Go back to sleep."

Fat chance, thought Karen. The story Audrey had told her earlier came back to her now in a rush. Karen had meant to find out more from Martha, but she had fallen asleep instead, on top of her bedspread, still in her clothes, exhausted from the day's events. What a day! Leaving Mark—how long ago was that, really? It couldn't have been just yesterday morning. And then finding Martha and Terry together—going out to Ralph's with Martha—putting in a good eight hours at Vinnie's—the drink at Annie's. No wonder she had zonked out.

"Where are you going?"

"Don't worry, I'm OK."

"Have you slept at all?"

"I tried . . . a little, maybe. I thought I might as well get up."

"You're going out to look for him now?"

"Go back to sleep," said Martha, and she was gone.

"Christ!" muttered Karen. "Goddamnit. Fuck!" She pulled the goose-neck lamp toward her and turned the switch. Its hundred watts blazed in her eyes. "Shit!"

Patches of incandescence bounded blindingly before her retina, but Karen made out the door and rushed toward it, flung it open, and yelled to Martha's back, which was about to turn the corner to the elevator. "Stop! Wait for me!"

Good. She was already dressed. Sleeping in one's clothes saves time, Karen remarked to herself. It pays to be a sloven. She sat on her bed, grunted, grabbed up her wet combat boots, stuck in her feet, and laced them in a fury.

Martha was standing before her when she straightened. "Don't be ridiculous, Karen. I can't allow it. It's my insanity, not yours. I don't want to involve you anymore than I have already."

Karen looked up into the face which had come to seem so lovely to her in the last two weeks: the lines etched around the eyes, the strong set to the mouth, the white wisps that framed it, the wisdom that marked it. "Shut the fuck up," she said to it, and grabbed her Persian lamb.

*T*hey were on their way to Port Authority. Martha said he would be there. She was certain she would find him there. She and Michele had been there earlier and not found him, but she knew he was there now.

The night was even worse than it had been earlier. You are making a serious mistake, Karen told herself as they pushed themselves out the Arcadia's front door. It was a barbaric night, a raw, wet beast, savage and dark. The two women made their slow way to the corner. Martha's sturdy black umbrella blew out forthwith. But did she immediately abandon it curbside? No. She carried it with her, though it threatened her eyes and railed against her and pulled her back. She carried it with her until she came to a wire basket where she stuck it beside two of its disabled, rent-ribbed kin. So like Martha, Karen could not help but muse, before a gust hit her broadside. They were soaked through, bone cold. Construction scaffolding over the sidewalk provided a brief respite from the rain, and they walked under gratefully.

But they were not alone under the plywood.

"Uh! *What*? Oh . . . no!" wailed Martha suddenly, terrified, and grabbed Karen's shoulder so urgently that Karen's heart stopped dead, even before her feet.

"What is it?" Karen hissed.

"*A person*," Martha sobbed, but Karen knew even

as Martha managed to get this out, because a living bag of dark and wet was rolling onto the toes of her boots. It was a man, and the moan he emitted just then seemed to be what set Martha off, to cause in her a turbulence as deep and dark and dreadful as the night they were out in.

Martha could not move. Karen urged her to move, but Martha stood there, weeping wantonly; indeed, it seemed to Karen almost indulgently, as though her lamentation were a luxury, something precious she had been holding back on, a gift she hadn't given grief before. Karen heard her and felt a kind of envy.

"C'mon, Martha," she said tugging at her. No use. She grabbed Martha and held her. She felt the deflated down of Martha's coat, flat with wet. She held her cold cheek against Martha's. "Please, Martha, let's go. There's nothing we can do about him, you know that."

"I c-can't. I can't walk over him, I can't walk past him. How can we do that, Karen?" Her voice in the dark was high and unfamiliar.

"We have to. You want to find Terry, don't you?" And Karen thought, as she had so often before, that dealing with Martha was like dealing with a child. Promise her anything. Promise her Terry. "Look, we'll call the police when we get to a phone. That's the only thing we can do, the best thing we can do." She tugged at her. "Please . . . we'll go find a phone."

It convinced Martha. Heaving and sobbing, she stepped over the man. She managed to collect herself somewhat by the time they came to the phone on the next corner. She was breathing heavily, but she was calm. A yellow "Out of Order" sticker covered the change slot. They moved on, across Park.

305

They jumped away from the curb after a hellbent southbound truck passed too near and sprayed a filthy puddle over their legs. Karen considered whether it would be better to be naked than so waterlogged. You couldn't be any colder if you were naked. You would be lighter. You could move faster. Maybe someone would pick you up and wrap you in a blanket and take you to a nice cozy insane asylum. Maybe they would anyway. She looked up the canyon to the Pan Am Building, barely visible through fog and sleet. *The Pan Am Building has an inside*, she thought with reverence. It would be heaven to be there, under the Pan Am Building, on one of the pews in Grand Central, chomping a Snickers from the newsstand.

WALK flashed greenly at them. An order or a reminder, Karen wondered. She took Martha's elbow and prompted her. "How you doin'?" she asked gently as the elements wreaked havoc upon their heads.

"Oh, I'm doin' OK," said Martha brightly, catching a sob. "But look, let's stay here . . . this'll be the best place to get a cab, yes? . . . cars going by both ways."

The innocent faith with which Martha spoke of this implausibility, this remote chance in thousands of coming by a cab at 3 A.M. on a night like this caused Karen to laugh out loud even as the wind blew up through the wide sleeves of her jacket to numb her armpits.

"You mean you don't think we will?" Martha asked meekly, and laughed, too.

Karen looked at Martha's shocked expression and laughed even louder before Martha joined her. They were giggling helplessly as they made their way to the BMT, buffeted by a backwind.

*   *   *

*A*t Martha's insistence, Karen dialed 911 as they waited on the subway platform. She put a finger in her ear to block the noise of the train departing on the opposite track. After several rings a young woman answered, the boredom and annoyance in her voice apparent even through the roar of the receding train. Karen removed her finger and cupped her raw reddened hand around the receiver as she gave the precise location of the man they had stumbled upon. "We'll send a car when one is available," the young woman intoned snottily. Karen slammed the receiver down violently. She knew it had been no use to call.

"Maybe it's the Police Department . . ." said Martha. Karen looked at her quizzically. "You know, why so many pay phones are out of order in New York." Karen nodded. It sounded right. The train was coming at long last.

*F*ive women who had begun their lives in the Ukraine, but who now probably mopped up the World Trade Center by night, were hurtling home huddled together at one end of the heatless car. Faces more purely Slavic than Karen's, wholesome and wide and unrefined. Two were in the short seat next to the conductor's booth. The three across from them were sitting beneath the gorgeous sleek body of a beautiful black woman emerging from a green sea. The black woman was wearing a near-transparent white T-shirt that said IT'S BETTER IN THE

BAHAMAS in clean blue letters. The Ukrainian women were bundled more sensibly in plaid wool babushkas, zip-up, lined waterproof boots, thick socks over dark tights, clear plastic folding raincoats over winter coats. They were still dry, Karen noted. They had, no doubt, come direct on the elevator from the 102nd floor, through the huge arcade past Alexander's and Waldenbooks to the down escalator and the token booth. They might not have been able to see the storm in the dark sky from the 102nd floor. But they would have heard of it on the transistor radios they took with them from office to office. They knew what they would face when they made their ascent into Astoria. The youngest of them was carrying a well-worn Bonwit Teller bag with its trademarked violets. The black woman above her was smiling radiantly. The woman with the Bonwit Teller bag wore a more subdued, resigned expression. The Ukrainian women said little to each other. One was nodding with sleep. One was reading *The Star*.

Across from Karen and Martha a slim and elderly black man in a soaking trenchcoat, a face worn with work and worry, blew warmth into gloveless hands. A "Get Goetz" graffito covered the glass over the subway map behind his head. Above him was a commuter poem, containing morning glories, brought to them by the New York State Council on the Arts. Karen liked the poem, though she wasn't certain what it meant. At the far end of the car there was no one, only an empty fifth of cheap vodka rolling dolefully in the doorway.

Karen had jumped into her boots and come with Martha without thinking, but now, in the relative tranquillity of the RR, she considered her motives. Or, rather, what she said to herself was: Why the *fuck* am I here? But it wasn't rational, why she was here. None of this business was. Some crazy wild goose chase to Port Authority. She was here because Martha was here, because nothing would have kept Martha from going out, and she couldn't let her go out by herself, on this night, at this hour. She was here because the boy was by himself somewhere, alone, and because Martha thought there was a chance of finding him. Karen looked at her reflection in the window across the aisle. She always looked older in subway windows, and sadder somehow. Subway windows showed her with hollows and shadows that she didn't really have.

Maybe, in some way, she was the cause of his leaving. Michele had said that. It was probably true. She had accused him of taking her mother's ring, and though she had not found it, she was sure now that he hadn't. She had lost it the way she had lost so much else, just by being sloppy. She felt very bad about that, about accusing him, not about the ring. And then she had freaked when she saw them in bed together—or had she? A normal enough reaction, freaking, given the circumstances. Still, she knew she had scared him badly.

She liked Terry. She was worried about him, too. She remembered Mark's words: "It's up to you . . . do you want to help this kid or not?"

"You told them all he was your son," she said to Martha, loudly, to be heard. She couldn't let Martha slide on this, she just couldn't.

Martha looked at her, surprised, and a little annoyed to be called on this, as though Karen were being somewhat petty, nattering on about mere facts. She shrugged. "You know what it is . . . he's a son, right?

And I'm somebody's mother. It confuses me, some-times, I must say. Where you stop, or should stop . . . don't you see?" She paused, then dismissed it with, "Anyway, I was probably upset." She leaned back on the metal seat and stared without seeing at the com-muter poem.

Karen considered Martha's words, then warned herself: You are losing it, darling, when Martha and Vinnie start to make sense. Or is it just that you are freezing to death? Her feet didn't feel anymore. Her fingers couldn't bend. A major cold was seizing her system—she felt an ache in her back, her throat was scratchy and sore, and her deviated septum was further screwed up by pre- and postnasal drips. She wiped it with the back of her wrist. The train pulled into the Thirty-fourth Street stop. The black man exited and the doors closed behind him. Karen sneezed and swallowed sputum.

"God bless you," said Martha beside her.

"Goddamn you," said Karen to Martha, and they both laughed.

From the subway, they walked through a tunnel a city-block long, stinking with urine and lined with ads for the School of Visual Arts, *Penthouse*, *Dreamgirls*, and Murjani jeans, and ads against kinky hair, aging, drug abuse, and AIDS. I WANT YOU TO HAVE MY CHILD, said Ed Koch, in one poster, a tasteless, ill-conceived cam-paign for foster children. "*Yuk!*" said Karen, "Can you believe it? As though he gave a damn. So obnoxious! That man is really Ordinary Ed." She wished she hadn't lost her "This Exploits Women" stickers in one of her moves.

But Martha wasn't listening. She walked directly

310

through the tunnel, turned right, then right again at the entrance to the bus station, past Walgreen's, Zaro's Bread Basket, Jo Ann's Nut House, then left up the escalator. Karen hadn't been in Port Authority in some time. It was looking good since its renovation, even now, at 3:32 A.M. Brighter, cleaner, a little jazzier, with its play of crisscrossed piping high above them, its vivid violet, fuchsia, and turquoise pennants hanging, and its brick walls bright red. It was freezing in here as well, but at least it wasn't outside. Right off the escalator, then through the arch to the other building, past the bagel stand . . .

Oh, God, let her find him, said Karen, though she didn't necessarily mean God. Just let him be found so that I can be done with them both and go home to bed. After this thought there was the dawning of another thought concerning home and beds and the fact that Martha and the boy, if he should be found, had neither. This thought, which was not yet fully formed in Karen's head, involved that Vision Realty bag that was still on her floor and those clothes of Terry's that had no place to go. Though not complete, this thought had begun to disturb her in an amorphous way, because there was a corollary to it, also incomplete, but which had to do with the fact that Karen's own sleep would be further delayed if this crazy little pair didn't have home or bed. "Shit," Karen muttered, and bumped into Martha's back, because Martha had stopped walking.

"Terry!" Martha said.

He was sitting there, on a wooden bench across from Gate 319. He was wearing the jacket and plaid flannel shirt Martha had bought him, his blond hair hanging over his eyes. His clothes appeared damp, but

311

not soaking. There was a newspaper on his lap, and Karen thought he had been reading, but his head jerked up so quickly when Martha spoke his name a second time that Karen realized he had been sleeping, using the paper as a front.

"Terry."

He looked at Martha and smiled broadly. But something crossed his face when he saw Karen. Karen saw it, quite definitely, though she wished she hadn't.

He stood up. "Hi, Martha . . . hello, Karen." He looked back at Martha and shifted his feet. "I didn't have any money. I was just sitting here awhile." His lower lip was taut against his teeth.

Martha embraced him tightly, then pulled away and studied his face. "You weren't here earlier," she said. Karen thought it was almost as though it were an unspoken agreement to meet at Gate 319. Was this search for him part of a little masque the two of them were enacting? Or perhaps he had come to this spot as a test, to see if she would look for him. "Where were you before? I was *so* worried!"

"A man took care of me. A black man with a foreign accent. He was outside when I left, by the Square. It was really rainy, and I didn't know what to do. He said he could tell that I was in trouble, so he took me to a warm place, the Alcoholics Anonymous. I rested there awhile, a couple of hours. He gave me a peanut butter sandwich and a token to get here. He was OK to me, you know?"

Martha sat on the bench, then pulled him down next to her and shook his shoulders lightly. "You stay with me now, OK? Don't go away again, you promise?

312

At least not for a while." He nodded. She stood up. "So come on now, let's go, OK? Let's get out of here!"

Karen's eyes met Terry's. "Um, Martha . . . where are you gonna go?"

"Oh, yes," said Martha matter-of-factly. "Yes . . . where?" She began to laugh and sat back down. Karen sat down, too, Terry between them. "Where shall we go, Terry? We sure can't go back to the Arcadia, can we, and we can't get into our house for another week." She laughed again. It was bothersome, an inconvenience, but no great worry.

Karen leaned across Terry and looked at Martha. "Your house?"

"Well, yes, Karen . . . I bought a house! In Jersey City. The first half of my divorce settlement came through and that's how I used it. Victorian. I think you'll like it. You will come and see us there, I hope. It's going to be wonderful once we fix it up, which should take forever." She sighed as she said this, not unhappily.

Karen didn't respond for a moment. "You and Terry?" she asked.

"Oh! Me, and Terry—and Michele, too, for a while, a few months maybe, until the summer, when she starts with that fat-cat law firm. She's going to pay me off in sweat equity, you know." Karen didn't know, and felt a little hurt at being unincluded, even in a scheme she would never go for.

Martha saw her surprise. "I didn't tell you because I didn't think you'd approve. The place really needs work and the neighborhood isn't great. I attach a lot to what you say, and if you didn't like it I would have had

313

second thoughts, when, really, I just wanted to get it done. You're so sensible, Karen."

It was meant as a compliment, Karen knew.

"A little common sense would come in handy right now. I wasn't counting on getting kicked out, you know. We only had to make it till next Wednesday and the closing. I'm getting a second check, but not right away, and meanwhile there's gonna be closing costs and who knows what all else. So! Any suggestions?" she asked brightly, looking across at Karen. "You know the city so well."

A line was forming near them, mostly senior citizens, getting an early bus for Atlantic City. Karen thought about it for a moment, about who could take them in. "I think I know a place," she said.

It was, happily, a recently renovated phone, marred by only one graffito: "Polyps for Reagan." She dialed the only person she knew in the city with an extra room, knowing he would not refuse, knowing his promise from his words. *You like this kid, right? You want to help him. It's up to you, if you want to or not.*

And he answered her direct from sleep, glad it was her, no matter the hour. Like an AT&T ad, thought Karen as she smiled into the receiver, like everyone's dream of welcome. "Bring 'em on," said Mark Pitofsky when she told him. And she did.